THE EMPIRE
SECRETS
AND
PROPHECIES

BOOK 1

BY
RANCH BARLOW

MILTON & HUGO L.L.C.
4407 Park Ave., Suite 5
Union City, NJ 07087, USA

Website: *www. miltonandhugo.com*
Hotline: *1- 888-778-0033*
Email: *info@miltonandhugo.com*

Ordering Information:
Quantity sales. Special discounts are granted to corporations, associations, and other organizations. For more information on these discounts, please reach out to the publisher using the contact information provided above.

Library of Congress Control Number: 2024907413
ISBN-13:   979-8-89285-074-2   [Paperback Edition]
                  979-8-89285-073-5   [Digital Edition]

Rev. date: 03/19/2024

Prologue

How did the world come to this, oh how far the residents of Earth have fallen. Callus thought to himself looking up at the ceiling of his war room. Earth, vast and beautiful as it was, or mostly beautiful anyway, some places were quite horrendous all things considered. The world was so torn apart that it was basically at war.

Politics. Callus thought. Politics are pretty dumb, like the ideas that some of them, or most of them, think of are just stupid. He continued thinking to himself. *Stupid like the one that Vasilldir proposed at the World Senatorial Meeting. "I believe that all non-magic users should be shown the way of magic so that we may think considerably more like one another and all contentions will end." Vasilldir said.*

"That idiotic elf." Callus muttered, shaking his head still looking at the ceiling. "What was that?" Asked Hevtur.

Callus looked over to the pale white wind dragon laying down in his designated spot while visiting. He was about average size for a dragon, but like average sized dragons he was rather large compared to Callus, a human, Callus stood at six feet tall to the top of his scalp and he stood to the height of just more than half way up Hevtur's leg. Hevtur was about fifty feet in length from the end of his snout to the tip of his tail. He wore the crown of Jurrunt that was the colors of light gray and dark gray in a diagonal line from the right to the left side of his body with the light gray on top.

Hevtur was there studying the map of the Earth and what to think of psychotic dwarf armies huddling near the dwarf kingdom of Zulkbar's borders, and where to position their own forces to immediately counter any threats that loom near their own borders with Callus, if need be.

"I was just remembering what Vasilldir said at the World Senatorial Meeting." Said Callus, looking away from Hevtur and back at the map.

The nation he led was the Imperium of Praetoria which was bordering the dwarf Kingdom of Zulkbar to the northeast more to the north than the east though, the human Kingdom of Corinos almost directly to the east just slightly south, the human Republic of Farrius to the west, the dragon Kingdom of Jurrunt to the northeast between Zulkbar and Corinos, which was where Hevtur was from, matter of fact he was the king of that kingdom. To the south a river that led to the ocean bordered Praetoria and on the other side of the river were marauders and barbarians. To the northwest the Imperium of Praetoria, a vast ocean that stretched between the continent of Drakenmor and the continent of Luminarch, where they resided.

"You were paying attention?" Asked Hevtur. "Yes for that part at least, after I woke up a little more." Callus responded, stroking his chin and jawline where his facial hair used to be before he shaved it.

"You continue to stroke your face as if you still had your beard. In fact, why did you shave off your beard in the first place, it was finally beginning to grow on me. Made you look nice." Callus looked at him concerningly with his brows forming a line. "What do you mean it made me look nice, what, were you going to fall head over talons for me if I kept it?" Callus continued. "I don't think Mirada would like that." Hevtur looked at him. Callus looked into his icy blue eyes as if he was amused, even though he was.

"How is Mirada by the way?" Callus inquired, looking back at the map table. "She's good. Well, at least most of the time that is. She makes suggestions, good ones too, but everytime I say I'll try to do what she suggests, I forget, or at least most of the time I do. I believe she might be going insane." Hevtur replied, looking at the map as well. Callus smirked and almost, almost laughed. Hevtur continued, "Are you ever going to find a wife? You're the only one of us, I think, that hasn't got one yet, if you ever do get one."

"Uhhh, I hope so, but I'm not going to marry a back-stabbing woman that is just going to poison me when she gets the chance."

Callus replied, looking at Hevtur then back to the map. "Ahh, I see. I would feel the same way if I was a human." Hevtur said, amused at his comment. Callus just stared at him. At least Callus had the decency to stop and not absolutely insult Hevtur, much less his whole race, but they were friends after all. So he probably should insult him all he can.

After a moment of silence passed Callus said with a demanding tone, somewhat irritated. "When is that guy going to show up?" Agamemnon was the King of Corinos, who was allied with Praetoria and Jurrunt along with Farrius. In most ways Agamemnon was full of himself, usually he was less late than this, but again, he was pretty proud of himself. Daentious, who was the head of the Republic of Farrius's military board, could not make it to this meeting and henceforth he was not going to show up. "One may never know, including him." Hevtur said in a sarcastic voice. Callus barked out a short laugh.

There was a knock on the door. "Yes." Callus asked, and the door was opened by a guard which was just shorter than Callus and wearing lorica armor.

"King Agamemnon is here, my Liege. Shall I permit him to enter?" The guard asked. "Yes, let him in." Callus replied, and the guard stepped out and to the side, and Agamemnon strode in. One of the guards closed the door behind him.

"Good day Callus, Hevtur." Agamemnon said in a lazily confident voice.

Agamemnon was just taller than Callus with dirt brown hair that was a few inches in length from his scalp, he wore a cape with the white and royal blue colors of Corinos in a diagonal line from his left shoulder to the opposite corner of the cape. He had a smooth black shallow beard forming on his jawline and around his mouth.

"Good day to you too." Hevtur said, Callus repeated right after.

"Please excuse me for being late... once again... you see... I had to take care of some..." He mused on what to say and continued, "Dispute in the waters that could not wait." Agamemnon said, walking over to the table that hosted the wine and other beverages. "Well at least you're here, finally." Callus said and continued, "May I ask what kind of dispute this was and where it was? Was it in the Alzeirs river?"

"It was a civil dispute near the port of Kalados. Nothing to be concerned about." Agamemnon replied, as he finished pouring his choice of wine and swirling it around in its cup.

"Where is Daentious today?" He asked as he walked to the map table in the center of the room. "It would appear that he is out in the field today." Hevtur said.

"'It would appear'?" Agamemnon asked, raising an eyebrow.

"Gaius Seplomus said that he was inspecting their troops on the northern front. Not that that means he is actually doing that alone." Hevtur responded.

"I see." Agamemnon said, nodding his head. "I also see that the pieces that represent the forces of Zulkbar are on the map near their borders." Agamemnon said, looking at the map.

"Yes." Callus said and added, "According to our information, King Folkhem has positioned his armies there, as if he's preparing for war."

"Mmmm." Agamemnon hummed.

"Now that you're here we'll tell you about what we were thinking." Callus said to Agamemnon. "I will be placing Legio III Attis at the Chechian Crater to match this army." Callus said, pointing his stick near the northernmost area of Praetoria where one scarlet banner piece and one blue and black banner piece stood next to each other. Callus continued, "I will also be placing Legio VII Donnious at the Plaxident Valley near his other army that resides near my borders." Pointing at another pair of scarlet and blue and black banner pieces.

"This part I was waiting for you to show up to discuss, I want to pull Classis II Oceanianic out of Courous from the Alzeirs River, and station it up north with my other fleet in case of any naval attack. What do you think of it if I do and you take up full responsibility of securing the Alzeirs?" Callus asked, pointing at the Alzeirs River on the map. Agamemnon inhaled and said, "That can be done. Do you really think that if a war breaks out that they will attack in such a great force to call two fleets to one sea region?" Agamemnon asked, taking a sip from his cup of wine.

"Anything is possible, maybe they have a reserve fleet hidden away somewhere." Callus suggested, folding his arms and resting on his heels, looking at Agamemnon. "Very well, makes sense." Agamemnon responded. Then he turned to look at Hevtur, gesturing to him to speak.

"Since I border more potential enemies, I do not want to station my armies in a particular spot where they can be avoided in some way, so I was going to hide them away and put scouts on my borders near where their armies are to watch and see their first move." Hevtur said, pointing at the map with a claw.

"Good enough, I'll probably keep my armies in reserve in case any of my unfriendly neighbors decide that they think they're invited into my lands, and so that if any reinforcements are required they'll be ready to march as soon as possible." Agamemnon said, stroking his beard, looking at the map. "That sounds good enough." Callus said, looking at the other two.

"Sure does, I'll see you next at our next standardized meeting at Corinthius in three months." Hevtur said, nodding once at both of them.

"Yep, see you there." Agamemnon replied, nodding once back at Hevtur and Callus.

"Alright, see you then." Callus nodded once back to both. Agamemnon then gulped down the last of his wine, walked over to the beverage table, put his cup down and strode out of the room. Hevtur then turned to the archway that was big enough for him to fit through. The door that was shut within it was opened and Hevtur walked out to the landing platform and took off toward his home.

Callus stared at the banner pieces with his brown eyes for a moment thinking to himself. *A possible world war… I would rather not, they take forever to end. Any war takes forever to end… usually, but wars on this scale. Much longer, war weariness gets to basically an all-time high, and the death toll is much more catastrophic than those of regular wars, then again if a world war starts we either win and those idiots like Vasilldir will shut up, or they won't ever speak again, which would probably be better. Or we lose and I still don't have to listen to Vasilldir's voice ever again, it's almost like a win–win, though one win is better than the other.*

He then removed the banner pieces from the map board with a long stick that had a large blunted end and put them away in a drawer on another table across the room from the beverage table before calling, "Guards!"

The guard that knocked on the door before wearing his lorica armor and his tyrian purple cape opened the door and walked into the room with three more guards behind him also wearing lorica and tyrian purple capes. He stopped ten feet from Callus, crisped a hard salute to his heart and said, "My Liege."

"Dowse the torches and close the dragon doors then return to your post." Callus said, nodding once, sharply, to him before turning and walking out. "Right away, my Liege." The guard returned. The guards then began dowsing the fires and closed the doors with help from a few fellow guards that came in with him.

Callus left the room and walked down the hall to the exit, his cloak of scarlet trailing behind due to the speed he walked. One of the guards wearing lorica and a cape of tyrian purple opened the door and banged out a salute to the heart, the other guard did the same. Callus nodded to them and walked out of the hallway and turned to his left and walked away. The guards then closed the door behind him and returned to their original positions on either side of the door.

PART ONE

Chapter

1

Three months later

"GET IN LINE, YOU FISH!" Snarled a centurion. "WAIT, ACTUALLY, YOU'RE WORSE THAN A FISH, BECAUSE EVEN A FISH WOULD HAVE BRAINS ENOUGH TO FOLLOW ORDERS, OR AT LEAST LOOK LIKE AN ACTUAL SOLDIER!" The centurion added.

"Yes sir, sorry sir." replied the new recruit. "OH, YOU'LL BE SORRY WHEN BEAT YOUR BRAINS IN, FISH!" The centurion yelled back.

Legio IX Lavidica was founded just about a week earlier to this day with new weapons, new armor, and new formations. A theory really, to see how fast they could be trained and how well they would be in the field.

A legionary practicing a vertical thrust from his knee to the chest and throat of his potential enemy. His gladius slipped from his grasp and tumbled to the ground fifteen feet away and right next to a centurion. The centurion looked down at the sword and then looked at the legionary whose gladius it was and said, "WHAT WAS THAT! DID YOU FORGET HOW TO USE YOUR HANDS AND FINGERS!"

The centurion bellowed again, "OR MAYBE YOU'RE DUMBER THAN YOU LOOK!" The centurion picked up the gladius and threw it back at the legionaries' feet and said, "PICK IT UP YOU IDIOT!"

The sorry legionary bent down and picked up his gladius and continued practicing as if nothing happened.

"I never knew how funny it is to spectate training like this, seeing fish become legionaries. I always did hate having my ear drums be basically shattered by a centurion though." Said Crassus. "Basically gives me nightmares, but at least when they're through they're one of the best fighting forces in the world, and if not, the best fighting force in the world. Don't you agree, your Majesty?" Crassus asked Imperator Callus.

"Yes I do, others try to copy it, but it just doesn't work out for them as well." Callus answered, looking at General Crassus.

"How are the new technologies turning out general?" Callus asked.

"The bolt throwers are excellent, the legionary crews are getting quite good at using them. They've been hitting stationary targets from five-hundred yards away, sire, dead center." General Crassus replied.

"And as for the pilums, excellent compared to what you wanted. They've been doing what they were made for." Crassus said, looking out at the training camp and back to Callus.

"Compared to what I wanted? What do you mean?" Callus asked.

"They've been doing what they were made for, bending on impact rendering them useless to the enemy, but they've just been a pain to get out of the targets, which is what they are made to do." Crassus answered.

"I see, well other than that, how have they been?" Inquired Callus. "Perfect, our medics say that one hit from one of those can knock a soldier out of combat for the rest of their life, if they're not dead already." Answered Crassus.

"Good, very good." replied Callus.

"FALL IN, FALL IN!" A centurion shouted. "YOU'RE NOT A BALLERINA, AND YOU'RE NOT AT BALLERINA LESSONS EITHER! YOU'RE IN THE LEGIONS!"

Callus chuckled a little bit at that last one. *A ballerina huh? That's new, and I don't think that it's going to leave for a while. Not from the insults and definitely not from the recruit.* Callus thought.

"Well I must be on my way, I've got somewhere to be in a few days, probably don't want to be late." Callus said, turning toward Crassus. Crassus banged out a salute, and Callus nodded once in response.

"Uh, if I may, your Majesty?" Crassus asked, looking straight with his shoulders. Callus looked at the man, he was a few inches shorter than Callus with black hair and blue-gray eyes. "Go ahead, what is it?" Callus replied.

"Rumor has it that war is brewing on the northern front, is it true?" Crassus asked, looking at Callus.

"Where did you hear this?" Callus asked, turning to look at Crassus squarely.

Just overheard some fish from that way chit-chatting with each other, sire" Crassus said.

"Hmmm, well I'll tell you this much, tensions are high, and don't tell anyone else about it." Callus said with a matter of fact tone. "Of course, your Majesty." He saluted again, and Callus nodded again and strode out the door where his bodyguards were awaiting him.

In the background as he was walking to his coach that awaited him he could hear a centurion bellow, "TEAMWORK YOU IDIOTS, TEAMWORK!" Then another one said, "I'M BEGINNING TO THINK THAT THE REST OF YOU ARE BEING STUPEFIED BY ROSTERUS OVER HERE! YOU ALL ARE BEGINNING TO ACT LIKE HIM!"

As he climbed into his coach he saw his bodyguards mount onto their horses. He looked at the driver and said, "Alright let's go."

"Yes, your excellency." Replied the coach driver, and the coach began to move.

The coach was like a regular wagon, but it had a steel rim and doors into the back where the passengers would sit, it was covered in wood planks with windows in the doors, there was one door on each side and two bench like seats in the front and the back with cushions on them, large enough to fit a maximum of three people on each bench, that was is they weren't either scrawny like a twig or just fat, and it was covered with a roof.

As they began to leave he heard another centurion yell, "YOU WON'T BE COMPLAINING WHEN I'M DONE WITH YOU, YOU SWINE! DO YOU EVEN KNOW WHAT THAT MEANS?!" Callus supposed that the poor legionary said no, or just didn't say anything at all and froze because the next thing he heard was, "IT

MEANS PIG, YOU FATSO! NOW GET BACK IN THERE AND WORK OFF SOME OF THOSE FAT ROLLS!"

Callus smirked at that one. *These centurions are coming up with whole new insults, almost as if they were just waiting for the perfect time to say them, even though they thought up the insult a few weeks ago, or maybe months. Just had them brewing in their mind for a while so that they could get some seasoning or maybe tenderness to their insults when they said them, or more like bellowed them, at the new recruits.* Callus thought.

He inhaled slowly and continued thinking, *a long day, or a very long several days because I'm going to Corinos for the next meeting and that's a few days' travel, then the meeting, then the next few days on the way back.*

He looked out the window at the landscape, there was a forest in the distance and grassland with a few shrubs and bushes here and there. It wasn't perfectly flat, it had a few small hills and ditches, but one could definitely see that spring was blooming quite well that year.

One could see the birds above the trees flying around looking for a good spot to land, and there hadn't been snow for about a week, which was a relief. It was still nice and early in the morning and that meant one's nose would freeze and fall off, but the sun was in just the right spot to shine through the doors window and into his eyes though making him change to another seat.

The grass was green and beginning to grow and the flowers began to bloom and the bees were hunting for pollen to bring back to their hive for food. The sky was blue and a hint of faded purple with the morning sun. He could also hear the running of a river nearby, they were about to cross over the bridge. He straightened his back to his seat, leaned his head back, and closed his eyes to sleep. He didn't go to sleep immediately, he sat there with his eyes closed for a few minutes thinking. He lifted his legs to rest on the opposite bench of the coach, folded his arms and went to take in deep breaths and blow them out again, slowly. A few minutes passed and he fell to sleep.

Chapter

2

Calpos Daentious, the head of the military board of the Republic of Farrius, Daentious was walking to the senatorial court in Zamos, the capital of Farrius, he was a tall slender man with a short cropped red haircut and a closely shaved red beard.

When he arrived at the court he bowed his head and said in a stern voice, "You asked for me, your Honesty?"

"Yes, we have received the letter we have been waiting for." Volkar said. Volkar was the representative or speaker of the senate. He sat front and center in his deep purple robes, which was the color of Farrius, and was an older man reaching the end of his late prime.

"We want you to take this scroll to the next standardized meeting and get an answer before you return. Bring the answer back to us as soon as possible, we believe things are in motion that will change the world forever." Volkar said, gesturing towards the scroll and a silver plate brought by a servant.

Daentious picked up the scroll and bowed his head again and said, "It will be done." Then he walked out of the court and to his carriage that awaited him in front of the building, the carriage was dark purple, just like the senator's robes.

The carriage driver opened the door for him and nodded his head once firmly. "Sir." said the driver. Daentious nodded once in return saying, "Thank you." He then stepped into the carriage and sat in the back seat, still holding the scroll in his right hand. He then put the scroll on the seat opposite of him and folded his arms staring at it. It bore the stamp mark of Senator Volkar, with a purple ribbon keeping it rolled up.

The driver shut the carriage door and walked over and hopped up onto the driver's seat of the carriage, picked up the reigns and secured them tightly and whipped them once and the horses began pulling the carriage out of the courtyard and to the city gates which were in sight of the senatorial courts front doors, being directly lined up with each other. The driver directed the horses around the fountain in the center of the courtyard and down the street heading for the gates of Zamos.

As Daentious sat looking at the scroll for a moment he mused, *I wonder… what could be important enough that it had to come to the standardized meeting of the military leaders of this alliance? Much less be this much of a secret that I was called to pick it up personally to take it there, and then to report back as soon as possible.*

He shrugged and looked out the carriage window, which was right next to where he sat in the carriage. One could sit upright and look straight to his/her left or right and see out of either of the windows. There were a total of four windows on this carriage, two in the front and two in the back, each window was about one foot by one foot.

From inside the carriage he could hear the chattering of citizens outside on the street, the horse's hooves upon the stone ground pulling the carriage. The sun was high in the sky around noon in the spring and there were storm clouds in the distance.

As they pulled up to the gates the carriage stopped and a guard walked up to the window to the left of Daentious, Daentious was on the right side of the carriage. The guard walked around the rear and up to the window nearest to Daentious, looked at him and said, "Open the gates." He then looked back to Daentious and nodded his head saying, "Sir." Daentious returned the gesture and then the carriage began moving again.

He had four days until the meeting, just barely more time than needed to get there by sea, which was the route he was going to take. He never really liked the sea, which was probably the main reason he was head of the military board instead of the naval board.

The carriage passed through the gates, and the gates closed a few moments later as they came to a crossroads where they turned south towards the river Alzeirs, and the port settlement of Foreseus.

Daentious decided that then was the time to catch some sleep. He slumped in his seat, kept his arms folded, closed his eyes, and bowed his head. It took him longer than he usually does to fall asleep, but that may be due to the long rest he had on the way back to the capital from the military outpost of Tharshatus.

He was on inspection tour for the last three months and dealt with more fresh recruits than he would like to ever meet, but he got them into proper shape, eventually, before he would go to the next bunch of freshies.

He repositioned himself and tried to fall asleep again and then the carriage hit an odd bump in the road, rattling him out of the comfy position. After recovering from the unfortunate bump, he tried again to sleep. He found a decent position and went almost right to sleep.

He awoke a few hours later he assumed, as it was getting dark and he leaned his head out the window and asked the driver, "How much longer to the docks?"

"About one hour sir." The driver replied, and Daentious slid back into the carriage and looked forward at the message on the seat in front of him. He folded his hands and began staring at it again. He licked his lips and inhaled.

After a moment of blankly staring at it not being able to think of anything, he put his elbow on the rim of the carriage window leaning his head on his hand, with his index finger just under his nose covering his mouth. He stared out the window looking at the sky, studying it. It was turning red with the sunset and darkness was setting upon the ground around him.

He leaned out the window a little bit and looked forward ahead of the carriage, where he saw Foreseus and the wide Alzeirs River, it was glistening red and orange with the reflection of the sun upon its surface. He could see boats and ships in the water. Some had their sails down and others didn't, he saw one ship rolling up its sails and preparing to dock.

By the time he arrived it was almost pitch black, except for the torches and candles lighting the streets and houses. His carriage pulled up near one of the piers and stopped.

"My name is Scalious Phoco, and I'm here on Senator Volkar's orders to bring Military board leader, Sir Calpos Daentious to a ship for passage to Corinthus." The driver said to one of the piersmen.

"Alright, you're at the right place, we'll take it from here Phoco." The piersman replied. Someone looked into the window that Daentious sat next to and nodded his head once and said, "Good evening, Sir."

"Good evening." replied Daentious, nodding once back to the man. The man opened the door and stood aside as Daentious got up, picked up the scroll and walked out onto the ground and began to stretch his legs as the driver and piersman exchanged some words. The carriage door shut behind him and the carriage went off. Daentious exhaled slowly as he walked slowly around.

"Sir, as soon as you're ready we'll depart." The man said, standing to attention.

"Alright, I'll board in a moment." Daentious said, looking at the man. The man nodded his head once firmly, turned around and began giving orders to the others to make ready for departure.

Daentious looked up at the dark sky, not a lot of stars were in sight because of the light being illuminated from the docks and streets of Foreseus. He could see the moons though, there were both moons this night one being a shallow crescent and the other a near half lit moon, the one half lit was larger than the other and a little bit brighter, but maybe that was because there was more sunlight being reflected off of it due to its larger mass.

He continued to walk around in badly formed circles before turning and walking toward the man who he talked to before. "Alright I'm ready." He said to the man nodding his head.

The man nodded his head and said, "Follow me sir." And turned to lead him to the ship.

The ship was not a war ship, but it was not quite a merchant ship nor a fishing boat. The man walked past the plank that connected the ship to the pier and turned around and gestured up the plank. Daentious looked up the plank to the ship, inhaled sharply and began to walk up the plank to the upper deck of the ship. The man turned and began to walk up behind Daentious.

Daentious stepped off the plank and onto the ship and stepped aside for the man behind him to step onto the ship. "Alright, detach and let's get going!" He bellowed to the crew members. He turned to Daentious and lifted his right hand to the rear of the ship and said, "If you'll follow me sir." Daentious nodded and followed in suit toward a cabin near the stern of the ship, where the man opened a door and stepped aside for Daentious to walk through.

"Here's your cabin sir, and my name is Plaisdon, sir, I'm the captain of this vessel. Call for me if you need anything." Daentious nodded and said, "Thank you, Captain Plasidon." He then walked into the cabin and Plasidon shut the door behind him.

A candle was already lit and it looked like the cabin was also recently cleaned. Daentious looked to his left and where a bunk lay for him to sleep, then right in front of him was a desk facing the door where the candle lay lit on one side. Daentious walked over to the desk and put the scroll in one of the drawers, snuffed out the candle light and sat on his bunk. He then took off his boots and lay down on his back and went to fall asleep as the ship began to rock back and forth and the sound of waves crashing against the side of the ship got a little louder as the ship picked up speed.

He never really liked being on a ship over upon the waves, it always felt crowded even when it wasn't. The fact that there was really nowhere to run if the ship was under attack was no comfort either. It was either fight and win or fight and lose, which usually meant death. Granted the crew could turn the ship around before any physical contact was made, but if physical contact was made, it meant you basically fought to the death with your attacker. Other than that he didn't mind it, the rocking back and forth part kind of sucked, but it wasn't too big of a deal for him. It wasn't like he was going to get sea sick like others do, but it was quite annoying at first, until one got used to it.

He shifted his position in his bunk/cot thing within a moment or two, with his right arm over his forehead, bent at the elbow, and his right hand dangling by his left shoulder. His right leg was bent, and it slowly sagged down to the surface of the bunk, he fell asleep.

Chapter

3

Callus awoke to the sound of hooves striking upon the stone outside his coach. He began to sit upright in his seat and looked out the window on the door. He was nearly to the palace within Ecstallia, the capital of Praetoria, where he was to pick up another wagon that was filled with a bolt thrower and some pilums that he was going to take to the meeting.

Every four or five meetings, all members of the alliance would share any technology they wished to share and that they had. This technology could begin to reshape the world in Calluses eyes and would continue to reshape it for generations.

The coach stopped and the driver walked around to one of the doors and opened it for Callus to walk out through. The driver saluted and bowed his head upon seeing Imperator Callus and said, "My Liege."

"At ease." Callus said, stepping out of the coach. The driver then closed the door behind him and stood at the side of the coach.

Callus walked over to wagons that were being loaded up and asked, "Are you ready?" One of the engineers looked up, stood to attention, and saluted crisply and said, "My Liege, we're just finishing up."

Callus nodded and said, "Very good." Callus then turned around and walked back to his coach where the driver awaited.

Callus paced around the coach for a moment until the engineer that he spoke to before walked up and saluted, "We're ready my Liege." Callus nodded and looked at the driver, nodded his head and the driver opened the door to the coach, nodded his head and said, "My Liege."

Callus nodded his head in return and stepped up into the coach settling down on the same seat he was in before. The driver shut the door to the coach.

Callus sighed and relaxed a bit, lowering his shoulders and shutting his eyes. He opened his eyes a couple seconds later and a servant said, "My Liege?" Gesturing with a small plate of beverages. "For the trip if you'd like." Holding out the plate from outside the coach.

Callus reached for it and took it, setting it on the seat beside him and said, "Thank you." Nodding his head to the man. The man then strode off back to the palace from whence he came. The coach then began to move with the wagon behind them heading for the eastern gates of the city.

Callus looked down at the plate, it had a bundle of grapes, some bread, a few varieties of cheese and crackers.

Callus sighed looking at the plate and picked up a white slice of cheese and began to eat it, biting off a corner, or more like a half of it or so. After a few moments of snacking a spot on the silver plate was uncovered and Callus could see his reflection in it.

I should probably get a haircut. Callus thought, running his hand through his dark brown hair. His hair was groomed from front to the back and was a few inches thick. Since Callus thought himself a smooth shaven type of guy, he shaved about every one or two weeks.

It was a little disappointing to get used to little fuzzy hairs on his face then shave them off a few days later. He always found himself stroking from the top of his jaw to his chin with one hand as if he had a beard, but he never really let his beard grow out for more than about a month. When he did let it grow though it was brown like his hair.

As they reached the gate one of the guards stationed at it hollered, "Halt!" And the coach abruptly stopped, not that it was even going all too fast, it felt like it was actually going quite slow, but maybe that was just Callus. One of the guards walked up to the side of the coach and knocked saying, "Sire?" Callus leaned forward and peered out of the window to look at the man.

He was a younger man, probably in his mid-twenties. He had black hair and no facial hair, his hair was cut into a legionnaire cut. He was a little shorter than most and a little smaller as well.

He banged out a salute and said, "My Liege, we'll have you on your way soon." Callus nodded his head and the guard turned and began walking over to the gates, balling out orders to the men to open the gates. Callus poked his head out a little as his eyes followed the man.

That guy got to be new, didn't recognize him, or maybe I'm just too stupid to remember. I don't know. Callus mused.

"Sir, for the health of my own heart and the health of everyone else's, please retract your head from the window and sit back down within the coach." A mounted guard said to Callus. Callus looked up and one of his bodyguards was just ten feet from him still on his mount. Callus grinned at him and sat back down in his seat.

"Thank you sir." The guard replied to Callus's movement.

The gates began to open and the coach started forward again. The hooves beating upon the stone were almost in unison at first, then a moment later they all lined up perfectly.

Odd, how would that work, were they practicing behind my back or something? Callus thought, taking in the rhythm of the clicks and clacks from outside the coach.

He leaned his head back and blew out a sigh, looking up at the ceiling of the coach. He then looked back down at the silver plate on the seat next to him, and began plucking the grapes off of their vine.

It didn't take him long to finish eating the grapes from the plate, but once he was finished with them he went to the bread, breaking off piece by piece and shoving them into his mouth and eating them one by one. While he was eating the bread he stared out of the coaches' window at the angle he sat in the coach at. The sun was beginning to fall to the horizon and the air began to grow colder with the hour. Once he was done scarfing down the food from his plate he moved the plate farther aside and slumped down in his seat, folded his arms and tried to go to sleep. His body didn't quite want to go to sleep though, or maybe it was his brain blankly thinking, and was somehow someway keeping him awake. He repositioned himself in his seat, he stretched out his legs across the coach and crossed them, he then bowed his head more deeply and tried again. After a few minutes of waiting patiently in the same position, leaning against the side of the coach, he fell asleep.

Chapter

4

Daentious was sitting at the desk that was with the cabin that Captain Plasidon gave him. The boat rocked back and forth, not that it made him sick, but that it just wasn't something he liked. There was a knock at the door and Daentious said, "Yes?"

"Breakfast is ready sir. Do you want it in there or do you want to wait?" said a scruffy voice, almost as if he had a sore throat, but not quite like it. "Bring it in please." Daentious said back to the man. The door opened and a breeze that was just about on the verge of being unholy blew in and hit Daentious like an unpleasant hammer blow to the face. Daentious squinted his eyes so that it wouldn't seem as much like he was crying like a child. The man closed the door and walked over to Daentious's desk. "Here you go sir." The man said enthusiastically and panting a little bit.

There were either droplets of sweet or sea water on his face and black facial hair. He had dark brown hair that was all roughed up by the wind, Daentious supposed. His windows were closed through the night to keep out the weather as much as possible.

Daentious took the plate and nodded, "Thank you." The metal was warm to the touch and there was a lid covering the inner portion of the plate where the food was. "You're welcome sir... Would you like anything else?" The man said, blinking. By this point it wasn't just hard to understand what the man was saying but it sounded like it hurt him every time he talked and was beginning to hurt Daentious's throat just by listening to him, but he wanted to know something.

"Yes, where are we and are we near a storm?"

"Uhh. We are a few miles off the coast near Malos, and no we are not near a storm, but there is a storm to the west of us and heading toward us." The man continued, "We're out running it though thanks to its wind, it's a cold front by the way, so it's colder out there than usual, sir." The man said, nodding vigorously and grinning at Daentious. Daentious stared at the man for a minute before saying, "Thank you, that'll be all."

"Alright sir! Good day!" The man said, also being very vigorous with his words. He then turned around to the door, opened it and closed it as another breeze of unpleasantry came through and right into Daentious's face. Daentious flinched at the last one as if he was hit by a physical blow. He lifted the tray cover and looked down at the warm food on the plate, not that it needed to be hot, but it is probably better when it was hot.

The plate was of military standard dishing, two pieces of ham around five inches in diameter and two pieces of bread about three inches in diameter.

Daentious started with one of the ham pieces, ripping it into two pieces, one bigger than the other, and ate the smaller one first. As he sat there eating he was looking at military formations and equipment that were written upon pieces of paper on his desk. The first one was on new equipment that neighboring military soldiers were utilizing, it looked almost like a house with wheels and what looked like a battering ram covered within it. *A new version of the battering ram?* Daentious wondered. *It's got a roof like structure covering it from enemy fire, I'd think. How would it be used exactly? How would they move the heavy log that was the battering ram back and forth? Pulleys maybe, that would be the most reasonable explanation.*

He picked up the other piece of ham and began eating it.

The ship rocked harder than it usually did and Daentious heard men shouting from outside. He looked up and the ship rocked again and just as hard, sliding the plate and lid to his left, almost falling off of the side of the desk. He grasped the plate and lid and repositioned them in the center of his desk, putting the lid back over the food and pressing the plate down upon the papers and to the desktop.

Men continued to shout and scream, as if they were in the midst of battle, shouting out their defiance towards the enemy. He could hear heavy footsteps, and a lot of them on the deck of the ship. Then he could hear metal clashing on metal and more shouting and yelling.

He stood up, picked up the plate of food, placed it on the ground, grabbed his sheathed sword, belted it on and sped walked to the door of the cabin. He opened the door and unsheathed his sword and strode out of the cabin onto the deck.

The sky behind the ship was dark gray with a storm and the sea was rough with high waves. There was a black painted ship to his left or the port side of the ship as he faced the bow. Men were jumping onto the ship he was and were assaulting the crew members of his ship, no not just men, but women too. Their ship was fastening itself to the one Daentious was on with ropes as thick as one's forearm.

Other than the storm behind them it was a sunny day. One of the mob like attackers, pirates most likely possible to be mercenaries, went after Daentious. The attacker screamed out his warcry and swung his sword at Daentious. Daentious parried the blow to his right and swung his sword at the man's neck, severing off of the rest of his body, and he dropped to the deck boards. Daentious now covered with blood on his right side. He glided forward toward the next one nearest to him, who was fighting with a crew member of the ship he was on. He reached him and cut his arm off at the center of his forearm with a downstroke of his sword, and let his momentum carry his sword into the assumed pirate's leg near his knee, cutting into his knee but not severing it. The attacker screamed in high-pitched agony and fell to the deck. The friendly crewmember thrust his sword into the pirate's abdomen.

"Why thank you sir!" Said the friendly crew member to Daentious, as a smile grew on his face. "What's your name, and what's going on!" Asked Daentious looking down to the friendly crewmate. "Shaetus Coursus sir, and we're under attack by marauders from the south sir!" Answered Coursus.

Thunder rumbled in the distance as a few more marauders cut through an outnumbered crewmate and moved towards them. Daentious moved towards them and Coursus followed in suit. Daentious blocked the first invader's attack, threw it to the side and thrust his sword into his throat, drawing nothing but a gasp from the man and a long spray of blood and he withdrew his sword and the man fell to the deck.

Coursus moved in and blocked a stroke aimed at Daentious's throat and then pressed the attack on the marauder. The other marauder moved in towards Daentious with a ferocious scream and thrust for his stomach. Daentious parried the attack, and landed a blow to the marauders face with his fist. Coursus continued to fight the other invader. The marauder swiped at his upper arm and nicked his arm as Coursus felt a burning sensation in his left arm where the swipe got him. He faltered a step and backed into the railing on the port side of the ship. The marauder saw and took the chance, thrusting his sword at Coursus's heart.

It took Daentious a moment more of fighting before he saw that his nemesis was a woman. He faltered as well but recovered his balance in time to parry at swing for his lower abdomen and seized the marauders arm with one hand and gripped the womans hand hard loosening the marauders grip on her sword, she cried in pain falling to her knees as Daentious thrust his sword into her throat near the larynx. Blood shot out of the wound and all over his right arm putting another coat of blood on him as she choked on air due to his sword being in her windpipe.

Daentious whipped his head up to a cry as he pulled his sword from the dead woman's neck and saw the other marauder's sword in Coursus's chest and then saw Coursus shove his sword up through the marauder's body from his nape to his upper back drawing a agonizing scream as he let go of his sword and fell to the ground with Coursus's sword still in the marauder's body. Coursus also fell down to the deck dying. Daentious looked at Coursus's dying body and wiped his sword on the woman's clothing and continued up to the bow of the ship.

More thunder cracked and rumbled in the distant storm as it grew closer. They weren't moving and the storm was closing upon them very quickly. Another uncontested marauder locked his gaze upon Daentious and strode toward him with an ax in his hand instead of a sword like the others he had fought, but it was of no concern for these marauders did not know how to properly fight, not against a trained military. The crew of this ship was outnumbered, but were holding well enough. They wouldn't hold against as many attackers as there were though. They would fall eventually. Most likely before that storm got within range to swallow their ships into the waves though.

Are we not within the Alzeirs River? Do we not still control it? Where were the fleets of Corinos and Praetoria? Daentious thought, moving to attack the invader in front of him. The marauder whirled his ax in his hands and bolted towards Daentious. Daentious sidestepped the marauders initial stroke, and swung his sword at the man's guts, slicing open his lower abdomen allowing his intestines to fall out upon the deck boards.

The ship rocked hard enough again to throw Daentious off of his feet and to the blood stained deck. Then something ruptured out of the waves below and the attacking ship to the port side exploded out of the water and into the air into two main parts and splinters ranging from the size of a toothpick to as big as ones the size of a man's arm flying in every direction.

A piece of wood flew and landed on Daentious's left arm pinning it to the deck. He cried in pain and went to pull it out, and with another cry of pain, pulled the piece of black painted wood out of his arm and threw it scrambling to cover behind the railing as more wood flew and fell down all around the battle warped deck and sea around him.

Cries went out among the ships, all of terror and to the port side of the ship where Daentious resided, a shape appeared and web-like talons with deep blue scales grabbed onto the deck, not crushing the planks, just holding its balance to look over the ship and down at Daentious with dark blue eyes and sniffed.

"You are not of the stench of these marauders. Who are you and what is your purpose in these waters?" Asked the water dragon, eyeing Daentious intensely.

"I am Calpos Daentious, Head of the Military Board of the Republic of Farrius. I am enroute to Corinthus of Corinos for the Alzeirs Alliance's standardized meeting." Replied Daentious.

"Mmmm." Hummed the dragon as another thunderous explosion erupted from the other side of the ship near the bow and more cries of terror went out, then they were drowned out by howls of defiant victory and glee.

"You and your ship will follow us there. Tell your captain of this, or show him unto my direction or show me unto his." The dragon said, looking from the area of the explosion, to the storm, and then back to Daentious. Daentious nodded and the dragon fell back under the surface of the water.

"Sir! Sir, are you alright!" A crewman shouted running towards Daentious. He looked at the crewman and nodded, lifting his arm to grab onto the crewman's arm and lift himself up with the help of the sailor. He winced as he stood up to his feet and asked, "Where is Captain Plasidon? I need to see him immediately." "He's on the bow of the ship, I'll take you there." Said the crewman.

A moment passed as Daentious and the crew member stalked toward the ship's bow to the Captain. Another moment passed before they found Captain Plasidon wounded in the right arm, just a slight cut on his upper arm, and his left cheek scarred with a single cut opening up his cheek from chin to ear lobe.

He was barking out orders to all his men. "Captain!" The crewman with Daentious called. Captain Plasidon turned and looked at the pair of them and shouted, "Medic! Get this man a medic!" Pointing at Daentious.

"Captain, there is a water dragon that wants to see you off of the port side. He says to follow him through these waters." Daentious said to the Captain. Captain Plasidon nodded once, turning to the port side and began walking over to that side giving what looked like his second in command an order and continued walking over to the port side.

A man bearing a medical bag at his side took a hold of Daentious softly and led him to sit by the railing on the starboard side and began tending to his wounded arm.

Captain Plasidon reached the port side and looked up and down the ship and then spotted the water stirring near the ship and the dragon from before arose to face him squarely, "Are you the captain of this ship?" Asked the dragon. "Yes, yes I am, and who are you?" Inquired Plasidon, raising his chin at the dragon. "I am a protector of these waters, and if what Calpos Daentious said is true then you shall follow me and my companion to Corinthus." Said the dragon, looking down at Plasidon. "How do I know that you will not betray me and my crew and send us to our deaths?" Plasidon asked, raising an eyebrow at the dragon. "I give you my word." The dragon returned.

"The word of a dragon who will not tell me his name is not a word I want to willingly trust."

The dragon inhaled, "Very well, Captain." The dragon continued, "If I give you my name will you trust in my word?"

Plasidon inhaled as well, then exhaled slowly. "To the best of my ability, I will. Only because you haven't shown aggression towards my ship and crew."

"Very well, my name is Zorok, and I am aligned with King Agamemnon of Corinos," said Zorok. "You are aligned with King Agamemnon?" asked Plasidon, looking up at Zorok. "Yes, we have so far asked to remain hidden." Zorok answered, looking at the storm coming in from the west.

"There is not much time left to waste Captain, we must go now." Zorok said, leaning forward towards Plasidon, his voice deepening from his regular mildly toned voice to a near growling voice. "I couldn't agree more, Zorok, lead the way." Plasidon said, nodding once at Zorok. He then turned and walked toward the stern of the ship. Zorok slipped back into the river and forward to the bow of the ship with a little bit of his back poking out of the water.

Daentious was returned to his cabin and laid down upon his bunk. He lay there looking up at the ceiling of the cabin thinking. *How long have these pirates been terrorizing these waters, where was the Praetorian fleet? Where were the fleets of Corinos? And that dragon, I didn't know that there were dragons in these waters. They're usually farther out into the ocean.* He inhaled slowly, "Huh." He said, licking his lips in thought.

Plasidon stood at the stern of the ship upon the conning tower, looking out at the river. He saw Zorok and made eye contact, he nodded once and Zorok nodded once back turning his head forward, and beginning to worm forward through the water. The sails fell down on the masts of the ships and caught the wind moving the ship forward. Starting almost unnoticeably slow, then began to pick up speed with the wind of the storm at their backs propelling them forward. He looked down at the deck at the bodies that still lay dead on the boards, the crewmen throwing them overboard into the water to decompose.

He frowned, staring intensely at the corpses that lay strung out like scattered grain upon stone, the deck planks soaked with blood and guts, stenching up the air that the wind blew it to up at the bow of the ship. Not many people would probably be up at the bow of the ship because of how bad it would smell. Plasidon inhaled, and exhaled shortly after looking up at the now darkening sky due to the storm closing in upon them.

"Spallius." Beckoned Plasidon. A short, buffy man strolled up to Plasidon, stood to attention and said, "Captain."

"Take over for me, if anything important occurs, or if a dragon comes asking for me, get me immediately. Got it?" Plasidon asked, turning towards Spallius. "Yes Captain." Spallius returned. Plasidon turned and moved out of the spot he occupied and Spallius stepped in his place.

Plasidon walked down the flight of stairs that connected the bridge and the deck below and went to find the medic that attended to Daentious earlier, or really any medico for that matter. He found one near the center of the ship tending to an injured man.

The man's arm was broken and the bone of his forearm was sticking out like a needle through a cloth while the cloth was being mended. The medic got the man to his feet and began walking him to a nearby cabin, where they kept the rest of the injured men, until they were healed.

The medic saw Captain Plasidon walking towards him and said, "Sir, do you need something?" Plasidon looked at the broken arm and then looked at the medic and asked, "Yes, where is Sir Daentious and may I speak with him?"

The medic said, "He's back at his cabin, sir." Plasidon nodded his thanks and turned toward the stern of the ship where the cabin that Daentious occupied was.

He reached the cabin and knocked on the door asking, "Sir Daentious, it's the Captain. May I enter?" He heard some shuffling and then a voice said, "Yes Captain, come on in." Plasidon opened the door and saw Daentious laying on his bunk, with his left arm bandaged up where the wood shard impaled him.

"Are you alright Sir Daentious?" Plasidon asked, looking at Daentious. "I'll live, what do you want?" Daentious asked. "Sorry for the delay, we are now renewing our course towards Corinthus for your meeting Sir Daentious." Plasidon said, folding his hands behind his back.

"Thank you Captain, will that be all?" Daentious asked. "I also just wanted to say thank you for your help on the deck today." Plasidon replied bowing at the hips just slightly. "No problem." Daentious said. Plasidon shut the door behind him as he left the cabin, turned to his left and towards his own cabin.

Chapter

5

So far only one storm has passed over Classis II Oceanianic on their long voyage out of the Alzeirs river and to the north, destination: Port Reaver. Goal: Join up with Classis I Glacius and await further orders. Admiral Bortus was in his cabin on the flag ship of the fleet, a Tower Trireme, a vast war vessel with three banks of rows and approximately one-hundred and twenty feet in length. The sails bore the scarlet colors of Praetoria along with the purple flag design of a legionary shield and a curve on either side of it as if they were protecting the flanks of the shield in the center. They lost two ships in the storm and another one was crippled slightly, not enough to sink it, but enough to slow it down.

Bortus was eating his breakfast as they passed through the Alzeirs river, on the southern coast of the Corrue Peninsula, where Praetoria and her allies stood near the inner tip of the river Alzeirs, where the Alzeirs flow out of the mountains and towards the ocean.

Their course took them around the peninsula and to Port Reaver on the northern coast of Praetoria. Luckily the worst of the sailing was behind them as they were now entering mid to late spring. They had the wind to their backs for now, but that would change when they turned east up the coast. When that happened the slaves would do their part rowing the fleet toward its destination. There would be wind, but not as much as they were having while they were heading west. The slaves were resting for the moment to keep their strength up, but every hour they would be brought out of their sleeping holds and stay warmed up and active in case of an emergency. They would row for a half hour before being permitted to rest again.

The slaves did well for their tasks, it wasn't like they were condemned to slavery for life, although some were. Imperator Callus and his fathers before him made the law system to fuel the slave market. If one committed a minor crime, they would be sentenced to three years in slavery and if they did anything foul within slavery it just extended their sentence. If one committed a major crime, like stealing very valuable items and a lot of them, they would be sentenced to a few years to several years depending on how large the crime was or how much items they stole. If one committed an Imperium offense, like murder, which is killing with probable cause or just cause in all, they were sentenced to life in slavery. So the ones who killed on purpose before were harder to deal with than the ones who accidentally killed or just committed a lower level of crime. Most of the slaves were very good listeners and did what they were told, if it was reasonably within the jurisdictions of the law, and then they would be free after their sentence.

It wasn't really a good thing that there were a lot of slaves, because that meant there was a lot of crime in Praetoria, but it is also a good thing meaning they would most likely never run short on slaves to row their ships across the waves. In time of war though there were still plenty of slaves whenever a battle was won. A slave master would never have to worry about accidentally putting one of the very insubordinate slaves down like a dog, there were still repercussions for the slave waster that did it though, but most officers didn't care all too much as long as it was one of the troublemakers.

The vessel rocked back and forth to the waves as Bortus finished up his meal, and stood up to walk out onto the sunny deck, he thought anyways, he really hoped that it was sunny. Not like blistering about to melt your skin off hot, but warm and welcoming. Granted the blistering sun that decided to show up every other day on every other week. He opened his cabin door and poked out for a brief moment, checking the temperature before deciding whether to walk out and check on his fleet or to just wait in his cot until something arose to his attention that would pull him out of his cabin.

It wasn't cold, but it sure wasn't warm enough for just the thought of a smile. The sun wasn't out, just behind about fifty different clouds it felt like. He put on his overcoat and walked out onto the deck, he could hear the oar headers, the soldiers that maintained the rhythm of proper oar strokes from the slaves, beating their mallots down upon the wooden stand in front of them when they looked down the ship facing the slaves. They were beating out the rhythm for a steady pace, and the oars followed in suit moving the ships ahead at a steady pace, the wind made the ships go a little faster than the regular steady pace the slaves would move the vessels at.

Bortus walked over to the rear tower where he usually stood when looking over the fleet. He reached the stairs and the guards stationed there stood to attention and saluted, fist to their heart. Bortus nodded once and climbed up the ladder to the upper level of the tower. The guards went back to their at ease stance and kept their eyes peeled, not that there were any threats or dangers in the past few weeks, except for that storm, they stood almost on their toes as if something was about to happen and they were just waiting to spring into action.

Bortus reached the top of the tower and looked out at the fleet upon the vast blue ocean. The guards on the tower saluted as well with the rest of the men up there, Bortus came to his feet and nodded, looking at one then another then another, all the men relaxed and one said, "Good morning sir. Hope you have a good night and a tasty breakfast."

Bortus turned and looked at the front of the ship and said, "Yes I did have a good night's rest, and the breakfast was excellent." The wind blew steadily at his back, from the southeast to the northwest, and punched into the sails and blew them out in a just more than slight curve.

"How is the rest of the fleet?" Bortus asked, still looking forward. "All reports say that all is well sir" The man who talked previously replied. Bortus was just beginning to think walking outside his cabin was a worse idea than he thought. He debated about turning around and climbing back down the ladder and walking right back into his cabin, where it wasn't really house warm, but was warmer than up there. "Very well." Bortus said and added, "I'm going to go back into my cabin to do some things, knock if something major occurs."

"Yes sir." The man said, saluting. Bortus turned around and walked over to where the ladder was near the back of the tower, leaving enough room for a few men to walk past in case they ever needed to. He climbed down the ladder and the guards at the bottom saluted again. Bortus nodded once and walked off toward his cabin.

He opened the door and closed it behind him. He stood there for a moment before blowing out an exhale and walking over to his desk where his candle still held onto life, quite well actually.

He sat down at his desk and looked to a drawer on his right side. He opened the drawer and pulled out some letters. He put them on his desk, picked one up, and leaned back in his chair and opened up the letter, or more like reopened the letter because it was already opened. The letter said, 'To: Admiral Bortus, From Basous Orias.' He pulled out the paper that was contained in the envelope. Then he moved his chair so that he could see the writing in the light of his desk candle and put his right elbow on the right side arm of the chair and put his right hand over his mouth as if he was resting his head upon his thumb, using his arm as if it was a support to hold his head upright, almost, and sighed deeply then began to read the paper in his left hand.

Chapter

6

The sun was setting in the west as Calluses' coach and bodyguards neared the border between Praetoria and Corinos. They stopped to let the horses rest and to stretch their legs, his bodyguards didn't really stretch their legs though, they more of just watched him stretch his legs, they probably don't even have real legs, they probably have manikin legs, because they seemed to be unbothered by sitting on a saddle atop their mounts for days. Even then they didn't let him leave outside of twenty feet of the coach, as if they were his mother and he was a three year old toddler that didn't know any better. Every time he went a little too far from the coach one of the guards cleared his throat and just looked at him and then said, "Sire, please stay by the coach, for your safety."

And they said that exact line every time, with almost the same soft/stern voice resonating from each one of their mouths separately, almost as if they just had set lines that their vocabulary was set to and they were all spoken by the same guy just from the different mouths and bodies. It wasn't annoying, but it was definitely boring. They all acted this way, like it is their job and all, but it was still boring.

A few more moments passed before the driver said "Your Majesty, whenever you're ready." Callus turned around and looked at the man because the tone he said it in almost sounded like he was standing there for a while, and he could have been. Callus stood in the same spot for about ten minutes looking in the same direction, stroking what used to be his small prickly like beard before the driver spoke.

"Alright, what time should we be there if we leave now and make no more stops?" Callus asked, folding his hands behind his back walking towards the driver.

"About nine O'clock tomorrow morning, sire." The driver answered, opening the coach door for Callus to enter.

"Alright, thank you." Callus said, nodding once to the driver.

"No problem sire. Will there be anything else?" The driver inquired.

Callus shook his head and climbed into the coach without another word, he sat in the back most part of the coach, on the bench that looked forward in the direction the driver faced. The driver shut the door and walked over and up to his seat of the coach clutching the reins in his hand and urging the pair of horses forward along the road. His bodyguards formed back up around the coach and mainly behind it and began following the road as well.

Callus leaned his head back, looked up to the ceiling of the coach and thought. He licked his teeth and pursed his lips, he then lowered his head back down to look straight forward, sitting straight in the seat he occupied with his hands on his knees. He then folded his arms and relaxed and, thanks to the growing darkness, fell asleep.

He awoke a few hours later, or more like several hours later, because the sun was rising in the east, or so he thought anyways, he couldn't know for sure since he was in an enclosed coach with only two windows, where he had to lean forward to see out the window nearest him, but as for the other window, all he had to do was look almost straight to his left and he could see almost perfectly out the window where the darkness was retreating and the light was replacing it.

He supposed it was morning due to the blueish purple light illuminating the ground outside, the cold ground nonetheless. He was pretty cold this morning unlike the other mornings, but it was spring after all and the weather seems to act like it doesn't know whether to be warm, cold, or just in between. It was almost never in between, it was usually just cold, freezing cold, warm, or somehow hot, almost like the summer sun.

He leaned forward and looked out the window at one of his guards. He, like the rest of the guards, wore a purple cape with a scarlet underside. Feathers, also scarlet, were embedded in a little metal piece of the helmet that stuck out about two inches and was roughly six inches long to hold the feathers in properly, they weren't like chicken feathers, they were like the feathers found in pillows, all fluffy and soft. "Guard." Callus said, looking at the man. The guard turned to his left to look at Callus and asked, "Yes, your Majesty?"

"What time is it, do you think?" Callus asked, repositioning himself to look out the window more comfortably. The guard looked toward the east and back at Callus. "It looks like the sun is about to rise, I can see Corinthus in the distance." Callus nodded his head and said, "Thank you, wake me up before we actually reach the city." "Yes my Liege." The guard said, saluting and bowing his head. Callus leaned back into the seat and closed his eyes again.

After a few moments of sleep, Callus awoke to a voice saying, "Your Majesty we're just outside the gates, a few more minutes and we'll be standing in front of them." Callus opened his eyes and blinked, looking up at the voice and he saw the guard he talked to earlier. Callus yawned, "Thank you." And straightened in his seat.

The guard leaned back upright and nudged his horse back to its position alongside the coach. Callus stretched all he could, which was everything, his legs his arms and his back mostly, and straightened back upright in his seat smacking his lips silently, it felt rather hard to keep his eyes open, but he managed it, barely, and folded his arms leaning back against the back of his seat looking out the window to his left.

It was much brighter now than it was before and it almost hurt his eyes just to have them open, much less looking at the brightness. He rolled his shoulders and relaxed a bit. After a minute of staring straight forward at the other side of the coach, a man said, "Stop!" And the coach came to a stop. He heard what sounded like one of his guards say, "We are here protecting our Liege, and he is here for the alliance's meeting." The guard on the wall above the gate inhaled. "What is in the wagon behind the coach?" The Corinosian guard asked. "Some new technologies that I wish to show King Agamemnon and the others later today." Callus said within the coach. One of his body guards that he could see looked at him then at the other one that spoke earlier then back to the gate and the Corinosian guards atop the wall, the one that spoke earlier also looked at the coach and then back at the Corinosian guard atop the gate walls. "Very well Imperator Callus, we'll have this gate opened momentarily." The Corinosian guard said, turning his head around to the guards before and hollered, "Open the gates!" And the gates began to open and the coach began moving again along with the Praetorian guards surrounding it, and the wagon behind them also started to move.

A few moments passed and a guard yelled, "Open the gates! Imperator Callus is here for the meeting!" One of Corinosian guard escorts shouted to the others on the inner wall. The gates opened and the mini convoy passed through and the gates closed shortly after the last of them cleared.

The coach stopped and the driver stepped down off his seat and opened the door nearest Callus. Callus stepped out of the coach and the driver saluted, Callus set foot upon the ground and nodded his head at the driver. The driver removed his arm from his heart and closed the coach door behind Callus. "Imperator Callus, if you'll follow me." A Corinosian guard said, bowing his head and at the waist a little bit, gesturing to his left towards the doors of Agamemnon's palace. Some of the Praetorian guards dismounted and gave their reins to another guard and walked over behind Callus. Callus nodded at the Corinosian guard and the guard began walking and Callus followed with his guards behind him.

They walked down the great hall and turned to their left and walked down another smaller hallway before stopping and the Corinosian guard knocked on the door to their right in an odd sequence and the door was opened by another Corinosian guard wearing linothorax and a white and royal blue cape and soft feathers on his helmet like the ones on the Praetorian guard's helmet but white and royal blue. The guard leading Callus and his men said, "Imperator Callus is here for the King and their meeting today." The other guard nodded and shut the door.

About a minute later the door opened again and the guard on the other side said, "Come in, Imperator." bowing his head to Callus. Callus walked in and his guards stayed outside and stood near the walls out of the way so people passing by could walk through. The other guard shut the door behind Callus and the one that greeted him led him to another doorway that was guarded by another two guards and turned back to the other door that he was guarding before and one of the guards by the next door opened it, stepping out of the way for Callus to walk through. Callus stepped into the war room of Corinthus of Corinos and saw King Agamemnon standing near the beverages table that was within the room.

Agamemnon's war room was much like Calluses, with a moderately large map table in the center of the room and a large archway for dragons to pass through. The archway for the dragons wasn't much larger than a dragon like a door was for a human. Agamemnon turned to look at Callus after pouring himself a cup of wine and the guard that opened the door for Callus shut the door and walked off back to his post by the door. "Callus!" Agamemnon said gleefully, "Do you want any?" Agamemnon swished his cup of wine around implying about what he was exactly asking Callus. "Yes, I think I will have some wine this time at this moment." Callus answered walking over to him.

"You're here a little earlier than usual." Agamemnon said, grabbing another cup and pulling it closer to the edge of the table near where he was standing. Callus walked over and stood next to Agamemnon and looked at the different wines on the table. "Yes, the technologies that I wish to share with everyone were loaded by the time I got back to Ecstallia, so I was quicker than I anticipated." Callus said, finally seeing the wine he was looking for and grasped it in his right hand and poured some into the cup Agamemnon retrieved for him.

"Technologies? How many did you figure out?" Agamemnon asked, raising a brow at Callus and picking up his cup to begin drinking. "Two, and I believe that they will prove to be a great advantage to us in any war that presents itself, if one ever does." Callus said, putting the wine bottle down and picking up his cup of wine to drink. "Two huh? Are you going to make me have to present an advantage to hold on to my spot of popularity?" Agamemnon asked, taking another sip of wine.

Callus chuckled a little and said, "Only if you want to keep it from me." Agamemnon barked out a laugh and turned fully towards Callus. Callus turned towards Agamemnon as well, shifting his wine cup to his left hand. They traded grips with each other and Agamemnon said, "Callus old friend, or should I say young friend since we are not too terribly old as of yet?"

Callus and Agamemnon laughed. "So, were you going to keep me waiting until the others show up?" Agamemnon asked, still grinning at Callus. "I believe it won't hurt their feelings if I show you now. I am quite eager to show you and the others." Callus replied, still smiling at Agamemnon.

They turned for the door Callus walked in from and started for it, walking side by side. "I see you're still shaving your beard quite regularly. Do you just not like looking as manly as possible or what?" Agamemnon asked, looking at Callus. Callus turned to look at him, they were the same height and Agamemnon was allowing his beard to grow longer. "Maybe one day I'll give it a chance." "And maybe one day you'll forget you said that and shave it again." Agamemnon replied, grining. They began laughing and Agamemnon said in a near smug like tone, "Guards, open the door." And the door opened.

They walked through and the guard shut the door behind them. The guards at the next door opened the door and stood to attention, stomping their feet as a form of salute. The Praetorian guards outside the door along with a matching number of Corinosian guards along with them stood to attention, the Praetorian guards slamming their fists to their hearts and the Corinosian guards stomped their feet in suit. Both Agamemnon and Callus nodded their heads in an 'at ease' movement. They turned and the guards lined up in single file behind their corresponding leaders and followed them out of the hallway to the great hall.

"So, where are these technologies you promise?" Agamemnon asked, still looking forward. "Outside, wherever your guards took the wagon and coach that came with me." Callus responded, as the door to the great hall opened and they walked into it. "Alright." Agamemnon said, turning to look at another guard, "Guard tell Arros to bring the Praetorian wagon to the... Where is the best spot for these technologies, do you say?" "For looking at them almost anywhere, but for using one of them, outside. The other can be used inside." Callus answered. "I see. Tell him to bring them to the war room and to leave them there." Agamemnon told the guard he beckoned earlier.

"The engineers with the wagon will need to go with to set up one of the items within it." Callus said, looking over at Agamemnon. "Very well, allow them to set it up in the war room where it fits, assign a squad of guards to them so that they won't incidentally do something rash." Agamemnon said, looking from Callus to the guard. "Yes my Liege." The guard said, stomping one of his feet to the ground before speed walking off. "I wish to show you something while they get your technology ready." Agamemnon said, looking at Callus. "Lead the way." Callus replied, the guards behind them continued to follow them through the palace. Agamemnon looked at one of the guards and said, "Get a coach ready at the southern inner gates." The guard saluted and hurried off.

A few moments of walking through the palace and they turned up at the southern end of it, walking out the door and onto the stone of the southern courtyard. The guards stomped out a salute and the citizens in the courtyard in front of them, nearest to them anyway, turned and saw them walking towards them. One of the guards said in a louder than normal voice, but not quite a shout, "Clear a path for the King." And all of the citizens in the courtyard turned to look and then scurried to get out of the way and fell to one knee with their heads bowed down to King Agamemnon.

One moment the whole courtyard was full and busy with people going about their day and the next, it was quiet and there was a path from the doors to the palace to the inner wall gates. Agamemnon and Callus strode through the empty space and out the reopened gates to a waiting coach with the white and royal blue colors of Corinos.

A guard held open the door to the coach and saluted as they passed and stepped into the coach, the guard shut the door and hopped onto the upper passenger seat next to the driver who urged the horses forward down the street. Callus and Agamemnon sat opposite of each other. "So, what is this thing you wish to show me?" Callus asked.

Chapter

7

It was a warm sunny day, or a warmer than usual sunny day, in the mountain range under the control of the Kingdom of Jurrunt. There were no clouds overhead for miles upon miles, and the wind blew at a slight breeze. The mountain range itself was referred to as 'The Screaming Spires' due to the wind always blowing throughout them. The mountains themselves weren't too high in elevation, like it rained more than it snowed, until it was winter, it snowed a lot in the winter.

Down on the rocky plains a couple miles from the base of the mountains was a black spot in the brown rock, an army of dwarves to be precise, and they were camped and quite lazy for an army in the open. The guards that were stationed were yawning regularly and were leaning on their shields, spears, swords, and axes. Their armor was in terrible shape, rusted and stained with what looked like... not blood, but something else Hevtur didn't want to know about, it was probably something like stomach fluids, which would be very disgusting.

Hevtur stood to the left of a rock platform where one of his scouts lay watching the dwarven army from behind cover. Hevtur was just peeking around the rock, using a form of wind magic that bent the light into the desired form to create a sight like a magnifying glass would. He was still waiting on his scales to shift color to blend in with the mountainous landscape around him before stepping closer to the other dragon.

"Keep watching them, Sades, let me know if something drastic happens." Hevtur said, turning his gaze from the army to Sades, the other dragon, crouching down so that it was a whisper, to a dragon anyways. "Yes, my Liege." Sades bowed his head in response. Hevtur backed up and stood straight again before turning to leave for the King's Peak, what the dragons basically called a palace, and walked a few more paces into the mountains before lifting off to fly low to the Kings Peak.

Some of a wind dragon's magic attributes were that they were the fastest dragons at flying. A magic attribute was that they could, in a way, bend the light, so that they could see farther or closer, so to speak. They can bend the light for others to see in magnified detail as well. Another one of their magic attributes were that they could summon the wind, like making it blow hard or softer when they wished. Another one of their magic attributes was that they could create a soundproof barrier around them when they wished, meaning what they said couldn't be heard outside of the barrier they created, but they couldn't hear anything outside the barrier while they were in it. Granted one could just walk through the barrier and to the other side of it, they could see through the barrier to the outside and others could see into the barrier at them. Another magic ability was that they could camouflage their scales to blend in with their surroundings. It took time for it to happen, about five minutes which isn't too much time, but it can be the difference where one's caught or not. They had to wait that long so that their scales could, in lack of a better word, mirror their surroundings, after that they could move and still be blended in with the landscape around them. Part of the camouflage is that a wind dragon can change into any color of its desire, and they didn't have to blend in with the environment. They could simply turn their scales to gray when they were surrounded by any other color than gray.

Though using wind magic, like using any other magic, it takes a toll on the users mind weariness, making them tired or giving them a headache, if they used too much or used it for too long.

All wind dragons that were of pure wind dragon blood, or mostly pure wind dragon blood, were white like snow or a cloud. Their eye colors were usually certain colors for the breed or type, or maybe race, of dragon that they were. Wind dragons would typically have a lighter blue, a light green, a light purple, or white rounded with a dark trim to separate their iris from the white of their eyes, as their iris, black, like normal, for their pupils over the white of their eyes and their pupils, like all other dragons, were round like a human's eye.

All water dragons that were also of, or mostly of pure water dragon blood, were royal blue to navy blue and all other shades in between those two. The irises of their eyes are a random shade between and including royal blue and navy blue. Water dragons, unlike the other races of dragons, had web-like talons and gills. A water dragons magic attributes were: 1: they could breathe underwater with their gills and outside of water like a regular living creature above the waves, 2: they were very fast swimmers due to their webbed talons and strong tail, not that they needed them to be faster at swimming than the other dragons, and their wings weren't all that special, but they did help them swim, like all other dragons could do in the water, or could do if they knew how, 3: they could see in the dark, which made sense because they could swim down to some of the deeper levels of the ocean. They could also talk underwater, but it wasn't very private since the water carries sound a lot easier than air. Another magic attribute they had was that they could move the waves, like a tide, raising the water level or lowering it, they could also create currents within the water. They could remove water from any place and they could also place water in a place that was dry in the first place. This basically means they can either make one thirst to death, or they could drown one while he/she was on dry land.

All earth dragons that had mostly pure blood were just about any shade of brown, like the dirt of the earth. They could also be gray, like the rocks of the mountains, or pale yellow like sand, they weren't green like vegetation though. Their irises could also be the same shade of their scales. Not the exact same, although they could have the same color of eyes and scales, it wasn't really uncommon, it was just more likely to be unlikely to happen. Magic attributes for them were that they were much stronger, on average, than any other dragon and they had a bigger bite force than other dragons, they were also a bit bigger on average than the others. Another magic attribute was that they could, literally, reshape the earth. They could raise mountains from the ground and form craters or valleys into it. They couldn't create dirt, just like all other natural magic users. They just misplaced it. An earth dragon's tail was usually littered with spikes near the end.

A fire dragon was any shade of red to orange, like fire, and so were their irises. A magic attribute to them was that they are naturally warm just to be next to, because of the heat radiating off of their body. They could also illuminate their scales in the dark, glowing in the dark scales, in any shade between the shades of red and orange. They were also more heat resistant, or more like completely heat resistant. Another magic attribute was that they could breathe fire, they didn't have to wait to, in lack of better words, recharge. They could just start breathing fire and almost not even stop, the only reasons to stop would be that they were just done breathing fire, like they got done what they wanted to get done, or they lost concentration because of a headache or dizziness, or if they got too cold. They could get sore throats if they breathed fire for too long and then it would hurt immensely to breathe fire again. They did have to, in a way, power up to breathe fire for a long period of time. Fire was like their breath. In order to breathe fire for a consistently long period of time they would have to take a deep breath. Some fire dragons though were hatched with less fire, or heat, than others or they could be hatched with more fire than others. The ones that are hatched with less fire aren't stripped of any attributes besides the ability to radiate heat off of their body, and the glow in the dark ability, even then they weren't stripped of them, they were just weaker. And the ones hatched with more fire just have them even more than the rest, usually the fire dragons hatched with more fire were too hot just to touch for creatures besides other fire dragons.

Metal dragons that are mostly of metal dragon blood, are usually some shade of some kind of metal, like iron, copper, gold, any shade a metal could be, a metal dragon could be. Same with the colors of their irises. A magic that a metal dragon has is that it has much stronger scales than other dragons. Another magic attribute for metal dragons is that they can warp any metal, can turn any solid into a metal, but it takes a lot of energy, and they also have a poisonous bite and scratch from their teeth and claws.

Those are the main five dragons anyways, there are others that form their own element, so to speak. There are also two main types of magic, natural magic and unnatural magic. Anyone could use either or. Dragons were just hatched with natural magic of any element that they had in their blood and which element they were hatched in, but a dragon that did not have a specific element could not hatch and survive within that element. Like if a pure fire dragon egg was in any other element besides a fire element. They would die when hatched, or they wouldn't have any magic if they survived. An adult dragon, when in the same place for a long enough period of time, would eventually begin to change the place that they resided into the element that they were. They didn't have to stay there continuously, they just had to be there for intervals throughout almost every day. If a wind dragon was taking a certain cave for residence, the cave would eventually have a steady breeze somewhere near it or within it. Wind dragons never went too far into the ground because they would be too far for their element for too long and would grow insane.

On the lower two thirds of the peak was an enclosure, a place like a courtyard for the citizens to walk around in, also to shelter many in a time of war, which was the main reason there were courtyards within palace walls and within the King's Peak enclosure. The walls down in the enclosure were formed of regular stone and other natural materials formed under the mountain. The walls on the uppermost part of the mountain, or the peak of the mountain, was the King's layer. The walls up there were lined with gold and other metals of value, there were gems within certain spots on the walls and pillars. The King's Peak and the largest peak in the kingdom, so that the enclosure below could fit as much as possible if needed.

Hevtur arrived at the King's Peak and the guards, one was a wind dragon and the other a fire, outside the cave's main entrance to the King's layer stood to attention, and lowered their heads and crouched on their front legs in a bow. Hevtur walked past the guards and into his layer. The guards stood back upright and relaxed a bit. Hevtur continued into the layer and to his left through another warn down archway into another subsection of the cave. He looked down into the cave at a stump looking stone that he usually used as a table, no, they used it as a table for eating together.

Some cooked meat lay upon a platter in the center of the stone, at one end another wind dragon sat straight up, as if to pay attention, with her tail covering her talons.

A female dragon most always looked different from a male dragon. A female dragon had smaller horns and was usually more slim.

Hevtur stopped and inhaled quietly looking at his situation, this looked like one of those, 'We have got to talk', moments. Granted he was up and about on the front almost all morning, but the morning wasn't over yet. It was a few more hours before mid-day, but Mirada, the dragon next to the table-like stone, didn't really like it nonetheless. She always wanted him to eat something before he went out anywhere. She was his wife, the queen and all, but sometimes it felt like she was his mother, suggestive and all. Not that he didn't appreciate her insight, he did, but it got bad when he said he would try what she suggested and then didn't. Duty calls though, he was the king and he had an obligation to his kingdom, to protect it.

She turned to look at him and he stiffened a bit at her stare.

Yeah… she's not happy. Hevtur thought, staring back at her.

"Are you going to eat?" Mirada asked, gesturing to the meat. Her voice was soft and gentle like it usually was, warm and welcoming.

"You have your meeting later today, and you'll need a full stomach to make the flight." She added, looking straight forward again, almost like a statue.

"I'm sorry, I forgot again." Hevtur said, with a humbled voice. "It's okay, just eat." She said, looking at him. Her whitish eyes fixed upon him.

He moved as quietly as possible toward the empty side of the table stone, sat and looked into her eyes, as she continued to stare at him. She wasn't psychotic or anything, though she was probably on the edge of being so, she was actually very calm and gentle, almost the very opposite of psychotic. It was why he loved her so much.

"I'm serious though, I am very sorry about it." Hevtur said in a sober voice, looking down at the food. "If you're soooo sorry, then I'd suggest that you eat some food right now." Mirada said in a rye voice, the corner of her mouth twinging up into a slight smile. He stared at her while his own smile began to grow on his face.

"Very well, at least I'll be able to do something right for you instead of forgetting it within an hour or so." He replied in his own rye voice, looking down at the cooked meat. She chuckled a little, and turned to look at him saying, "You remember more than you think."

"I don't know about that, seeing how I don't remember whether that's true or not." He replied, reaching for a small piece, or smaller piece than the largest, which was about a mouth full for a dragon.

She laughed a bit harder before sobering and asking, "So, how does it look? The border near Zulkbar." Hevtur froze and the question for a split second before continuing to swallow.

He inhaled then said, "Nothing has happened as of yet."

"Then why were you out there this morning? You know it's dangerous as well as I do."

"It's not as dangerous as you may think." Hevtur replied.

"Yes it is, all that has to happen is one of those dwarves getting in over their heads and trying to kill the king of Jurrunt. That ends up one of two ways. You either injure one of them, if not killing one of them, or them killing or injuring you. Either way a war breaks out, but with one of those routes the kingdom is possibly without a ready king, me without my husband." Mirada said, leaning forward towards Hevtur.

He inhaled and said, "Mirada, I will assure you again that neither of those possibilities will present themselves. I will be fine. You will be fine. The kingdom will be fine."

She wrapped her tail back over her talons and sighed deeply, looking down to the ground saying, "You're probably right. I'm probably worried over nothing."

Hevtur tilted his head, looking at her concerningly. "I'm sorry if I got carried away with that. I appreciate the concern you show me, but sometimes it's just a little excessive." He said, with a comforting voice. He stood up and walked over to her and touched his snout to hers saying, "I love you, Mirada."

Mirada inhaled slowly before answering, "And I you, Hevtur." She continued, "You didn't eat all of your breakfast."

He let out a short laugh, inhaled and said, "Never going to get off too easily, am I?" A rye tone coming to his voice, moving back to look at her more fully.

"Hevtur, I'm still concerned about the possibility of a war. A few days ago, while you were meeting with the generals, I was over near the western plaza and I saw that Callus had stationed a legion near his border, almost mirroring King Folkhem's army there by the Plaxident Valley. I'm afraid." Mirada said, looking up at Hevtur with worried eyes.

Hevtur returned the look and said, "I'm afraid too. I'm afraid for the lives that will be lost if a war should start. I'm afraid, for if one does, what will happen if our enemies overwhelm us. I am terrified of the thought that something may happen to you if that should happen."

He moved closer to her, intertwining his tail with hers and touching snouts again, bowing their heads more deeply. They stayed there for a moment before breaking off. "If I am to arrive at the meeting in time, I've got to go momentarily." Hevtur said, looking down at her. She looked up at him and nodded and asked, "Yes you do, but will you at least have a few more bites before leaving, and will you also say goodbye to Hierion before you go as well?"

He looked at her and responded, "Yes I will." They touched snouts again and she departed the room, or cave, depending on how you thought about, leaving Hevtur alone with his thoughts.

He took a few more bites before closing his eyes and taking a deep breath. He blew it out and walked over to the same exit Mirada used to leave, which was straight forward from where he ate about twenty feet on the other side of the archway that led to the great hall of the peak.

He walked through the archway and around another corner to find Hierion laying on a rock platform fifteen feet off the base of the worn down floor of the layer. Hierion was about a half Hevturs age and not much smaller than he, other than that he was basically a complete remake of Hevtur. Granted he was his son, his heir, the prince to the kingdom of Jurrunt, but it was still remarkable how similar they could look.

"What time is your meeting today?" Hierion asked with his head still resting on his front legs. "About halfway through the afternoon today." Hevtur replied, looking into Hierion's icy-blue eyes. "Where is it this time?" Hierion asked, waving his tail slightly back and forth. "Corinthus." Hevtur replied.

"Will there be a day where I can come with you, like how you said grandfather took you to some of those meetings?" Hierion inquired.

"Yes, there will be, but just not this time. Most likely next time and if your mother is okay with it." Hevtur replied, looking at Hierion. Hevtur knew that Mirada would almost certainly not be okay with it while tensions were this high around the world. A young heir out in public was an ideal target for other royal families and factions that looked to end Hevtur's bloodline.

Hierion exhaled deeply and said, "You know she'll never be okay with it. She always says that it's too dangerous out there."

"And she's right, therefore you cannot come until you are older and are more attuned to the threats that will come for you outside this kingdom's borders." Hevtur said. "Okay." Hierion replied, exhaling while doing so. Hevtur nodded once and turned around to leave saying, "I'll see you tomorrow."

"That's if you make it back." Hierion said, looking after Hevtur. Hevtur stopped dead in his tracks and turned his head around to see Hierion looking at him square in the eyes. He almost looked amused by what he said, as if he either planned on Hevtur not coming back, or was just picking up on Mirada's paranoia. Hevtur stared back at him, suppressing a laugh and a grin. Hierions tail swagged back and forth in small slow movements. He was joking, he just made fun of his mother, and did it well.

Hevtur didn't know whether to shoot an angry glare at him and say something like, "Don't make fun of your mother" or whether to begin laughing uncontrollably. Instead he just said, "See you tomorrow, son." and left for the exit of the great hall.

He walked out onto the platform where he landed earlier and saw four more guards, all wind dragons, at the ready, he nodded once to them and said, "Let's go." and they lifted off the ground and to the air heading south for Corinthus. It would be about an hour before they reached the border and then another one to one and a half to reach the port city of Corinthus, thanks to the swift flying offered to them by their element of wind. They began to shift the color of their scales to match the sky to hide them from the view from spectators on the ground below. He actually always wanted Hierion to come with him, but Mirada wouldn't allow it, and for good reason too. If his heir was injured or killed, that could bring heavy consequences toward Jurrunt. So it was best to keep him safe for now.

Chapter

8

Agamemnon and Callus arrived at the naval wharf of Corinthus. The door to the coach opened and Agamemnon stepped out first, followed by Callus, and onto the stone and wood docks of Corinthus's naval wharf, where the fleet was stationed when one of them was in port.

Agamemnon led Callus up to an overlook of the wharf and said, "This is what I wished you to see." Callus caught up and stood next to him, looking down at the vast number of war vessels in the harbor. Every single docking spot was occupied by a ship, from what Callus could see, and they were massive. Callus looked down at them, noticing that they weren't Triremes. They were bigger.

All ships were of the same look, most likely the same class of ship for what looked like almost five hundred of them. Each ship was bigger than a Tower Trireme, like the ones in Classis II Oceanianic, the flagships in Praetorian fleets. Instead of three banks of rows, they had four, they were about one hundred fifty feet in length and around twenty feet wide. They had two masts, and a sail on each one that were rolled up onto the top of the masts. They were painted white and royal blue, which were the colors of Corinos. The rams on the ships were huge, about ten feet from the bottom tip of the bow made to damage opposing ships. Along with the metal ram head was, halfway up the bow of the ship. Another skewer made for a great chance of actually sinking the enemy ship by cracking the hull open.

"Beautiful isn't it." Agamemnon said, looking at Callus with a smug face, and his hands folded behind his back. "A new model of ship?" Callus asked. "Yes, they're called Quadriremes, and with them Corinos will dominate the Alzeirs, and if not, the ocean itself." Agamemnon replied, looking even more smug.

"What about any water dragon that sees it fit to try and stop you?" Callus asked. "Another thing I want you to see." Agamemnon said, turning for the stairs that led down to the stone wharf. Callus followed him to the edge of the wharf, and they followed the edge of the wharf out to the outermost part of the harbor.

"Stay here for a moment." Agamemnon said, lifting a hand for Callus to stop. Callus stopped and Agamemnon walked forward and around a corner. Callus heard the water stir and some whispering around the corner where Agamemnon went. The water stirred again and silence fell for a few moments before the water stirred again and more whispering followed. Agamemnon then turned around the corner where he first walked away and gestured for Callus to come to him. Callus walked to him and followed him around the corner to a deep section of the river near the river bank. Agamemnon stopped and Callus went to stand next to him.

"Interesting water isn't it?" Callus said, with a wry voice. "Just wait a minute, not everything happens within two seconds of you appearing." Agamemnon replied sarcastically. Callus chuckled, looking out to the vast river beyond the harbor of Corinthus where he stood.

A moment later and the water stirred again and a water dragon of navy blue scales and queen blue eyes. The dragon positioned itself to look at the men squarely. "Queen Cora of the Kingdom of Alzeirs." Agamemnon said, bowing at the waist with one arm on his stomach and the other on his lower back.

"King Agamemnon." Cora said, bowing her head towards Agamemnon. Callus blanked out for a second before realizing that he was taught manners as a child and bowing at the waist towards Cora saying, "Queen Cora, I'm afraid to say I have never made an acquaintance with you."

He stood back up straight and looked into her eyes. "And I with you." She replied, bowing her head towards Callus. "Your Highness, this is Imperator Callus of Praetoria." Agamemnon said, gesturing his hand towards Callus.

"Ah, from what Agamemnon says, you're one to be remembered." Cora said, looking from Agamemnon to Callus. "He may have been exaggerating. And as for you, this is the first time I have heard of you, and your kingdom." Callus replied.

Cora inhaled and said, "Yes, it would appear that Agamemnon has kept his promise, and very well at that."

"Promise, may I ask?" Callus asked, really both of them. "It took a lot of persuading to get her to finally meet at least you, maybe even the others as well." Agamemnon said, looking at Callus and back at Cora.

"After the death of Harox, the late king of Alzeirs, I asked to be kept from the knowledge of the world by Agamemnon and his father. I did not want what happened to Harox to happen to the heir, my son. But now it would appear that the world is growing colder and closer to war, and I'm afraid if we do not act together, we will fall to destruction." Cora said looking at Callus.

Callus studied the dragon queen. Callus didn't mind that Agamemnon kept an entire civilization from him, or the others, but he wondered why they would want to stay hidden from the rest of the world. Maybe it was a hasty decision on Cora's part, or maybe there was something she didn't trust or like about what the world had to offer, but that was behind them now.

"What makes you think that the world is on the brink of a war, I mean Agamemnon may have told you about what's going on at the World Senatorial Meetings, but other than that, what else could give you the idea that war is so close? I mean no offense by the question." Callus said, folding his arms and looking curiously into Cora's eyes.

Agamemnon looked at Callus confused, as if he was trying to figure out what Callus just said. "A day ago, some scouts encountered three ships in the river near the southern borders of Farrius and Praetoria. Two of them were attacking the other, the two attacking were marauders from the other side of the river and the other was from Farrius." Cora paused breathing in while Callus and Agamemnon looked at each other bewildered. Cora continued, "Sir Calpos Daentious, from what reports say, was on the ship from Farrius, and on his way here. I believe that that was no coincidental attack because they have never attacked lone vessels with more than one of their own vessels. Zorok, one of the ones who were there, said that the marauders weren't just attacking, but more like searching for something, and once they saw Sir Daentious, the ones that saw him tried to converge on him from what Zorok could see, before he got to one of the marauders ships and sunk it."

Agamemnon inhaled and asked, "You believe he may have something important?" Cora turned to look at Agamemnon and nodded. Callus looked out to the large river, pursing his lips thoughtfully.

"If he does have something important, then why wouldn't Volkar send someone else, unless Volkar didn't know that Daentious had this information?" Callus asked in a low murmur that the others could barely hear. "I don't know, but I'm sure it will play a big part soon in the coming time." Cora said, looking at Callus.

"Huh. Well, is Daentious still alive?" Agamemnon asked, looking at Cora. "Yes, he was injured, but not severely." Cora returned, looking back at Agamemnon. "I guess we'll see whether your assumptions are true and how important his information could be, later today." Agamemnon said, putting his hands on his hips and turning from Cora to Callus.

"I guess we will." Cora said as she bowed to each of them and they returned the gesture, then slipped back under the surface of the river and out of sight. Callus turned to Agamemnon and said, "Alright, we have some new toys to look at." Drawing a smile from Agamemnon and they prodded off back to the awaiting coach.

Once they got to the coach, the guard opened the door and stomped his feet in a Corinosian salute. Agamemnon stepped up into the coach first and Callus followed. "I hope you're not disappointed that I kept such a secret right under your nose and you never saw it." Agamemnon said with an extremely rye voice, after they sat down into the coach in the same spots they occupied before.

"No, I'm not disappointed, I'm more confused about what Daentious could have that could be so important." Callus replied, putting his hand over his chin looking at Agamemnon. "We really don't have any other choice, but to wait and see if there's something and what it is." Agamemnon said, looking back at Callus.

The rest of the ride was mostly quiet besides some jokes made here or there. They arrived at the palace and the door to the coach opened again and again Agamemnon led, stepping out onto the stone courtyard first, with Callus a few steps behind. Agamemnon slowed so that he and Callus would walk side by side and talk while they made their way up the stairs and to the palace doors. They were dropped off at the palace's base instead of where they were picked up before, probably because the coach was requested on such short notice before than it was just now.

The guards at the doors opened them and saluted, stomping their feet. They walked into the palace and towards the war room. Callus' guards stayed in a particular spot where Callus told them to wait for him to return, they protested of course, but he got them to subside and wait there for him to come back.

The Corinosian guards that followed Agamemnon before were there as well, and it looked like the four Praetorian guards were actually socializing with the Corinosians as if the Praetorian guards were actually humans and not a puppet that just read certain lines aloud when they fit. The Praetorian guards stood on one side of the hallway and the Corinosian guards on the other, facing each other, only a few feet from one another. As they got closer to the guards, their voices became clearer.

"So, this bolt thrower thing is like a bow and arrow, just enlarged?" One of the Corinosian guards asked.

A Praetorian said, "Yeah, so what it looks like is a enlarged bow bolted to another piece of wood, which is attached to the base of the weapon, making the bow lay on top of the base of the weapon horizontally, and a massive arrow, or the bolt is put into it."

"I don't quite get it, do like five men hold the string back while another one or two aims the bolt thrower?" Another Corinosian guard asked.

The same Praetorian guard from before said, "Not quite, you see, there's a hook that the crewmen of the bolt thrower latch the string onto, and then they put the bolt in and aim."

"Oh, I see now, and what exactly is the purpose of it? Does it split apart into shards after losing it, and hit the enemy ranks like a volley of regular arrows?"

Another Praetorian guard cut in and said, "No, it stays as one solid bolt as it flies through the air at its target. I guess it's almost more of a prototype for a larger one, so to speak." "Yeah, it might be powerful enough to go through some less developed walls, can tear through ranks like paper, and I'm willing to bet that it can also pierce dragon scales." The original Praetorian guard added.

"Ohhh, okay. That could be pretty valuable in a battle." One of the Corinosian guards said.

They stopped talking as Calluses and Agamemnon's footsteps approached, they rounded the corner to find all eight guards looking at them.

The Praetorians were on their right side and the Corinosians were on the left side of the hallway as they walked down it. The closest Praetorian had his right arm folded over his lower chest and his left arm vertical with his left hand holding his chin, and he was resting on one leg, the Praetorian guard behind him was leaning backwards with his arms folded to see who was coming, and the Praetorian behind that one was shifted to the side and looking down the hallway at Callus and Agamemnon, as for the other Praetorian, he was barely in sight, poking his head over the other three to see down the hallway.

For the Corinosian guards however, the first one had his arms folded and was leaning his back against the wall, the one behind him was leaning forward holding onto his spear with both hands, the one behind him was standing straight up to look over the second guards slightly arching back, and as for the forth, he was standing similarly to the third Praetorian guard, in about the center of the hallway, leaning on one leg looking down the hallway at Callus and Agamemnon.

Upon seeing the King and Imperator, the guards formed up and stood to attention. The Corinosian guards saluted with stomping their feet once in a Corinosian type salute, and the Praetorian guards banged their fists to their hearts in a Praetorian style salute.

Both groups stood to either side of the hallway, Corinosian guards holding their spears up tight against their body as Agamemnon and Callus strode passed, trying their best to keep a straight face at the situation that they just walked into. Once they walked past the guards, the guards followed after them in the single file lines like before, each line of guards behind their corresponding leader. They continued to walk through the palace towards the great hall.

Ahead they heard a guard say, "Yes your highness, I'll let him know as soon as possible." A female voice said, "Thank you, Plubion." They heard the guard salute and walk off through the palace. Agamemnon slowed a little bit, grimaced and began to look around for another exit besides the one the voices came from. There was no other way out, except for the way they came. Light footsteps sounded like they approached the hallway and a woman walked out from behind the corner of the wall of the other hallway that they were headed to.

She looked down the hallway and Agamemnon sighed. "Ah, there you are, I'll have to find Plubion again to tell him I found you." She said in a smug voice, raising her finger at Agamemnon. Agamemnon drew out a smile and reached out his hand to take hers. "Thessisana." He said.

Thessisana was Agamemnon's wife, the Queen of Corinos, and was just shorter than Agamemnon himself. She had moderately long blonde hair and blue-green eyes, she was slender in a beautiful way. She never really liked the perversions of women like the rest of the world, and neither did Agamemnon. She was one of probably the few, in Calluses point of view, that a man could actually trust and rely on to do just about anything you asked, as long as it was appropriate, and she was quite smart. Not easily fooled.

She reached out her hand as well and allowed Agamemnon to take it and gently kiss it. "If I didn't know any better, I would think that you're trying to avoid me today." She said with a wry smile on her lips.

"Oh, you know I would never attempt such a thing on such a smart gorgeous woman as you." Agamemnon replied, straightening his back to stand straight again looking her in the eye. "Mmmm. I would, wouldn't I, but I would also know if you were lying as well." She returned. Callus looked back at the guards behind them, and if HE didn't know any better, they were suppressing laughs and smiles, just like he was. Callus turned to look forward again and caught Thessisana's eye. He gulped.

"Oh, maybe you weren't trying to avoid me, maybe Callus over here has something I don't?" She asked looking back at Agamemnon. Callus and Agamemnon made eye contact for a second before Callus turned around to look at the guards one more time because he thought he heard a short chuckle slip through, but again there was nothing but straight faces among them. Callus turned back to Thessisana and said, "Thessisana." bowing his head to her. She raised her hand and he took it in his and kissed it gently.

"Well, yes he does have something you don't, he has some technologies that he's going to show me." Agamemnon said, looking at Thessisana. She turned and looked at Agamemnon and then back at Callus saying, "Oh really?" Agamemnon then said, "Yes, and we were just on our way to look at them, so if you don't mind…" She cut him off, "I still have something to say to you."

Agamemnon looked at her and she signaled to him to go somewhere private and he followed. Callus and the eight guards stood there in the hallway waiting for his return. A few moments later Agamemnon came walking out of the private room they just walked into with Thessisana just behind. Agamemnon walked towards Callus and the guards and Thessisana walked back out the way she came.

"Sorry about that, shall we continue?" Agamemnon asked Callus. Callus gestured to the open walkway in front of them and they began walking again.

They reached the war room not too long later, and Callus and Agamemnon told their guards to stay out in the hallway and walked into the miniature hallway to the war room. The Corinosian guards opened the door saluting and Callus and Agamemnon strode into the room. When they entered the room, some Praetorian guards and the engineers were sitting next to the bolt thrower along with some Corinosian guards talking with each other. The guards and engineers stood to attention and saluted, Praetorians Praetorian style, and Corinosians Corinosian style. Both Callus and Agamemnon nodded their heads once and the other men dispersed out of the room and through the hallway that led out of it.

Agamemnon stared at the bolt thrower in wonder. It looked like an enlarged crossbow that sat upon the ground with wheels in the front and a brace in the rear to keep it from moving when a shot was loosed at a target. The wheels were there so that it could be repositioned by hand. It wasn't loaded, but the bolts were lying in a crate next to it. Each bolt was four and a half feet in length and a coi[le inches in width. The bolt thrower itself was only five feet in length itself and stood at just under chest height off the ground. The bow that lay on its side was about seven feet in length.

Agamemnon continued walking towards it and asked, "Is this the bolt thrower that the guards were talking about earlier?" Callus nodded to him in response. Agamemnon stopped next to it looking at it from forward to back, taking in every detail.

He looked down and saw the opened crate of bolts, crouched down and picked one up in his left hand. He examined it for a few seconds before saying, "I'm willing to bet that this weapon has enough power behind one volley that it could pierce right through dragon scales." Callus stepped forward to stand next to him and replied, "It could teach some ignorant minded fools about what humans can accomplish if needed." Callus glanced at Agamemnon.

"How does it work exactly?" Agamemnon asked, putting his hands on his hips. "You pull the heavy string back here." Callus said, moving his hand over the bolt thrower and continued, "You hook it onto this hook here, then you put the bolt in like this." Callus picked up a bolt and pretended to feed it through the loop at the front of the bolt thrower that straightened the shot as much as possible, and continued, "You then aim at your target and pull this rope that is holding the hook in place." He said, lifting up an inch thick rope at the rear of the weapon. He continued, "The bolt is launched from the thrower and you place the rope back into its slot, repositioning the hook as well and repeat." Callus finished and glanced at Agamemnon then put down the bolt and reached down into another crate and picked up a pilum.

A pilum looked nothing quite like an ordinary spear or javelin. Instead of having a nine inch head, it had about a foot long head, and also unlike a javelin which was eight and a half feet in length, a pilum was seven feet in length. The regular javelin head was flat like a knife on its metal head, where a pilum's metal head looked like a very lengthy pyramid type shape and was barbed. When a javelin was thrown, it would pierce the enemies' armor and flesh staying intact and keeping its integrity. When a pilum was thrown on the other hand, it would pierce the armor and bend into the enemies flesh, making it almost impossible to pull it out with one hand and very hard to throw back at the original thrower. The bending part was originally an accident.

Agamemnon grabbed the pilum and inspected it. "A new version of the javelin?" Agamemnon asked, looking back towards Callus. "Yes, it has been issued to all legions to equip them, each legionary will carry about one of them into a fight, throwing it into the enemy ranks before making contact." Callus said, folding his hands behind his back. "May I test it?" Agamemnon asked, picking the pilum up off the ground and laying it horizontally in his hands.

"Why yes, it is partially the reason why they're here. Just don't test it on me." Callus replied, pointing at Agamemnon on the last part. Agamemnon grinned at Callus and looked around the room until he found two beams that crossed each other above the door to the hallway. He gestured at it and said, "There."

He picked up the pilum in his left hand, angled his body, and threw the pilum across the room and into one of the beams that lat above the door, it didn't land where the beams crossed, but it hit with a thud and the pilum went into the wood and bent downwards, leaving it hanging on an angle above the door. Callus picked one up himself, positioned it in his right hand and launched it towards the cross beams. It hit the other beam above the door about the same distance away from the crossing of the beams as Agamemnon's throw had. It bent up with a thud as it went into the wooden beam, it waved there for a moment settling into its spot before going still.

"Are they prototypes?" Agamemnon asked, looking from the thrown pilums to Callus. "Yes, but no, we're still looking for a lighter more agile javelin, but they will suffice until then, and if you're wondering about the bending that occurred, that's supposed to happen so that the enemy can't pull them out of their own bodies and throw them back." Callus said, looking from the pilums to Agamemnon.

"Oh really?" Agamemnon said, his eyebrows raising a touch. "Yes, it's bad enough having to worry about being outnumbered than to worry about them throwing your own tools of destruction back at your men." Callus said.

"Smart." Agamemnon said with a tone of approval in his voice. "What about this bolt thrower, can I keep it to try it out?" Agamemnon asked, walking back to the bolt thrower as a gesture. "I don't see why not. Unless either Daentious may want to take it back to Farrius or Hevtur to Jurrunt." Callus replied, folding his arms. "Hmmm, you know I just thought of something. I'm going to try it out and let you know how it goes." Agamemnon said, stroking his beard. "Okay, what is it?" Callus asked. "I'll let you know whether it works or not." Agamemnon used this as a reply.

"Well, Thessisana asked me to ask you whether you wanted to eat something before the meeting. That is one of the things we talked about earlier. So do you?" Agamemnon said, turning around in place and raising a brow. "Why not, food sounds rather delicious as of the moment." Callus responded. "Okay, let's go." Agamemnon said, gesturing and walking to the door. Callus walked beside him.

Chapter

9

Daentious's transporting ship arrived in Corinthus at just past noon. When they got in sight of the harbor, they could see the fleet of Quadriremes docked there, all five hundred of them. They were massive compared to the small transport ship he was on.

Their dragon escort departed not two hours ago after they were close enough to the city that they wouldn't be attacked. Daentious stood at the bow of the ship looking forward at the Corinosian fleet of warships, taking it all in as they went. A few moments later, they docked and he began walking towards the center of the ship, in hopes of finding Captain Plasidon. It took him a while to find him amongst the other crew members, but when he got to the Captain he asked, "When is it safe to leave the ship?" "In one or two more minutes sir." Plasidon said, inspecting rope knots that the crew had tied. "All they have to do is secure the ship and the boarding plank, and you're all set to leave sir." Plasidon added, feeling one of the knots. "Alright, thank you Captain, for the trip." Daentious replied, nodding his head once in approval. "Anytime sir." Plasidon said.

A moment later the boarding plank was set down on the ship and dock they were to empty onto, one of the crewmen went first to make sure it was steady and secured, once he got to the wooden dock, he signaled the others that it was good. Daentious went next and he was greeted by several Corinosian guards and a courier. "Greetings, Sir Daentious. I am Kasos Minore, and I am here to ensure your safety on the walk toward the palace. Whenever you're ready sir." The courier said, bowing at the waist a little. Daentious looked at the courier for a couple of seconds. The Courier, or Kasos Minore, was a short man, almost as if he was still a growing boy. He had short black hair, thick brows and dark gray eyes.

"I'm ready now." Daentious said to the courier. "Alrighty then, if you'll follow me." The courier said, turning down the dock to the pier, gesturing with his hand and began walking. Deanitous followed as the guards stood to the side and followed behind them, shields and spears in their hands.

Maybe they heard of what happened. Or maybe something else happened. Which could be the reason this fleet was in harbor and not on patrol, or maybe I'm just thinking too much about it. Daentious thought, walking behind Kasos Minore. Daentious felt to his side where a pouch lay holding the scroll from Senator Volkar making sure he had it on him, as if he hadn't done that five times already. It hurt to move his left arm, or not move it, but use it in a physical way.

When they reached near the end of the pier, a coach was awaiting them. The driver stood near the door and opened it for Daentious and the courier, bowing at the waist slightly to both with one bow. Kasos stepped up into the coach first, sitting on the right side of Daentious, or the front side of the coach. Daentious stepped up after him sitting on the left side, or the rear of the coach. Two of the guards stepped up after them and went to the other side of the coach, one sitting on the front bench with Kasos, and the other on the rear bench with Daentious.

The door then shut to the coach and the driver and one guard stepped up onto the top of the coach, the driver grabbed the reins and urged the horses forward and the guard sat next to him. The coach got under way and just a few moments later they arrived at the Inner southern gates, where the coach stopped and the guards atop the gates opened them for the coach to pass through. The gates closed after the coach cleared them and the coach stopped several seconds later at the palace stairs. The driver and the guard dismounted and the driver opened the door for Daentious and the others to get out. The guards went first and then Kasos, and then Daentious followed onto the stone courtyard of the palace of Corinthus.

The driver then shut the door and got up to the top of the coach and urged the horses forward again, taking the coach to where Daentious thought to most likely be where they kept the coaches. "Right this way sir." Kasos said, gesturing up the stairs. He began walking and Daentious followed him up the stairs and into the palace with the three guards just behind them.

The doors opened and they walked into the palace, the doors closed as they entered and they walked through the southern great hall. The ceiling of the great hall was almost sixty feet high and the walls were forty feet across from each other, they went up more stairs to where the four great halls of each direction met on a square platform of forty feet by forty feet, and a mosaic of the flag of Corinos lay on the ground there.

The ceiling retained its sixty foot height and they heard other footsteps and chattering from one of the four hallways that were connected onto the platform on its corners. From one of the doors in front of them, Imperator Callus and King Agamemnon stepped onto the mosaic followed by eight guards, four Corinosian and four Praetorian. Callus and Agamemnon were talking to each other as they entered, and they both saw Daentious.

"Sir Daentious. I'm glad you're alright, or alive anyways. I heard about what happened out there and I want to give my apologies. I hope you're well enough for the meeting." Agamemnon said, walking over to Daentious and gripping his right arm with his. "I'm fine enough, if it wasn't for those dragons, we may have won and survived, but not as much as that did though." Daentious replied, as he and Callus gripped hands.

Daentious bowed to Callus and Agamemnon at the waist grimacing and said, "We have urgent matters to discuss." "I agree." Agamemnon said, looking from Daentious to Callus, he continued, "Shall we?" Agamemnon nodded once to Kasos and the courier left with the three guards that followed him and Daentious into the palace.

They walked through the palace and into a hallway that branched out into another hallway that led to the war room. Callus and Agamemnon ordered their guards to wait out in the original hallway and the three men walked into the war room where a wooden contraption stood along with a couple crates of what looked like large arrows and javelins, one of each. Daentious eyed them intently before looking forward to see Callus and Agamemnon looking back at him with smiles on their faces.

"Look pretty?" Callus asked, grinning at this point. "What are they?" Daentious asked, looking from Callus to the weapons and back. "They're new weapons that have just been created and I am now showing them to you all." Callus replied, turning around near the table and gesturing with one hand to them. "Go ahead, try one of the javelins, they're called pilums by the way." Callus said. Daentious walked over to the crates of weapons and picked up a pilum. He felt its weight and tossed it up and down in his hand. He looked at Agamemnon and Agamemnon gestured a hand at the beams above the door and said, "Go ahead, they're quite interesting."

Daentious turned to see two of the pilums embedded into the wooden beams above the door they just entered. He balanced the pilum in his hand, angled himself, and threw the pilum towards the beams. He winced in slight pain as he threw it. He hit the dead center of the two beams where they crossed, the pilum wobbled and bent up at almost a forty five degree angle. His eyes widened at it.

"Don't worry, it's meant to bend like that." Callus said, leaning on the map table with his arms folded. Daentious looked at him puzzled. "It makes it where the enemy can't throw it back, or it at least makes it much harder for them to do so." Callus added. Daentious blinked with a realization. "How long have you had these, Callus?" Daentious asked, with a hint of ryeness in his voice, regaining his posture.

"Just about a week and a half, I have just implemented them into my legions, the legions on the front should be receiving them within a week or two, maybe three depending on the weather. You can take some back to Farrius with you if you'd like." Callus said, gesturing at the pilums before continuing, "As for the bolt thrower, Agamemnon here has already claimed it for an idea of his." He gestured at the bolt thrower. Daentious turned and looked at it inquisitively before asking, "What does it do, like what is its main purpose?"

"Its main purpose is for war, one could say, but its main target is anti-large, like cavalry and dragons." Callus said, looking at the bolt thrower. Daentious studied it a bit longer, nodding his head before asking, "How does it work?" Callus told him how it worked and once he was done, Daentious put his hand to his beard and began stroking it saying, "I see, that brings me to what I brought to show and tell today. I guess we're just waiting for Hevtur?" "Yes, he should be here any moment now." Agamemnon said, looking at the map with his arms folded.

A few moments later a knock on the door sounded and Agamemnon asked, "Yes, what is it?" "King Hevtur of the Kingdom of Jurrunt is arriving, my Liege." The voice said from outside the door. "Very well, thank you, that will be all." Agamemnon replied, and then continued after he exhaled, "It's about time. Or well, I guess he's actually on time, you guys were early." Callus chuckled.

A minute later Hevtur and his escort landed on the platform outside the war room and one of the Corinosian guards looked up at him before nodding once and moving out of the way for him to walk through. Hevtur's guards stayed where they were and began to rest, while he was in the meeting. The door opened for him and he walked in to find the other three standing around the map table looking at it.

"Good day, Hevtur. I hope you had a pleasant enough trip." Agamemnon said first, then Callus said, "Good day." Bowing his head slightly along with Agamemnon. Hevtur looked at them and then to the equipment to the side and back at them and said, "Good day to you too, and yes I had a good enough trip." He bowed his head slightly as well.

Daentious waited for his turn before greeting Hevtur, bowing at the waist instead of just the head. Hevtur bowed his head to Daentious in response. "May I ask what that is over there?" Hevtur asked, gesturing to the equipment.

"Yes, you may. That is some new technologies that my researchers and engineers have made about two weeks ago. The wooden toy here is called a bolt thrower, it's an artillery piece, and the crate nearest to it is the ammunition for it. The other crate is full or almost full of a new model of javelin called the pilum." Callus said, walking closer to the equipment, gesturing at it and continued, "We haven't tested the bolt thrower here, but we did test the pilums, if you'll look at the man door." He gestured to the man door and Hevtur saw three pilums embedded into the wooden cross beams, one on the horizontal beam, one on the vertical beam, and the other dead center of the crossing.

He noticed that they were bent and said, "Just a prototype?" Gesturing at the pilums in the beams above the door. Callus turned to look at them and said, "No, they're supposed to do that so that the enemy can't throw them back at the one who threw it. It is also barbed so that it inflicts maximum damage to the target."

"Oh, I see. And what about this contraption? What does this do?" Callus told Hevtur about the bolt thrower, and Hevtur didn't look the least bit excited. A weapon that was made to kill your own kind by a friend from another kind. He understood that it wasn't to kill him or any other dragon he knew, but it just reminded him of how it would become hard to protect his people and family if such a weapon existed.

"Interesting." Hevtur said, looking from the bolt thrower to Callus. "I know it may be… uh… offensive in a way, a weapon almost deliberately made to kill dragons, but that is not its intended purpose. Its main purpose is to help us stay ahead of the curve on technology." Callus said, then added, "It can also puncture through walls, not heavy siege walls, but almost any wall raised by an enemy force."

Hevtur nodded and turned to the map laying down so that he could see the map a bit more clearer, not that it wasn't clear in the first place, just that it was easier to see what the others saw like that. The others huddled around the map table as well. It was then Hevtur realized that Daentious was injured and asked, "Sir Daentious, what happened to your arm?" Daentious looked up at him then back down at his arm, as if he hadn't known that it was bandaged. "On the way here some pirates or mercenaries attacked the ship I was on, but they were taken care of." Daentious said, looking back up at Hevtur. Hevtur raised a brow at him then at Agamemnon. Agamemnon sighed, lifted his chin and said, "I said I was sorry, does that make you feel better Hevtur?" Hevtur eyed Agamemnon more intently saying, "Pirates in your waters? That doesn't really sound like something you would allow to go unchecked."

Agamemnon inhaled and said, "I guess this is the best time to tell you about my secret of the deep. She wants you to know anyway." Agamemnon paused to breathe then continued, "I have been hiding the kingdom of Alzeirs for the last ten years after my father gave me the crown, and he hid it from the world for about five years before that. I will show you after the meeting today if you'd like to see." Hevtur looked like his heart skipped a beat, Callus already knew and Daentious almost found out the hard way. "I'll hold you to that Agamemnon." Hevtur said after regaining the little posture he lost. "Indeed you will." Agamemnon said, then continued, "But first let us have our meeting." They all nodded in agreement.

Chapter

10

"First, before we get talking about whatever we will be talking about, I have some information to share with you all." Daentious said, reaching into the pouch at his side and pulled out the scroll. Callus and Agamemnon gave each other a look and then looked back at Daentious. Hevtur watched the trade off, then turned his gaze upon Daentious as well.

"Here in my hand is something that Senator Volkar has deemed highly important, and he wished me to bring it to this meeting." He broke the wax seal on the scroll and unrolled it, clenching his teeth in a slight pain from his arm and read it to himself before reading aloud, "This message is between Senator Volkar of the Republic of Farrius and King Lithimir of the Kingdom of Thraldilis." Agamemnon looked almost completely shocked, as did Callus and Hevtur, Agamemnon then asked, "What does a high elf want to do with any of us?" Daentious looked up from the paper and looked at Agamemnon and said, "I'll get there in a moment."

Daentious then continued to read the message to the others:

> "Senator Volkar of the Republic of Farrius, I am to understand that you are the man I should talk to for a treaty, so I ask you what you would say of a treaty between our people? And what I mean by that is, I wish

to form an alliance between our two alliances to create one standing alliance.

Now before you answer, we both know that trying times are upon us, so I would ask you to consider your answer before you make a mistake in it. I want you to understand that I do not think that I thought you were going to say no, just that I do not want any rash decisions being made in such a fragile time as we are in.

So I ask, do you agree to my proposal of aligning ourselves together to make a stronger alliance between you and the other three that form the alliance that you are a part of and the three within the alliance that I help form.

Sincerely, King Lithimir of the Kingdom of Thraldilis."

Daentious ended and said a split second later, "Senator Volkar gave me this scroll to bring to you three for your opinion, so what do you think about it?" A moment of silence fell before Agamemnon said, "I would have never thought, but then I never gave the thought of high elves becoming an ally." He finished looking up at the ceiling. Callus inhaled and said, "I do not see a problem with it, we'll just have Senator Volkar reply saying that we will accept to meet with them at the World Senatorial Meeting and further discussions about it will be done there in about three months."

Hevtur nodded and said, "I agree with Callus on the matter. A possible ally is better than a possible enemy." Agamemnon looked down from the ceiling and at the other three before saying, "Yeah, I think that that's the best way to go about it for now, but first I believe we should be having this discussion with someone else as well." Callus and Agamemnon's eyes locked as Daentious and Hevtur looked from them and at each other then back to them.

"I agree." Callus said, nodding his head slightly. "Who else will we be talking to about this?" Hevtur asked, raising a brow at Agamemnon. Daentious stood there musing for a bit before it looked like he understood what they were talking about and said, "If that is what they said to you, then yes I believe that they should be allowed in on this matter." Hevtur looked at Daentious, then back at Agamemnon with confusion and asked in a rye voice, "Does everyone know of this secret besides me, or am I just the unlucky one that wasn't there to see it myself one day?"

Agamemnon chuckled and said, "Stay here and I will return in about a half an hour, or maybe you can come with me." He looked up in thought then said, "I believe you can all come with me to the port."

"Where exactly?" Hevtur asked. Agamemnon looked at him and then seemed to remember that Hevtur was a dragon and couldn't fit in a coach. "Oh, right… uhhhh… one minute." Agamemnon said, turning to open a drawer on the map table and pulled out a map, big enough for Hevtur to see clearly.

It was a map of Corinthus. Agamemnon pointed at a pier on the southernmost point of the city near the west side of the pier and said, "Meet us here." Hevtur studied the map and nodded once and said, "I'll be there." Agamemnon then folded the map and put it back in the drawer that he took it from and shut the drawer.

Agamemnon turned on one foot and walked out of the room, Callus and Daentious followed. Agamemnon opened the door and the guards on the other side stood to attention, stomping their foot in a salute, Callus and Daentious, almost walking side by side, walked through the door and after Agamemnon. Hevtur turned to the dragon door and walked outside to the platform, his escort awoke to his voice saying, stay here, I'll be back." His guards bowed and watched him go, looking at one another before finding another comfortable enough spot to lay down again. The guards shut the door behind them and the other two guards on the other side of the miniature hallway opened the door and saluted.

Agamemnon walked through the door and Callus and Daentious, on his heels, did as well. The door shut behind them, and the eight guards of Corinos and Praetoria got up from their resting places and followed them in single file lines like before. They reached the great hall and turned for the southern side. Agamemnon saw a servant and said to him, "You! Get a coach ready at the southern palace doors, immediately!" The servant bowed at the waist saying, "Yes, your Majesty, it will be done right away." And hurried off to get a coach as quickly as possible. The whole moment felt intense for some reason, like as if they discovered a secret from their enemy or they found out a plot of assassination and were hurting to foil it. They were beginning to walk faster due to the intense feeling of the moment and it began to feel like a race to the finish line and their opponent was Hevtur, Callus thought that if that were the case, they would most surely lose.

They reached the southern courtyard and a coach was awaiting them. *That's odd, how did they get here before us? It's only been like three minutes at a maximum.* Callus thought walking behind Agamemnon towards the coach, Callus then realized that their guards were still behind them, keeping pace with them the whole, not moving any faster, slower, or louder than what Callus heard the entire time.

Callus thought that maybe that their footsteps blurred with the intense moment and so he didn't really hear them. The driver of the coach hastily opened the door saluting to Agamemnon. Agamemnon climbed into the coach and Daentious followed after Callus gestured for him to go first, while that was happening, Callus turned around to the eight guards and told them to wait near the doors of the palace, he thought that the Corinosian guards wouldn't listen, but to his surprise, they did and all eight of them turned on a heel and went back up to the palace doors. Callus climbed in and the driver shut the door and hurried up onto the top of the coach and urged the horses forward at an immediate trot, and then once they were through the southern inner gates, they began to go faster and faster, almost to a full run, so basically a quick canter.

Hevtur surveyed the city below, remembering where the spot was that he was trying to get to. He closed his eyes hard and remembered, he opened them and looked at the palace, then to the south, and in the distance, not far distance, he could see the little peninsula that Agamemnon pointed at. He began flying at a steady speed towards it.

"What, are we going to war or something?" Callus said with a wry voice, looking at Agamemnon. Agamemnon smiled and said, "That was getting pretty intense, wasn't it?" Callus chuckled. "No, just trying to get there at around the same time of Hevtur so that he's not waiting for too long." Agamemnon added.

"Tell me, how do you… like… tell her when you're coming?" Callus asked, folding his arms. "Where you met her, was just because that was where she was at the moment. Where you met her is where I go to seek permission to enter her palace." Agamemnon said, looking intently at Callus. "May I ask who 'her' represents?" Daentious asked, raising a brow. Agamemnon turned to Daentious and said, "The pronoun 'her' represents the queen of the Alzeirs kingdom." Daentious nodded in comprehension.

Hevtur arrived at the spot where Agamemnon told him to meet them and didn't see them there, which was no surprise really, he expected to be there earlier than the others. He began to wonder, *She? The Kingdom of Alzeirs? Like the river? What could this kingdom be, as in what species could this kingdom be? It could be dwarfs underneath the surface, it could also be dragons. Those are the only two I can think of at the moment. And She? Does that mean her husband is dead, or does she also do some things for the kingdom while the king does other things? I would suppose since it is called a kingdom that their titles are King and Queen.* Hevtur sat and looked forward over the surface of the water. The river was so wide it was almost not even a river, but the waterfall that produced the river was also enormous in comparison to just about anything in the world. It was so large that one could not see across the river. One could see the other side of the waterfall that created it. The waterfall itself was around four miles in length and the river widened as it flowed to the ocean.

The coach came to a stop and the driver opened the door for them. Agamemnon stepped out first followed by Callus and then Daentious. They didn't see Hevtur there, and Callus realized that this was the same spot where he met Queen Cora.

"Where is Hevtur, I thought that he would've been here before us?" Daentious asked, leaning forward in anticipation of an answer. "It would appear that I purposefully told him the incorrect spot to meet." Agamemnon said, turning around to face the others before turning around the corner to where he went before to introduce Queen Cora to Callus.

"You told him the wrong place? Where did you tell him to go then?" Daentious asked. "I told him to go on the other side of this building complex here, I was just about to ask you to go and get him in a moment." Agamemnon said to Daentious, implying that he was going to ask Daentious specifically for the task.

"Well what do you want me to say to him, that you deliberately told him to go to the wrong place in the first place?" Daentious asked, raising a brow at Agamemnon. "Yes, matter of fact that was exactly what I wanted you to say to him." Agamemnon replied, raising his chin just a tad bit and continued, "But don't go yet. I'll tell you when to go get him." Daentious nodded once and walked to stand side by side with Callus. Agamemnon turned and walked around the corner and out of sight.

Water stirred in front of Agamemnon and a water dragon poked its head above the surface of the water and looked at Agamemnon. "Ah, Porthon, can you tell Queen Cora that I am here to see her and that I have brought what she wanted too." Agamemnon said to the dragon.

In a light voice, but not to light, kind of like a boy coming into the middle stages of his adult voice, Porthon said, "Right away, King Agamemnon. I'll be right back with an answer." And Porthon fell back into the water. Agamemnon then turned to walk around the two corners he did to get to the section of water and saw Daentious and Callus chatting with one another and said, "Sorry to interrupt, but Sir Daentious, will you go get Hevtur now?"

"Sure thing, be right back." Daentious said and strode off to the main road and turned to his left for the other side of the pier they were on.

There were no ships on this pier, it was like a private pier for Agamemnon to meet up with and talk to Cora on. Agamemnon turned around and went back to the section of water where he awaited word from Porthon.

Daentious almost got lost about two, if you count the time thought he saw something he didn't and went to follow it, but turned around before committing himself down that path. He found the side where Hevtur was and walked up to him and cleared his throat. Hevtur was still resting on his haunches thinking, he heard Daentious clear his throat and say, "Hevtur, it would appear that Agamemnon deliberately told you to fly to the incorrect place for the meeting, I am here to show you to the correct place." He ended on a slight bow at the waist and Hevtur turned to look at him, still sitting down, just turning his head around and said, "Really?"

"Yes, he asked me to come get you and take you to the right place." Daentious replied. Hevtur looked at him blankly, not moving from his original position and said, "He told you to tell me exactly that, didn't he?" "More or less, yeah." Daentious said, nodding with the last word.

"Where is the right place?" Hevtur asked, moving to face Daentious squarely. "Just over this building complex here." Daentious said, pointing at the section of buildings to the east.

Hevtur inhaled and said, "Take a deep breath." Daentious blinked, taken aback, and a split second later, Hevtur spread his wings, moved closer to Daentious with lightning quick speed and grabbed Daentious in his front talons, picked him up off the ground and into the air. Daentious had the breath knocked out of him as he thought he was just about to get squished like a bug, an extremely large bug. Hevtur had just picked him up faster than he could think and took him over to the other side of the peninsula type pier within a second or two.

Hevtur landed on his back legs, and gently put Daentious on his feet, before coming to a complete land. Callus turned around to see Daentious take a few steps as if he was drunk and wince in pain because of his injured arm, and almost fall over, but he reclaimed his balance in time to prevent it, besides Hevtur was there behind him with a talon ready to stabilize him if necessary.

Daentious's eyes were wide with shock and his right arm was extended to keep his balance. He was breathing slowly through his mouth and then took a few more steps before letting out a quick exhale. "Hevtur, you about gave him a heart attack or something." Callus said, walking over to see if Daentious was actually going to fall or if his arm was damaged any more than it already was.

"I came as quickly as I could, I even told him to take in a deep breath before I did so." Hevtur said, acting like he was innocent, which he kind of was, he didn't actually do anything wrong.

Callus stared at him for a second before laughing in front of Daentious who was just recovering from their endeavor and grabbing at his injured left arm. Callus crouched a bit with his hands on his knees and his head looking down still laughing. Hevtur was trying to suppress a laugh, but wasn't doing a good job of it as a smile began to creep up on him. Daentious could tell that Hevtur was holding his breath to help suppress the laugh, but knew that it would only increase the laugh once he stopped holding his breath. Daentious swung his right arm from left to right grimacing and began bobbing up and down on his legs making sure everything still worked.

Hevtur saw him and couldn't hold his posture anymore and began laughing. Callus was still laughing, but more quietly now that his initial breath was spent, he crouched more and lowered himself to the ground holding his hand over his eyes laughing. Daentious didn't really find it amusing, he thought he was about to die or something. Hevtur bowed his head in a deeper laugh and almost looked like he was going to fall over.

Agamemnon walked around the corner one more time and saw the situation. Callus and Hevtur laughing almost uncontrollably and Daentious standing them with his hands on his hips looking at them with an unamused look on his face. Agamemnon walked over to Daentious's side and asked, "Hevtur took you on a flying lesson, didn't he?" Daentious looked at him and nodded slightly and slowly, still feeling the extreme pain in his arm. Agamemnon began to chuckle and asked, "How fast did he move?"

"I don't really want to talk about it." Daentious replied, holding his left arm in his right hand and looked at the other two, still laughing. How were they STILL LAUGHING. They've been doing it for almost a minute now. Then it wasn't just them, Agamemnon began to laugh as well. Daentious turned to look at Agamemnon laughing with his head up to the sky.

Daentious thought, *I could cut this guy's throat open and leave before anyone knew what happened.*

They all finally came to an end to their laughter and Agamemnon said, "Okay, follow me." They all began to follow him and Daentious could still hear Callus and Hevtur whispering and chuckling behind him. It almost made him feel insecure about his personal safety of being on solid ground. He already respected being on solid ground, but now that respect was taken to another level. Daentious was about to begin to respect the ground as if it were his own life, which in a way it was. He couldn't fly neither was he a great swimmer.

They followed Agamemnon to a large building that had large wooden doors. The doors opened to them and they all strode into the building, the doors shut behind them and two water dragons guarded it. Hevtur reeled his head back in surprise and looked at Callus who was looking at him. Callus shrugged his shoulders and looked ahead at Agamemnon who stood next to a large pool of water that led to the river. Hevtur walked up to stand next to Agamemnon and asked, "Water dragons, you kept an entire civilization of water dragons from the rest of the world?"

Agamemnon shrugged and said, "I don't actually own the Alzeirs River, they do, I just label it under my flag so that others don't try to get greedy and attempt to take it in force." Hevtur looked at him and back at the guards behind them before saying, "Not bad, not bad at all, and when an invading force presents itself, they fight it and you take the blame."

Agamemnon looked at him and shrugged again saying, "Works like a charm, and when they need reinforcements, I send a fleet. It's also almost like a spy network. They figure something out and tell me about it, and then I take care of it on a world diplomatic scale." Hevtur nodded in comprehension and straightened back up and sat down again waiting, his tail curled around his talons and his wings folded in as much as possible to stay confined like he usually did in a new or unusual place, like at the World Senatorial Building during the meetings there.

Callus and Daentious stood side by side with Agamemnon and Hevtur. After a half minute if entering, the water in front of them stirred and two more water dragons crawled out of the water and onto the stone surface of the building, behind them Queen Cora emerged and stepped up onto the stone platform on the other side of the water where the other two dragons stood. She turned around and saw the four of them standing there waiting.

"Sorry if I kept you waiting, this was on short notice." She said, looking at Agamemnon. "No worries. Daentious, Hevtur." Agamemnon said, turning from Cora to look at them. "This is Queen Cora of the

Kingdom of Alzeirs." He continued, gesturing at Cora. As he did Daentious and Hevtur bowed to Cora, Daentious at the waist and Hevtur crouching his front legs and bowing head. Agamemnon continued, "Cora, this is Sir Calpos Daentious of the Republic of Farrius and King Hevtur of the Kingdom of Jurrunt."

Once he finished Cora bowed to them both and Agamemnon continued, "And you know Imperator Callus of Praetoria." Agamemnon said, gesturing at Callus. Callus and Cora exchanged bows. "I have called for you on such short notice because something has occurred." Agamemnon said to Cora.

"And that is?" She asked, gesturing for Agamemnon to continue. He did, saying, "Like you suspected, Daentious here has brought some rather important news, urgent matter of fact, and I thought it best if you knew as well before we made our decision." Cora stared intently at Agamemnon before inhaling deeply in something that almost looked like fear and asked, "And what is that?"

Agamemnon looked at Daentious as if telepathically telling him to speak. Daentious stepped forward and bowed again before saying, "Before I left Zamos, Capital of Farrius, Senator Volkar gave me this scroll." Daentious pulled out the scroll from the pouch still on his side, miraculously since Hevtur decided that Daentious wasn't perfectly fine on the ground, living life without having a single flying lesson, and unrolled the scroll to read it.

He held out the scroll, grimacing in pain once again for his arm and Cora saw it and asked, "That was from the skirmish on the ship?" Daentious looked at her in confusion and then remembered that his arm was bandaged and in pain, he nodded and read the message aloud again and Cora seemed to be taken aback as well from the request.

"King Lithimir is right, I also believe it to be for the best to align with them. If a war is to break out, we will want more allies than foes." Cora said, after a moment of thinking. "I agree, but in a time such as this one, one should never trust too easily, I say that we send a request to meet and talk it over at the World Senatorial Meeting." Callus said soberly.

"That would be smartest." Cora replied, then continued, "What am I to do with this? I do not go to the World Senatorial Meeting."

"You did say that sooner or later, more sooner than later, that you would like to become a part of this alliance, especially if a war were to happen, so that your coming would be less eye-catching." Agamemnon said, looking into Cora's queen blue eyes. She inhaled and said, "I did say that, but that does not change the fact that I am not recognized by the rest of the world, Agamemnon."

Agamemnon inhaled and exhaled then said, "You're right, it doesn't, I just wanted to let you know so that you weren't completely left in the dark, this was also a good chance to introduce you to the others." "Yes, you're right, and I'm grateful that you did include me in this discussion. I am also glad to have met all of you." Cora said, looking from Agamemnon to the others.

"So do you wish to be at the next standardized meeting?" Hevtur asked. Cora looked at him and said, "Yes, I would." "Alright, well the next one will be taking place in Jurrunt." Agamemnon said, looking up at Cora. She nodded in the affirmative and said, "Okay, I will be there. I hope I'll see you all then."

"Me too, I'd rather not die or have something else unfortunate happen to me between now and then." Callus said with a very rye voice. Hevtur caught a laugh in his throat and looked down at Callus with hard eyes. Daentious looked down for a moment as if he was trying to interpret what Callus just said. Agamemnon also gave Callus a hard look, but Callus could see a smile trying to widen his face, Cora also barely caught a laugh within her throat before suppressing it quickly with uncanny political skill.

Once Callus saw the smile begin to grow on Agamemnon's face, he turned to Hevtur and could see that he was trying his hardest not to smile, but it wasn;t working all too well for him, Callus then said, "Well, if that's how you guys want to play then, be that way." Hevtur coughed out a short laugh and turned away, Agamemnon looked down to the ground and his shoulders began to shake with laughter. Daentious appeared to finally get what Callus was trying to say and began laughing before being able to suppress it as quickly as possible, Cora chuckled a little bit and then said, "See you then, Callus." Chuckling as she climbed back into the water with her guards following in suit.

One of the guards swallowed hard and had a small smirk on his face and the other had his eyes shut tight and was looking at the ground and he reopened them and climbed into the water, with the other, after Cora. Hevtur turned to Callus and said with a small laugh in his voice, "You idiot, that was so stupid."

"I think it was rather great." Daentious said laughing and continued, "And if you didn't like it I'll be glad to talk to Callus about it on our way back, like you did on the way in here." Callus burst out laughing along with Agamemnon while Hevtur stood there staring at Daentious before closing his eyes and letting out a small chuckle of his own.

"Alright let's go back to the palace and resume our meeting." Agamemnon said, starting for the door. The two water dragons were chatting quietly with one another and laughing at something quietly as well.

They saw Agamemnon approaching and straightened up and opened the doors, there were still little smirks on their faces as they did so. The other three recovering from their laughter followed out the door and the dragon guards behind them closed the door.

11

Hevtur debated where or not he should take Daentious for another flying lesson or not, but in the end he decided not to.

"I'll see you guys there." Hevtur said, lifting off the ground and into the sky. The coach that brought Agamemnon, Callus, and Daentious was still at the pier where they got off waiting for them to return.

They reached the coach and the driver stepped down from the top of the coach and opened the door for them. He saluted and Agamemnon led into the coach followed by Callus and he was followed in by Daentious. Once they were all in the coach the driver shut the door and stepped up atop the coach, clutched the reins and urged the horses forward once again.

Agamemnon had a grin on his face and was looking at Callus and said, "I'll have to admit, that was pretty good." Callus looked at him and returned the grin saying, "That's just the way I am." Agamemnon burst out laughing along with Callus and Daentious put his hand casually over his mouth to cover up the smile that appeared on it. While Callus was laughing he choked and began coughing into his elbow, Agamemnon laughed even harder. Daentious was sure that the driver probably thought that they were drunk, and maybe just now the driver was thinking about having some booze himself, even though they weren't drunk.

Callus recovered from his coughing and said with a rye voice, "That was stupid." Agamemnon ceased laughing for the moment to say, "Yeah, it matches your profile." Daentious choked trying to hold in the laugh and began coughing. Agamemnon laughed again and Callus stared at him with an even look.

"Oh, so you think you're funny?" Callus asked, bobbing his head sarcastically. Agamemnon saw the look on Callus's face and laughed harder. Callus began laughing as well, not being able to hold it in any longer. Daentious was still coughing out the air he choked on earlier.

Hevtur was almost to the platform where his guards were laying and resting about awaiting his return. One of them saw him coming and warned the others to attention, and they all awoke and stood up to attention. He landed and nodded once for them to ease. He then turned to the palace and walked back inside and lied down in his designated spot while he waited for the others to show up.

The coach approached the southern inner gates and the gates opened for it. The coach then passed through and the gates closed behind them. The guards were talking to one another again as if they were a group of friends getting together as the coach pulled up next to the palace's southern doors stairs, and the driver hopped down from the driver's seat of the coach and opened the door.

The guards then stood to attention, in their corresponding colors and awaited the higher ups. Agamemnon, like usual, led the way out of the coach and onto the stone courtyard in front of the palace. Callus stepped out after him and Daentious out after Callus. They strode up the stairs quickly and the doors were opened by the guards that guarded it.

They walked through the doorway and the Corinosian guards that followed Agamemnon before followed him again and the Praetorian guards that followed Callus followed him again.

The thing was that Daentious never had any guards with him when he showed up for a meeting, nor did he wherever else he went. The only times Daentious actually had guards around him were when he was standing around any one of importance or when he was in the field, and even then they weren't even his guards and the ones he was around in the field weren't even guards.

Callus, Agamemnon, and Hevtur always thought it strange, but never questioned it after they asked him when they first met him, when he got his job, around the same time they all came to be crowned.

That part wasn't odd nearly as much as him not having any guards, it was almost like the senators of Farrius didn't care that much about their military leaders. Callus, Agamemnon, and Hevtur all thought that not having any guards around him was going to be what killed him in the end. It actually almost happened on his way here.

They often thought that the higher up military leaders of the Republic of Farrius didn't have guards because that way if the senators wanted the man gone they could pay for assassins to do the deed and have almost no worries of him somehow surviving the endeavor. Politics, they would say when they got done talking thinking about it, or anything that was stupid or unreasonable for the matter.

They reached the war room and the guards that followed Callus and Agamemnon around got used to being told to wait outside in the hallway, so when they reached the war room the guards stopped and waited in the hallway for the door to close before starting either another conversation with each other or picking up the same conversation from earlier and began talking to each other again.

The door shut behind Daentious, who was the last one in the room and the three of them walked over to the map table in the center of the war room. The map table was enormous compared to a human, much larger than a map table made for humans, so that Hevtur or any dragon for that matter could see it well enough, the table was a good height for a human or high elf, and where Hevtur lay the floor was lower so that when he lay down he could see the map at almost the exact angle a human could.

The map showed the continent of Luminarch, the continent of Drakenmor to the northwest of the continent of Luminarch, more to the north than the west, and the large island of Britone, which was just off the northwestern coast of Luminarch, more to the west than the north.

Between one to two thousand miles off the western and southwestern coasts of Luminarch was an entire spread of islands. Some were decent in size and others were much smaller and they were controlled by any faction that was on a bigger island closest to them, and some factions just had a few little islands as their territory. The wall of islands spread from about the center or level with Essilor's point and stretched to around near the bottom of the map... The wall of islands was called, well, The Island Wall, because it was a wall of islands.

"Well, let's get down to business. What are we thinking?" Callus said, clapping his hands and rubbing them together. "I was still thinking that you were stupid." Hevtur said in a rye voice.

Callus stopped rubbing his hands and froze, looking at Hevtur with a flat face. Hevtur looked up from the map at Callus with a smirk. Callus blinked idly at him before Daentious broke the silence by saying, "And I still think that it was pretty funny." Hevtur turned his gaze to Daentious and said in a sarcastic tone, "I didn't say that he wasn't funny, it was that it was so stupid that it was funny." Agamemnon laughed and bowed his head. Hevtur looked at Callus with a side-eye look, and Callus's lips were quivering with a laugh, but he was able to keep it in and at least look semi-serious.

Daentious replied with sarcasm, "It wasn't as stupid as your flying lesson though." Agamemnon laughed harder, and Callus couldn't hold in his anymore either and began laughing. Hevtur reshifted his gaze upon Daentious and said, "Well geez, apparently some people just can't be pleased." Daentious chuckled along with Hevtur and Callus and Agamemnon might not have heard Hevtur's remark because they were laughing so hard.

When they recovered a moment later Agamemnon said, "Okay, seriously, let's do this. Hevtur has anything happened on any of your fronts?"

"No, well actually, on my eastern front where the faction of Lashiduin lies, there have been some unnaturally intense storms happening and quite a bit of them as well." Hevtur said, looking at the map.

"Have any hit your borders?" Callus asked, wiping some water from his eyes after laughing so hard. "No, at least not yet." Hevtur replied.

"What about you, Callus? Has anything happened on your borders, granted you only border one other faction other than us?" Agamemnon said. "No, nothing has happened on any of my fronts. Classis II Oceanianic hasn't reached Port Reaver, but they're not planned to until a few more weeks from now." Callus replied looking from Agamemnon to the map.

"And you, Daentious? Anything you care to share?" Callus burst out a chuckle before repeating in a quieter voice, "Care to share." He put his fists on his hips and shook his head.

"Njori on the northwestern border have been acting a little weirder than normal, but that's not unusual for them. As for Glarlrel on the southwestern border, they have converted to using magic." Daentious said, stroking his beard slightly.

"Hmmm." Agamemnon said, scratching the left side of his face where his beard was with his right hand. "Well as for me, there are those marauders on the other side of the river and the ones bordering me by land are still on the sketchy side of all things. As for my eastern border, the dragons there don't seem to care about the sun or something, because none of my scouts ever see any. Maybe they're just hiding, and as for the dwarves they have not seemed to come out of their mines as well, but they never really do anyways." Agamemnon finished by folding his arms.

"Well I have one more thing to show you all." Daentious said, reaching into the pouch at his side and pulling out another scroll and placing it upon the table rolling it out.

It was a diagram of something that resembled a house-like structure with wheels and what looked like a large log sticking out the front and back. It had multiple of these diagrams, one of what looked like the front, another of what looked like the rear, and one of each side on the left and the right. There was one more picture of it at an angle from a focal point aligned with the corner and angled looking down at it so that the top of it was showing, another picture looked like it was from the top of the contraption, looking straight down on it.

"What is it?" Hevtur asked. It was a little too small for him to see it without bending the light to see more clearly and most things in the alliance were made for him to be able to see without having to resort to bending the light to see.

"Looks like a house with something like a battering ram sticking out the front and back of it, it has wheels as well." Agamemnon said, who was the closest to Daentious, looking down at the paper full of diagrams.

"Scouts reported seeing these in the land of Haxy in between the Njori, and the Garlrelians. It appears to be a battering ram encased in a shield of some kind so that it can be rolled up to the gates and begin to ram them without losing a single soldier in the process." Daentious said, putting his right hand knuckles to the table.

"A shielded battering ram." Agamemnon said, looking at the diagrams. Hevtur bent the light to see the diagram for himself and saw the drawings and said, "Interesting, but how exactly would it work? That doesn't really look like it has the room for the soldiers needed to push the whole of the machine and have the soldiers necessary to be able to pick up the battering ram and move it back and forth to hit a gate with it."

"I believe they use pulleys and ropes to use it, ropes hold it up and the soldiers within use pulleys to pull it back, let it go to hit into the gates and then repeat until the gates are destroyed." Daentious said, folding one arm across his torso and the other arm's elbow on the wrist of the other hand, supporting his arm that was stroking his beard.

"That's quite smart." Callus said, looking at the diagrams. "It would appear that everyone has their secrets." Callus added and continued, "We all know each one of us have a secret, and we all know that our neighbors have secrets and our neighbor's neighbors have their secrets as well." He looked at every other one in the room. "Don't even try to deny it." Callus added.

"I don't know what you're talking about." Daentious said, his tone all smug. Callus turned to him and said, "I told you not to and you did anyway." Hevtur laughed with Agamemnon, Daentious's lips were quivering with laughter, and Callus was looking at him intently, trying to get him to laugh before he did himself.

"Secrets are not mine to keep." Daentious said, almost laughing. "I'm just a messenger, I mean, I tell you what I'm supposed to tell you, you know." He added, gesturing with his hands in a shrugging like motion.

"No, I don't know, and what on earth do you mean, 'I'm just a messenger'?" Callus said, shrugging like Daentious did when he quoted him. Daentious winced out a laugh, and Callus was surprisingly holding one in himself, and Hevtur and Agamemnon laughed harder at Callus's imitation of Daentious.

"Okay, are we done here? I might need to go as soon as possible to deliver our response to the alliance request to the senate for delivery to King Lithimir." Daentious said, gesturing at the scroll in his pouch. "Yeah, I think we are unless someone else has anything to say." Agamemnon said, once he recovered enough to speak decently.

"Yeah, I'm good with ending this meeting the way it is." Callus said, rubbing his face. Hevtur regained his posture and said, "Yes, I believe we're done here as well."

"Okay, if you all will sign the paper, I can sign for you Hevtur, I'll be on my way." Daentious said, pulling out the scroll from his pouch and a quill from a nearby desk, and bringing them over to the map table for the paper to be signed.

Callus and Agamemnon signed it and Daentious signed it for Hevtur, because it was too small for Hevtur to be able to write. Daentious rolled the scroll back up and stuffed it neatly in the pouch at his side, walked over to the desk where he got the quill and put the quill back in the ink bowl that it lay in before he grabbed it. He turned and nodded once to the others before departing the room.

Hevtur then said, "I'll see you at the World Senatorial Meeting." Bowing his head and crouching his front legs in a bow. Callus and Agamemnon returned the gesture. Hevtur turned and the door opened for him, he walked out the door onto the platform where his guards were waiting, chatting with each other and the Corinosian guards on the platform as well.

"Let's go home." Hevtur said to his guards and lifted off, they followed him into the sky and blended in with the blue clear sky.

Callus then turned to Agamemnon and said, "I think that's my que to leave as well." He traded grips with Agamemnon and said, "See you next time." Agamemnon bowed his head in response and Callus strode off to the man door where the pilums were still embedded into the wooden beams. "What about your things here?" Agamemnon asked, gesturing at the equipment. Callus turned around and looked at them and said, "You can have them all if you'd like." Agamemnon blinked and said, "Alright, thank you." Callus nodded and walked out of the room and into the hallway where his guards were and gestured for them to follow him.

The doors behind him were shut by the guards who opened them for him and Agamemnon stood there in the room looking at the impaled cross beams above the door and thought, *Those are going to be a pain to remove. And as for my new gifts that Callus has given me, I don't know. Well actually I do know what I want to test with the bolt thrower.*

Agamemnon pursed his lips and called, "Guards!" And the door opened and all eight guards rushed into the room saluting. "Get this equipment to the engineers and get it out of here. I want that bolt thrower put on a ship for testing, and also pull those pilums out of the beams." Agamemnon said, pointing at the pilums above the door and continued, "Dowse the torches as well."

"Yes my Liege." One of the guards said, turning around to face his companions and barked out some orders. Agamemnon walked to the door and out of the room.

The history behind the name of the Chechian Crater was that one thousand years ago in the great war against evil, when the world came together to fight it, an earth dragon faction called the Chech were fighting an evil horde and were about to be overrun. The Chechians came together, or what was left of them, and fought at where the Chechian Crater is now, back then it wasn't a crater. One of the Chechians, probably the leader of that faction, called upon the earth, and with all his might, made the ground buckle and break and rollover onto itself and the evil that was upon it. It is said that such a strain on his mind from that much magic all at once, killed him, or her.

After the Great War, the world came together to create the first World Senatorial Meeting. Some passers-by must have seen the crater and remembered that that was where the Chechians were, and brought the information to the meeting, and from there on it has been called the Chechian Crater.

The Crater was still on neutral ground, neither the Praetorians nor the Zulkbarians owned it; it lay in between the two factions covering up to thirty miles in diameter and two miles deep, which was impressive for back then, even for now it was still quite a sight.

As for the history behind Legio III Attis, it was actually founded in the Great War itself by a man named Puveirious Attis. It kept his name, and the world, or most of the world still knows about the legion to the day.

Puveirious Attis was the leader of what used to be the tribe of Praevia, and he led this army's standard into battle against the great evil in the great war and won many battles against them. He was seen as a savior to most living things then and is still seen that way for some.

Legio III Attis was the third army that the Praevians raised in that time and was the last one standing once it was done. For a reward for his valiant efforts in the war he was given one of the biggest and best pieces of land. He was even offered the Chechian Crater, but he denied it in order to preserve the long lasting memory of the Chechians heroic defeat, or victory depending on how you look at it, by leaving it neutral for the world to see as a reminder of what they did.

Puveirious Attis never took a wife, and so his line didn't actually last that long. Fortunately, there was no civil war to claim the crown, most likely because everyone was done with fighting. Instead they all took a vote and decided that Craesious Hullious should take the throne. He accepted and began to continue in Attis's footsteps to build up the mighty faction that is now known as the Imperium of Praetoria. The name changed, and with the change of the houses from Puveirious to Craesious. The form of government changed as well.

The flag that Attis created stayed with a legionaries shield in the center and two long arcs on each side with a scarlet background and purple for the secondary color.

General Saveirious Plutoma, or just General Saveirious, was now the general of Legio III Attis until he stepped down, or was killed. He was respected by his men, or so he thought, and he was in his personal quarters reading a book, as he usually did when there was nothing to do, and was surprisingly almost halfway through.

He just received the book as a gift from his wife about three months ago right before he was stationed at the Chechian Crater. As he was reading it on his cot one of his guards said, "Sir messenger here to deliver a message." Saveirious looked up from his book and said, "Let him in." He put a piece of cloth in his book where he left off, and placed it down onto the cot. He stood and walked to the middle of the tent as a small scrawny fellow walked in through the tent flaps.

It looked like he was going to fall over by being hit by a tent flap, but he didn't and strode in front of Saveirious and saluted Praetorian style and said, "Message from Imperator Callus sir, along with new equipment." He held out a scroll in his left hand and Saveirious picked it up. He nodded and the messenger left the tent. Saveirious sat back down on his cot and broke the wax seal of the scroll and opened it. It said:

> "General Saveirious, this scroll contains an order
> to implement the new equipment that I have sent to
> your encampment near the Chechian Crater. I want
> this equipment ready and willing for battle if necessary.
> There will be engineers there to teach you and your men
> what they are and how to use them, there will also be a
> new century of legionaries that will be using some of the
> equipment. Ask the engineers for more details.
>
> Signed: Imperator Callus of the house of Craesious
> of the Imperium of Praetoria."

Saveiriuos stood to his feet and walked out of the tent, turned to one of the guards, who saluted him, held up the scroll and asked, "Where?" The guard pointed to his right and said, "Over there sir, they just arrived." Saveirious looked and walked off and towards the newly arriving convoy of wagons and came to a slight jog.

There were some legionaries who were just chatting around with each other and saw him and saluted, he jogged off past the and they looked at where he was going and saw the convoy, they looked at each other and walked off towards it as well talking with one another. Saveirious reached the road where the wagons were and came to a panting stop, he was wearing his legion lorica and cape, just not his helmet.

All the legionaries around the road saw him and saluted almost in perfect unison, some of them saw him later than others, and he nodded in approval to them and walked over to the first wagon. He controlled his breathing, looked to the driver of the wagon and asked, "Who's the superior officer on this convoy?"

The driver saluted to him and said, "He's back near the middle of the convoy sir, he was inspecting it on our way in, he should be on his way back up here." Saveirious nodded once in registration and walked back to the side of the road where the legionaries huddled and said,

"FORM UP!" And all of the legionaries found their spot and stood in it, forming the maniples of the third legion Attis.

The centurions got to the front and saluted followed by the rest of the legionaries. Saveirious walked over to about the front middle of the ranks and said, "You are all to stay here until further instructions." The legion saluted again.

The wind was blowing Saveirious's black hair around although it was short, his beard was shaved and he stood as a blocky man around just around six feet.

He looked at the wagons full of something, but there were tarps covering the cargo on each wagon. A moment went by and a man on a horse trotted up to Saveirious, saluted and said, "General Saveirious?"

Saveirious looked up at the man in legionary armor, but it wasn't the lorica that the rest of the legionaries wore, it was much different. Saveirious studied the man before responding, "Yes?" The man then said, "Sir, I am Centurion Scipio of the engineers that are to join up with your legion, I would ask for your orders on where to stop the convoy."

Saveirious looked at Scipio for another second and said, "That depends what is in the convoy." Scipio nodded and said, "There is new armor, like the armor I wear before you, new weapons that I do not wear on my persons.

Saveirious looked up at the man again thinking then said, "Set up your tents on the west side of camp, I'll see you there in two hours." Scipio saluted and said, "Yes sir." He turned his horse to the convoy and began barking out orders to the men. Saveirious watched him go and turned to his men standing aside the road and said, "Go get some rest, and in two hours I want every single one of you to form up and stand at the ready on the west side of camp!" The entire legion around him saluted and dispersed into the camp, heading towards their tents.

Saveirious walked back through the camp and to his tent where his guards stood guarding the tent. "Let me know when it has been two hours." Saveirious said as the guards nodded and held open the tent flap as he walked into the tent and let it fall behind him. He picked up his book and sat back down on his cot. He opened the black backed book and put the cloth down next to him on his cot and began reading again.

Two hours later one of his guards said, "Sir, it's been nearly two hours." And Saveirious picked up his cloth and put it between the pages where he was reading and closed the book. He put the book back down on the cot and stood up, he walked over to his armor stand and picked up his helmet and strapped it onto his head. He then walked over to the tents opening and opened the flap to the almost noon sun and legionaries were moving in their centuries toward the west side of camp.

He told his guards to follow him and they started through the camp to the west. A few minutes later they reached the engineers camp to the west of theirs and Centurion Scipio had his men at the ready waiting for Saveirious to arrive.

Scipio saluted Saveirious and he nodded his head in return. Saveirious looked to the sides of Scipio's century and saw crates and crates of javelins. There were more crates of what looked to be hide leather in cone-like shapes. There were also crates of chainmail among them.

"So what is it you bring to this legion?" Saveirious said, looking into Scipio's eyes.

"New equipment sir." Scipio replied, looking straight forward squarely with his body.

"Equipment?" Saveirious asked.

"Yes sir, armor additions like what you see on my men sir, weapon swaps and additions that you see around us on the ground and a new weapon that is behind us sir." Scipio replied, gesturing to the crates and then behind the mainple of men.

Behind Saveirious, thirty maniples of men stood at the ready for orders. And beyond that the two maniples of cavalry men on foot, as their horses were still in their corals.

"Very well, show me what this equipment is and how it works?" Saveirious said, folding his hands behind his back.

Scipio grabbed at his upper arms armor and said, "Chainmail has been added onto the armor for upper arm protection." He paused and grabbed down at his lower arm and continued, "Hide has been added onto the armor sets for lower arm protection."

"Wouldn't that hinder our ability to armor up in the morning for the day?" Saveirious asked, raising his chin slightly. "Not much sir, the chainmail just goes on before the lorica and as for the leather forearm guards, they slide on and are tightened by pulling this string." Scipio said, gesturing at the chainmail and then the leather guard, grabbing a string about the width of seven millimeters.

It wrapped around the front or the part closest to the hand and went back up to the rear of it, the part closest to the elbow, and back down again in integrating loops and paths. The string was covered by the leather so that the enemy couldn't cut it too easily.

"It is also loosened the same way." Scipio added.

"Elvish rope, or string in this case?" Saveirious asked, looking from the leather arm guard to Scipio.

"Yes sir." Scipio replied.

"Okay, what about the weapons?" Saveirious asked. Scipio gestured to one of the men to bring one and the man grabbed a javelin and carried it over to them and held the weapon up so they could see it and grab it with ease.

Scipio grabbed the javelin and said, "This is the new version of a javelin, it is called a pilum." He held the pilum horizontally with the ground and Saveirious grabbed it in one hand and studied it.

It was about seven feet long and moderately heavy, its tip was barbed and it had a longer metal head than a regular javelin.

"How exactly is it used?" Saveirious said, arching a brow at Scipio.

"Every legionary is given one and they throw it into the enemy ranks before contact." Scipio said.

"Okay, and what else is there?" Saveirious asked, looking from the pilum back to Scipio. Scipio gestured to his men and they moved aside and a few of them rolled a wooden structure forward and in front of them. They set it down and backed away, one was holding a heavy javelin, heavier than the pilum it looked like, and much shorter.

"This is called a bolt thrower, sir. It is an artillery piece." Scipio said, walking toward the bolt thrower to explain.

"How it works is that two crew members pull back this string..." Scipio said, touching the string, or cord based on the size of it, and continued, "and latch it onto this hook." He said touching the hook near the rear of the weapon. "Then another crew member will feed a bolt..." Scipio grabbed the bolt from the legionary holding it and continued, "Through this loop at the front and back against the string." He pretended to load the bolt onto the bolt thrower and went on, "Another crew member will then adjust the artillery toward its target and another will pull this rope…" He grabbed a rope at the rear of the weapon and picked it up for Saveirious to see before continuing, "And the bolt will be thrown through the air and to its target." He finished and gave the bolt back to the legionary that held it before.

"And your maniple is who will be operating these machines?" Saveirious asked, giving the pilum to a legionary standing nearby.

"Yes sir." Scipio answered, coming to attention. Saveirious nodded and said, "Very good, introduce this equipment to the head logistics officer and tell him what you told me. That will be all for today." Scipio saluted and turned around to give orders to his men to get going.

Saveirious turned around to his legion and said, "Tomorrow morning you will meet with Logistics Officer Garrus for armor additions and weapons. That will be all for today while the logistics officers sort things out! Dismissed!"

The legion saluted and turned to march back into the camp and towards their sectors where each maniples tents were pitched. Saveirious turned to his guards and said, "Let's go." Moving a hand in a gesture forward from his ear. They followed him and they walked over the rocky ground and back to his tent, where he was going to read his book for the next few hours and after that, go to the command tent for the officers meeting.

The place was desolate, devoid of almost all life. Grass and other weeds were growing here and there in patches, but it has been one thousand years and it was either barely beginning to grow or it was growing at an extremely slow rate. It was mid spring and gratefully it was a warm day, and there were no clouds in the sky near there.

13

There was nothing historically special about the Plaxident Valley, it was just a green, lush, and welcoming valley, or at least it looked that way.

It was twenty five miles long, one mile wide and about five hundred feet in depth on average. There were places with forests and scattered trees and others just grass plains. A stream here and there would join into a river that went down the valley to the north, away from the Kingdom of Jurrunt.

The valley stretched almost directly north and south and curved a little bit near the north end, if you were on the southern end of the valley. The mountains were in view and a few of the rivers or streams running through the valley started there.

It was a particularly sunny day, despite it being spring, and the wind was casually blowing. There were clouds heading to the east, but there always were since about two months ago. They just kept on forming and forming and kept on going over there as if they were being pulled there like a magnet being pulled from one's fingers to a larger magnetic item.

The Zulkbarian army that Legio VII Donnious was mirroring, or close to mirroring, never moved, granted like the Praetorians, they hid their camp behind the other ridge of the valley so that they couldn't be watched as much as they could be if they were on top of the ridge.

They could still get to certain points of the west side ridge to look down at the camp well enough to tell that the tents were still there.

The dwarves were too small, or short, to be seen from a great distance without magic, but every once in a while a dragon would come down from the mountains and tell them about something that happened that they deemed necessary to inform the Praetorians about.

It was helpful, one time they informed the Praetorians of dwarf scouts trying to move through the valley and onto the other side, which would have been trespassing, but the Praetorians wouldn't know about it therefore it wouldn't really be trespassing.

Chorrus Kasis, General of Legio VII Donnious, was in his tent when a guard outside spoke up, "General, messenger here to see you." Kasis looked up from his desk and asked, "From who?" "Imperator Callus, sir." The guard said. "Let him in." Kasis responded. The tent flap opened and what appeared to be the messenger walked in.

The messenger was tall and slender with blonde hair. His hair was cut short in legion style and his face was shaved. He bore a scroll in his left hand and saluted. "Message from The Imperator, general." The messenger said, holding out the scroll to General Kasis. Kasis took the scroll and said, "Dismissed." And the messenger left without another word.

Kasis opened the scroll and read the message within it. It said:

"General Chorrus Kasis, this message is to be read soberly. I have dispatched new equipment to your encampment to be implemented into Legio VII Donnious at once and to be ready in case of any violence.

Sincerely, Imperator Craesious Callus."

Kasis sat there in his tent a minute longer thinking about what the Imperator meant by new equipment then put the scroll down and stood up. He walked over to the tent flaps and opened them to stand outside in what was now a cloudy sky, and as always the clouds were moving to the east.

Greedy snots. Kasis thought, looking to the east at the dark gray sky. His guards saluted the moment he stepped out of the tent and he looked to the west and saw a convoy of wagons heading for the camp. He regarded them for a moment, pursing his lips before walking back into his tent and sitting back down at his desk to look at the papers upon it.

The legionaries looked at the convoy in inquiry as it pulled up next to the camp. The centurions there began to beckon the legionaries back into their tents and away from the incoming convoy. One of the centurions walked up to the nearest wagon and asked in a stern voice, "What is this and why is it here?"

The driver looked down at him and pointed to a man on horseback trotting to them. The centurion scowled at the driver and walked to the man on his mount. The horse came to a stop ten feet from the centurion and the rider of the horse asked, "Where is General Kasis?"

Centurion replied, "Not until you tell me who you are and what this is." The centurion had his baton in his hands resting near his waist.

The rider acknowledged and said, "I am Centurion Foollus Minus, and this is the new equipment that The Imperator has sent to be embedded into this legion." The other centurion looked up at him and said, "I haven't heard anything about this, how do I know you're not lying?"

Minus looked down at him intently and said, "Our messenger should have arrived earlier today or yesterday." The other centurion then said, "If you'll stay here, I'll see about your messenger."

Minus saluted as well as the other centurion and they went their separate ways. Minus began barking out orders to the convoy and the convoy began to move into ordered lines just outside of camp.

A few moments later, one of Kasis's guards said, "General, Centurion Bartus here to see you, shall I let him in?" Kasis looked up from his desk and said, "Yes."

The tent flap opened and Centurion Bartus, the centurion from earlier, walked in and stood five feet from Kasis's desk and saluted. Kasis nodded once and asked, "What is it?"

"Centurion Minus, who is leading that convoy out there wishes to meet with you claiming that a messenger was supposed to have arrived for them." Bartus said, standing to attention. Kasis nodded and said, "Yes, the messenger just arrived today. Tell him to come up here to meet with me." Bartus nodded once and saluted and walked out of the tent with long strides, like most centurions did, and back over to where the convoy had halted and began to form up.

Bartus reached the convoy and walked over to the nearest man he saw and asked, "Where is Centurion Minus?" The man looked at Bartus and said, "He's over there with the maniple, sir." Pointing at where a maniple was in formation. Bartus sharply nodded once and walked over to where the maniple was standing and Centurion Minus stepped out from around them and looked at Bartus.

Minus's hands were holding his baton behind his back as he walked around the maniple and towards Bartus.

"The General requests to see you in his tent as soon as possible." Bartus said to Minus. Minus nodded once and turned to his men and said, "Dismissed."

The maniple dispersed and Minus turned back to Bartus and said, "Thank you." Bartus stopped him and said, "I'll take you there, I would like to know any new centurions that are to be a part of this legion." Minus nodded and they started to go to General Kasis's personal tent.

A few minutes later, they reached the tent and Bartus said to the guards, "I'm here with Centurion Minus, here to see The General."

One of the guards leaned his head back and said, "General, Centurion Bartus and Centurion Minus are here to see you."

"Let them in." General Kasis said. One of the guards held out his hands and said, "Weapons please." And Bartus and Minus gave him their weapons and walked through the tent flaps that the other guard held open.

The two centurions saluted and Kasis looked up at them from his desk and asked, "Centurion Minus, I am to understand that you are here with new equipment and to be embedded into this legion as well?"

Minus said, "Yes sir. And I also wish that you tell me where to position the convoy for camp, sir." Kasis pursed his lips in thought before answering, "The west side of camp is best for now."

Minus then said, "Yes General, and also, when do you wish to inspect the new equipment?" Kasis folded his arms and said, "Now may be the best time for it while it's cloudy out. I will be down there shortly be ready for me to inspect. Dismissed." Minus and Bartus saluted and walked out of the tent.

Kasis continued to look at papers on his desk for several more minutes before standing up and walking over to the tent flaps and walking out of the tent. The guards saluted and Kasis said, "Get me a few legionaries for escort."

One of the guards said, "Yes General." And walked off to find some men. Kasis stood there and looked into the sky and the gray clouds above him, the air was cool and on the brink of being cold. He could barely see his breath when he exhaled, but it wasn't all that cold to him. Maybe standing outside in the weather for a while he would get cold eventually, but until that time came it felt rather pleasant to him.

After about one minute of standing there the guard returned with several legionaries and a centurion. Kasis turned to look at them before gesturing to them to follow him. They walked through the camp, Kasis drawing salutes from the legionaries that saw him, and arrived at the addition of the camp on the west side where the convoy had been a few minutes later.

Minus had his maniple formed up and waiting with him in front. They all saluted once Kasis became close enough and Kasis stopped in front of Minus and asked, "So, where is this equipment you brought?"

Minus said, "It is ready when you are General." Kasis nodded once and Minus gestured to a few men and they brought out two crates, two men on each crate, and set them down. The legionaries opened the crates and, from one pulled out leather couplings and from the other crate pulled out a javelin.

Minus held out his hand to the legionaries on his left and grabbed the leather coupling from his hand and said, "This sir, is an addition to every legionaries armor, it is a coupling made of hide to go around one's forearm. It is put on by sliding it over the hand and tightening these strings." He finished by sliding it over one of his arms where one already resided and grabbing onto the strings that went throughout it.

He then offered the coupling to Kasis and he took it. Kasis studied it for a second before sliding it over his hand and onto his forearm where it fit perfectly, one and a half inches from the inside of his elbow and the same distance from his wrist. He pulled the strings and the coupling tightened down on his arm comfortably. It didn't restrict him in any way. He looked up at Minus and Minus said, "It comes off the same way, it's made of elvish rope sir."

Kasis looked down to the coupling and tugged on the strings and the coupling came loose. He pulled off the coupling and handed it back to Minus saying, "What else?"

Minus then explained, "There are also chainmail half tunics that go underneath a legionary's armor and protect the upper arm while the coupling protects the lower arm."

Kasis nodded and gestured at the javelin saying, "And what about that?" Minus turned and gave the coupling back to the legionary and then held out his hand to the legionary that held the javelin.

The legionary gave him the javelin and Minus held it horizontally to the ground and said, "This is called a pilum, sir. Every legionary is to carry one into battle and throw it into the enemy ranks before engaging in close quarters."

Kasis's brows raised and he took the pilum from Minus's hands. He felt its weight for a second and turned his head towards the ground away from any people and gave himself space. He took the pilum in one hand, balanced it out and threw it at the ground. It struck the ground, impaling it, and bent almost straight up. Kasis raised an inquisitive brow and looked at Minus for answers as to why it bent.

Minus said, "Its tip is barbed to cause maximum damage to the enemy, and it bends like that so that the enemy cannot throw it back at your own men." Kasis raised his brows again and looked back at the pilum. It stopped wobbling and he could see that even if one could pull it out of a body without tearing out flesh along with it, they wouldn't be able to throw it all that well and not with good damage or accuracy.

Kasis turned and walked back to Minus and asked, "Is this all?" Minus shook his head and said, "No sir, there is one more thing. And it is the reason why this maniple is to be embedded into your legion."

Kasis gestured for him to show the reason and Minus did. He beckoned his maniple and they parted and a few men came forward pushing an item that came to just below chest height.

They stopped and put the machine down and took a step back. Kasis noticed that one of the men was holding a shorter and fatter than usual spear of some kind. Almost like an arrow but bigger in all dimensions.

Minus walked over to it and said, "This is called a bolt thrower. It is an artillery piece, meant to be easy to move onto and within the battlefield." Minus began to tell Kasis about the bolt thrower and when he finished he said, "Each one of these takes five men to operate, two to pull back the cord string, two to aim and load, and one to lose the bolt, and command the unit. We have a total of twenty four of these bolt throwers and two crates of ammunition for each."

Kasis nodded and said, "Very well. Get these pilums, couplings and chainmail tunics to the store house for the logistics officers to sort out, they will be implemented tomorrow." Minus saluted and said, "At once General." And turned around to give out orders to his maniple.

PART TWO

Chapter

14

Three Weeks Later

It was the beginning of summer when Classis II Oceanianic arrived in Port Reaver. The port was large enough to fit thousands of ships within it and still have space for others to sail in and out. Admiral Bortus was to meet up with Admiral Hethus of Classis I Glacius once everything was in order with his fleet. The men grew tired and weary on their long journey around the Courue Peninsula and Bortus had to ensure that they wouldn't go around and create trouble on their first few days of arrival at their new post.

Bortus was in his cabin when a knock on the door presented itself and the man on the other side said, "Admiral, are you ready to go?" Bortus was just finishing up some reviews on slave performance at his desk. He said, "Yes, I'll be there in a moment, Ghorstus."

Bortus stood up and put the papers in a drawer on his desk, he blew out the candle at his desk and walked through the dark cabin to the door. He opened the door and walked out. Ghorstus saluted firmly and Bortus nodded once in reply. They walked over to the boarding plank where the plank was connecting the ship to the dock and walked down the plank, Bortus led and Ghorstus followed.

The most fabulous thing is that it is mid-summer, and it is still cooler than it was in the south, granted it isn't as cold as other northern regions in the world, but it was still cooler than it was in the southern summers. I don't want to even think about how cold it would be in the winter. The winter's up here must suck severely, even though all winters now sucked greatly, the winter's up north would have been deathly. I wonder if children in the north even saw winter the same way as the child in the southern reaches of Praetoria. They must have seen it as well, hopefully no school, but considering how far north they were, snow days probably didn't really exist. Children in the south saw winter and holidays and snow ball fights and sled rides and snow angles or whatever they call those things they do in the snow with their arms and legs, laying on their backs, probably thinking, "Oh, how fun this is. Look, a snowball fight. Look a sled, let's go ride down the hill and", if you were a boy, "see who biffs it the hardest", and they'd be the winner with a bloody nose and split lip because there just happened to be a rock there or maybe a root or more likely something that another boy put there to make another suffer. If you were a girl... I don't know, I'm not a girl. They'd probably go on sled rides and build snowmen with the rocks of the playground. They'd probably even say, "Awweee, it's so adorable." They'd definitely hold out the adorable for as long as their lungs would allow as well. Dragons, elves, and dwarves probably looked at humans and were just concerned for their own stability of mind. Bortus thought as he and Ghortus walked through the town to the command building that housed the commanders who were stationed there.

It looked like a hotel of some kind, it wasn't fancy, but it didn't look quite like the rest in town. There was snow on the roof and it was about three stories high and what looked like ten windows across with equal spacing in between them. A sign stuck out and it read; "Command's Inn."

Bortus walked up the stairs behind Ghorstus to the door and Ghorstus opened the door, stepping out of the way for Bortus to enter. Ghorstus closed the door behind Bortus as quickly as possible and they walked to the front desk where some guards were stationed. The guards saluted and Bortus asked, "Where is Admiral Hethus?"

"Up these stairs and in the room with the double doors, sir." One of the guards said, pointing up the stairs. Bortus nodded once and walked up the stairs to the next floor where he saw a pair of doors leading to the same room and there were guards stationed there as well. The guards there saluted and one of the guards said, "Admiral Bortus of Classis II Oceanianic is here sir."

A voice from the other side of the doors said, "Let him in." And they opened the doors for Bortus to walk in. Ghorstus walked back down the stairs and out the door to the fleet.

Bortus walked in and the doors shut behind him. He looked forward to a desk squared on the doors and a man sitting at it. The man was a taller man and had light brown hair and blue eyes. He was beginning to get gray streaks of hair within his original light brown hair and he had short grayish brown whiskers on his jaw and chin and around his mouth.

He was standing and began to walk around the desk to meet Bortus. "Admiral Bortus." The man said, walking towards him. They shook hands and Bortus asked, "Admiral Hethus, how have you been?"

"Older and colder since the last time we met." Hethus said, releasing his hand from Bortus's. Bortus laughed for a short while and said, "Have you heard of what's been happening on the eastern front?"

"Yes, looks like a war's brewing. I supposed that that was why you're here." Hethus said, sitting back down at his desk. Bortus nodded and pulled up a chair to sit on the other side of the desk.

"Do you think we're going to fight soon?" Bortus asked, folding his hands. "Maybe, the World Senatorial Meeting is in a few weeks. Then will be the most likely time that a war will start." Hethus said, folding his arms and leaning back in his chair. "Yeah. It would be." Bortus replied.

"How's Orias? Is she well?" Hethus asked, leaning forward and putting his elbows on his desk with his hands cupped on his mouth. "Yeah, we just had a baby girl a few months before I left port." Bortus replied, looking into Hethus's eyes. "Yes, she told me about that in a letter, but I seem to have misplaced it." Hethus said.

Hethus was Orias's father and on good terms with Bortus, which is why Bortus was married to Orias. When Bortus asked for Hethus's daughter's hand, he asked Orias before okaying it.

"How old is your eldest, Merria?" Hethus asked.

"She's quite well now. She had a rough spot there a year ago, but she's moved on." Bortus answered.

"That's good." Hethus said before sighing and adding, "I want to see them again, but I've got a little more to do before I can retire. And this war, I don't want to leave this fleet in the hands of a new admiral who hasn't gotten used to the captains and their crews yet before a battle."

Bortus nodded in agreement and said, "Yeah, that wouldn' be too good. They also want to see you though, they'd always ask when they would see you again, but I never had a solid answer."

"What's the baby's name?" Hethus asked, looking at Bortus. "Basous Theirria." Bortus replied, looking up at Hethus from his slumped position with his elbows on his knees. "Beautiful name." Hethus said in reply.

"Well, should we begin military talks?" Hethus asked, standing up. "I believe we should." Bortus said, also standing up from his chair and sliding it back to its original position.

They walked to the door where two guards stood on the inside and the guards opened the doors for them to walk through and saluted. Hethus and Bortus nodded and walked through the doors and the guards on the other side of the doors saluted and the doors behind them closed. Hethus and Bortus walked up some more stairs, Hethus in the lead, and to the next floor where two more guards stood at their positions and saluted. They walked past the guards who opened another pair of doors and into a room with maps. The guards shut the doors behind them.

Chapter

15

Several More Weeks Later

"YOU'VE BEEN PRACTICING FOR MONTHS!!" A centurion bellowed. "HOW HAVE YOU NOT GOTTEN IT DOWN YET?!"

The legionary said, "No excuse sir."

"NO EXCUSE! OF COURSE THERE WILL BE NO EXCUSE! YOU'RE JUST STUPID!" The centurion shouted back.

The legionaries of the third legion were still practicing putting on their improved armor and new weapon at a good speed. They were able to do it in one minute and a half, but that wasn't fast enough for some centurions because of how quickly some other maniples were able to armor themselves and be ready for combat.

The original speed before the chainmail half tunics, leather couplings and pilum were added on was forty five seconds, which is a pretty dramatic jump in the wrong direction. The thing the legionaries were struggling most with was the feel of the chainmail armor underneath their lorica, many of them had to adjust their armor sizes a little bit to fit the chainmail in comfortably. Some of them still had this problem and just couldn't seem to fix it for some reason.

The bolt thrower maniple was doing fine with their practicing, granted they were already accustomed to the weapon and its tricks and gadgets. As for the practicing on throwing a pilum, it was fairly simple and easy to teach and most of the legionaries got it down within the first week or two of practice, others weren't as bright as most though when it came to that, but in the end all legionaries got it down in the first month.

General Saveirious stood in the command tent with his officers in the officer meeting. "So, we must keep an eye on the Zulkbarian army and make sure they don't try anything funny again." Saveirious said, pointing at his scouting officer who was in charge of the scouting maniple and making sure that they weren't being watched from now on.

They caught a dwarven scout a few weeks ago, or more like two and a half months ago and held him for ransom for fun, because that's just what you do when you're in the right and whoever you're teasing is in the wrong. The dwarves claim that they didn't send him to spy on us and that he snuck off and did it under his own inspiration, which sounded like the biggest boatload of a lie ever to come from any living thing's mouth, but it could still be the truth, although no one believed it. At times it looked like the dwarves themselves didn't even believe it, and they're the ones who said it was true.

"Yes sir." The scouting officer said, nodding his head once in acknowledgement.

Saveirious turned to the head logistics officer and asked, "How are we on food supplies, do we need anymore? And what about armor, some of them are still struggling with theirs?"

"As for food, we're good for another few months, we'll need to order some in about a week or so to ensure we don't run out. And as for the legionaries' armor, some of them just don't seem to be happy that it exists." The head logistics officer said.

Saveirious nodded once sharply and asked, "Well, does anyone have any complaints or suggestions?" He looked around and the head statistics officer said, "Do we have a plan if a war starts and we go to battle against the Dwarves?" Saveirious inhaled and said, "Not quite, I would like to speak with you and the other statistics officers privately and directly right after this meeting." The man nodded once in the affirmative.

"NO, NO, NO! TRY AGAIN! IT WASN'T FAST ENOUGH! I'M BEGINNING TO THINK YOU JUST DON'T HAVE THE BRAINS FOR THIS!" A centurion shouted from outside the tent. No one inside the tent spoke, they just shook their heads when Saveirious looked at them for any comments.

"Very good, dismissed."

The officers got up, saluted and walked out of the tent, but the statistics officers stayed in with The General.

"Okay, any suggestions about how to set up the legion for battle if necessary?" Saveirious asked, looking at the other officers. One of them spoke up, "I think we could try to use the Chechian Crater to pick off as many of them as possible." Saveirious looked at the man with a raised brow.

"I mean, position the bolt throwers in a way so that they can loose those bolts at them from across the crater." The officer elaborated.

"Our bolt throwers will be too inaccurate from that distance. We might be able to use them from a closer point if we can keep the dwarves on the ridge of the crater. We could loose the bolts into the sides of the crater and break off pieces and chunks of it as they walk on it." Another officer said with his arms folded.

Saveirious mused at that, but how would they keep the dwarves on the ridge? Fight them on an angle so that they would stay there while the bolts lodged themselves into the walls of it. It wasn't a bad suggestion if it was more solidified than that.

"We could fight the dwarves next to some of the looser rocks and use the bolt throwers to knock the rocks loose and onto their ranks, but that would put our own men in danger of being crushed as well." Another said, looking at the others in the tent.

"I say we think about this, and survey what would be the possible battlefields of this fight and pick this up next week when we have more information on our surroundings." Saveirious said, looking at the others and continued, "We have just received these weapons, they're brand new and haven't been used before in any fight. We don't know the best way to use them to maximum effect yet, so let's think about how we could use them to a greater effect than what they would normally cause, and if we can't think of anything. Then we use them the way they were meant to be used, loose the bolts directly at the enemy's ranks and disturb them as much as possible before physical contact is made." The others nodded in agreement.

"Okay, that will be all. Dismissed." Saveirious said, and the officers stood and saluted before exiting the tent.

"MOVE, MOVE, MOVE!" A centurion bellowed to his century as they practiced maneuvers, speed and endurance with their new armament on. They weren't slower really, it was just getting used to the feel of the additions of the armor and pilums they were issued. They were getting better by the day, and they were almost back up to their original speed with the new equipment. "COME ON, YOU SLUGS, MOOVVEEE!" The centurion shouted. The sound of footsteps almost sounded like thunder on the cloudy day.

There wasn't much mud or anything besides the rock and the other rock that was being weathered away by time and the wind and rain. It was relatively flat ground, with mountains around in particular places along with rocky hills that were not much more common than the mountains. The ground had little cracks here and there and there was grass and flowers sprouting out of most of the cracks in the ground wherever they could find an opening in the hard rocky-clay ground around them.

There were weeds, but whenever a legionary saw one he usually plucked it out when they weren't doing anything special, or stepped on it while they were drilling in the area where it was at. Some of the legionaries began to place bets on who would be able to find the most greens by the end of the day. They were going to do it weekly, but then realized that some of their older claimed greens were disappearing, or were withering away before the comparison at the end of the week making it where they were not believing each other that they actually pulled out living plants and not dead ones or using plants they pulled out the week before in the next week.

So what they began to do was come together at the end of the day after all of their drills were completed and compared their achievements with each other. After they compared they threw all of the pulled greens into a pile to burn for a fire. It was beginning to make the land bare again, but it almost looked better with no greens, making it look more like the desolate place it actually was.

Every once in a while they would see a lizard and try to catch it on their breaks and they usually succeeded in doing so. Sometimes they would lose track of where the lizard went and have to give it up. Other times the lizard got brighter and ran off as if it knew that they were after it to catch it, but most of the lizards just sat there and stared at them as they closed in on it and by the time it tried to run, it was too late.

Sometimes the men would see snakes, but after one encounter with a snake they decided to kill them instead of trying to capture them. Now that it was summer the birds were coming back and the lizards became more scarce, but some legionaries still saw them and took them captive before the birds could bring death to them.

Once, with the permission of The General, they got enough lizards and one of the legionaries thought of the idea of a race. It took them a little bit to figure out how to do it without the lizards running away, but they still got what they wanted and they, day to day, created a little race track for their lizards and had a race. It took them a little bit to find out how to get the lizards to move around the race track, but they again, figured out how to do it.

They got together and had their race, they betted on the lizards after they saw each one run individually the day before to see which one they liked most and betted on that one to win. They played cards and other sorts of entertainment. They didn't just bet with their military wages, they also used good looking rocks they found lying about and the better looking of the lizards they found and caught. It was interesting how they could find something to do when they weren't drilling.

Every now and then they would watch the bolt thrower maniple practice and would bet on which crew was the best. Some of the legionaries began to believe that the crews knew that they were being bet on and rotated who did the best. They probably flipped a coin on the matter to see which crew was going to not show up at practice and absolutely suck at their job of operating it.

When the logistics officers had nothing to do they decided that they could ruin some of the legionaries' day and had them draw sticks to see who would dig latrines and who would fill them in. General Saveirious had it where they drilled in intervals of three times a day to get used to the armor and pilums, and every other few days they would form up and march around the camp to get used to the equipment that way as well.

The most interesting thing was that since they've been there so long, the dwarves got a hold of their routine and did the same thing as the legionaries did. They would go on marches at the same time. At first each army didn't know what to think about it, but then they decided to be themselves and joke around with each other while they passed one another as they marched.

Once they came together and played some card games and watched lizards race. Then the dwarves caught their own lizards and brought them to the races and raced them against the legions and bet to see which lizard or lizards would win.

They also traded beer and other booze with one another and drank together in drinking games that the dwarves usually won. They never asked each other about their equipment and never talked about it either, it was part of the agreement they had with one another.

If a legionary or a Dawi soldier let something slip about their equipment the ones who heard the information could tell the corresponding general about it and receive a reward. Something like beer or a pet lizard, or some gold or silver. That never really happened though, so no one knew for sure what they'd be most likely to get, and no one wanted to try in fear of what the repercussions would be for the one who said anything.

After it rained once, the two armies got done with their drilling and found out during their drill that there was mud in certain places on the ground around the crater. They came together on a march and also found out that all of that marching and commuting they did on that large patch of ground was muddy, so they made bets on which ones would slide the farthest from one end to the other and also who would go the fastest.

It was pretty bad, when they got out of the mud the legionaries looked like completely different beings and the dwarven warriors had mud all over their beards, but they kept on doing it anyway. It was just too much fun to let it go because of a little discomfort and almost feeling completely stiff when the mud thought it was going to begin drying because someone was standing in the same spot almost not moving for a while.

Every once in a while one of either the legionaries or the dwarves would get mud in their mouths/nose and in their ears, but everyone else would have a good laugh out of it. When they had to clean out their armor though… that was a completely different story and was not just a physical strain, but a mental and social one too.

The centurions then figured out that when they wanted to punish a legionary, they would just either find some mud or make it and have the legionary, in full armor, get in and cover himself in it. They saw it as much easier than lashing them with a whip because the centurion didn't even have to move or anything, he just had to stand there and watch the legionary begin to change the color of his skin from white to mud brown, and then they made sure they changed it back from mud brown to white again. It was a much more excruciating process than being lashed ten times or so and it took much longer and was more humiliating than being lashed as well. For the legionaries, it was the worst, but for the centurions, it was a dream come true.

Legio VII Donnious, stationed at the Plaxident Valley, which was near the city of Plaxident that was about twenty-five miles away, wasn't on such good terms with the dwarves as Legio III Attis was. They were next to the dragons that were on good terms with them though. They used to keep an eye on the dwarven army by finding a good high point near them and squinting their eyes to attempt to see farther, but it never really did much for them, so they resorted to asking the wind dragons if they could spy on the dwarves for them and King Hevtur agreed and now there was a regular meeting with dragon scouts that would come down to report anything that was important looking in any way, or just came down regularly for a boring report.

Those daily reports got so boring that whenever the dragons came down to report, they reported and then stayed around for a bit, listening to jokes and also making a few themselves.

It, to the legionaries, was weird how funny a dragon could be when you weren't on duty or talking to a literal guard, which was boring no matter which factions guards you talked to they were all just, "straight faced and nonchalant as if they were any better than any of us reg's", as one legionary put it. The legionary did admit that they probably were better than any of the ones there, but still pretty boring to talk to.

They would say that when they were younger, seeing a guard was just about the coolest thing one could see, but as they grew older they realized that guards were almost more like statues than actual people.

As children they said they would always want to be a guard and then as they grew up and got smarter they realized that guards were the ones who were the unlucky of the rest of them. The legions got to see different places and landmarks on their tours, whereas guards basically saw the same thing everyday. It was like being in the same place day to day just sucked the enthusiasm out of them and left them with almost blank sober faces.

A lot of the jokes they made were about the dwarves and how the dragons would tease them every once in a while so that they could have something to laugh at the end of the day. Like how one "incidentally" fell over onto his face and even worse, or better depending on how one looked at it, fell into a latrine. That one was harsh and the dragon that did it said that he didn't see the latrine, which may have been a lie, and so when it happened they vowed to one another to not make them laugh on duty again because that could be pretty dangerous when ones commanding officer walked up behind them and saw that they weren't bored out of their minds and actually seeming like they have a life other than the army.

The dragons would sometimes get the wind to blow and make the legionaries' lives seem like they did something terribly wrong in life and now they were going to pay for it. They always said that it wasn't them or it was an accident of some kind, but everyone knew that that was such a lie that even a liar couldn't properly lie about that, because as much as they tried to say it wasn't them or it wasn't on purpose, they always looked as if they were about to explode into laughter.

It helped the legionaries feel how the dwarves felt being teased like that and didn't appreciate it as much, but was still funny to hear about how the dragons did it to the dwarves. Every legionary wanted to go up on the mountain and watch the dragons tease the dwarves in person, but legion regulations prevented them from doing so.

The drilling for the legionaries wasn't hard, but long and excruciating, the new armor additions didn't hinder their movements, but still took time to get used to. They got used to it though soon enough and they were almost back up to their original speed for putting their armor on and the pilums became almost a natural part of every legionary's persons.

The bolt thrower crews were ready and finished with practice because they were already trained on the subject and now were just getting used to being around the rest of the legion. General Kasis would have the legion form up and march around the camp in one complete circle before marching back into the camp and dismissing everyone.

When they marched there was no open spot in the circle, it was just one big circle around the camp. And every now and then he would have them stay in their circle for another hour before allowing them back into the camp, so while they waited outside the camp they would just stand there and watch the tall grass blow in the breeze, which they were sure was being tampered with by the dragons because it kept stopping and then starting up real quick blowing dandelion things into their eyes and dust followed if they weren't quick enough.

One time when the dragons came down for their report the legionaries asked about it and who, in their words, "needed to be taught a lesson", and the dragons would say, "It wasn't us, it was someone else", as if the legionaries would believe that. So the legionaries asked who else it could be and the dragons just said that it was top secret and all the legionaries would just scowl at that response.

It rained one or twice in the Plaxident Valley and one time it happened while the legion was on its practice march and that, to the legionaries, was most likely the worst day of their lives. Not only did they march in the rain, but they marched in the mud and the tall grass would somehow stick to their legs and arms giving them the want to scratch wherever the grass touched, and all the while the dragons watched from their hiding places, and then when they came with their reports, they were hiding some of the biggest grins known to man.

Every legionary could see it, no matter how much those dragons tried to hide those grins, the legionaries saw them right through their masks. The legionaries knew that they were there because if it were the other way around and the legionaries had the chance to see those dragons slip and slide in the mud, they would laugh uncontrollably.

"FALL IN LINE YOU MUD MAGGOTS!" A centurion bellowed at the legionaries attempting to stand in perfect rows and columns in the mud. "IN BATTLE YOU WON'T HAVE THE LIBERTY TO KISS THE MUD YOU LOVE SO DEARLY!" The centurion added.

As much as the insults could sting, they were still pretty funny, especially when it was directed at one particular legionary and not the rest of the maniple or even the rest of the legion for that matter, including that fact that the centurions would basically shout at the top of their lungs for every single legionary in the legion to hear, and not just them, but the dragons too.

"READY TO MARCH!" The centurions bellowed to their maniples. A trumpet blew and the centurions all in unison shouted, "MARCH!" And with that the legion began marching in a circle. Legionary footmen in the supposedly front followed by the legionary cavalry, and then they were followed by the maniple of bolt throwers who had to manually move their equipment.

When Legio VII Donnious first did that, the dragons said that the dwarves panicked and rushed to their feet to form their ranks and marched themselves to their ridge of the valley, and after a while of standing there, saw that the legion wasn't coming for them, but they also knew that the legion wasn't marching away either. The dragons said that they had never seen such confused faces on anyone before.

They said that the dwarves were looking back and forth at each other in utter confusion and when the marching stopped, they were even more confused. They said that even King Hevtur was confused as to what was going on and he came out onto the western most platform type rock thing that the lookouts were on and began chuckling at what he was seeing.

After a few times of that the dwarves thought that it was a scare tactic and so they did the same thing as well everyday at the same time, like the legion did just at a different time then the dwarves.

Other than that nothing really happened at the Plaxident Valley. King Hevtur did come down after they were done marching the first time and asked what that was about and General Kasis said that it was just a routine he was implementing for a few weeks or months, depending on how he felt about it, while the legion got used to the new equipment they had received.

The legion ended up marching so many times in the same circle that there was now officially a road there, it wasn't the prettiest road, but it was a road nonetheless.

"DANCE YOU MUD DOGS, DANCE!" Another centurion bellowed, now the legionaries' abdomens didn't just hurt with daily exercise, they now hurt with laughter as the legionaries withheld it from the centurions standing within their ranks.

"DO YOU THINK YOU'RE GETTING PAID TO WALK AS IF YOU'RE A BABY?!" Another centurion called.

They were almost done with their march and they couldn't let up now. Most would think General Kasis cruel for having the legion do this day to day, but in fact he also took part in the march right in the front maniple, his maniple, and he marched right alongside his legionaries and he would do so in battle as well, for that was just the kind of general he was.

He was the type of general that would say, "Hey leave some for the rest of us!" and then proceed to annihilate the entirety of the enemy force alone just so he would have the kills instead of anyone else. No one thought that he liked killing because they thought that if he did, he would've marched the legion right across the valley and into the dwarven army by now and wiped them clean off the map.

"MANIPLE HALT!" One centurion after another bellowed down the line in order, from front to back. The legion halted and stood in position awaiting the order from The General to either be dismissed back into the camp or to stand at the ready where they were.

General Kasis walked away from his men and looked up into the sky. There was some cloud cover, but not much. Kasis didn't really like drilling in any type of weather besides the weather that was present at the moment, but he also knew that the weather didn't care what they wanted for a battle and could throw any number of weather patterns at them. So, instead of having the legion drill for longer on the good days like this one, he decided that they would rest on these days and drill on the days that were most excruciating to deal with.

"DISMISSED!" Kasis said to the legion, or his legion since he was the general of it, and they all began to walk back into the camp in an orderly fashion.

This would probably be the last week we do this, as for the dwarves. I don't know. Maybe they'll stop once they figure out we've stopped or maybe they won't and they'll keep on doing it as if it actually affected the legion. The legion probably heard them marching and was glad that they weren't doing it themselves. Kasis thought as he walked back to the command tent to finish up on some reports.

A few hours passed and the dwarves began to march. It was quite thunderous like the legions' marches were. If one fell silent and still, they could barely feel the tremors of their march through the ground. From what reports say, the dwarves don't march in a circle like Legio VII Donnious does. Instead they marched back and forth in a solid line between two points, and they did it for as long as the legion marched, which was about fifteen to twenty minutes.

One of the best things that the legionaries thought about General Kasis is that, since he was an infantry general and preferred to be up on the front lines with his men, he would only eat whatever the rest of the legion ate. So every once in a while, when the officers' special food got piled up for long enough to be enough for the legion, which wasn't that long, the entire legion would have an officers meal.

Steaks, grapes, sometimes olives, maybe some pineapple, nice soft fluffy bread, and wine as the drink of the meal. Whenever one of these dinners were on for the day it was almost a brand new holiday for the legionaries.

They'd at least try to act civilized for it, but that was hard to do around such delicacies of great taste. The steaks were always around the size of one's hand, not like someone could fit it in their hand, but as big as their hand could span out from fingertip to fingertip. Whenever the dragons came down for their report and they saw what the legionaries got, the legionaries were sure that they were jealous, even though they probably weren't but still they better have been jealous to see, as the legionaries would call it, "royalty in motion in front of their eyes". This was one of those days.

Chattering went up from around the camp as the legionaries waited for the trumpet to blow so that they could get their food. They piled around in huddles of as small as four and as large as ten. Some would sit as they waited and others would stand there talking with one another about their day and their interests.

The sun was about two hours from hitting the horizon and the dragons usually came about two hours later when the sun was going down past the horizon. This gave the legion time to scarf down the food and talk about how delicious it was until the dragons arrived and then some, boasting about it in a semi discrete way. It was supposed to look discrete, but everyone that was there knew that they were doing it on purpose. The trumpet sounded and everyone got in a line to get food. Once they got their food they would walk to either a table or a flat enough, or comfortable enough, place on the ground and eat their food which was usually a steak as the main course, a cup of wine as the drink, some bread and one of the fruits mentioned earlier.

One legionary left to go get something halfway through his steak and the others finished theirs while he was gone.

The thing about guys is that there is no such thing as a limit to the amount or the size of a joke. Some jokes are uncalled for, but then that just gives another guy the reason to come up with a larger than life joke to get back at the guy who pranked him.

As the legionary was gone the others got the idea to hide his plate of dinner and wait until he came back to find out that it was gone. One legionary took the plate and swapped it with his empty plate. As they waited for him to come back they straightened their body postures and acted like they didn't just do what they just did. The legionary got back and saw that the empty plate was where he left his half empty plate and that the others were looking at him with slightly amused faces.

The legionary stood next to where the empty plate was and asked, "Who did it?" Looking at the other three around him. "Come on, tell me. Which one of you three faggoteers. Ate. My. Steak?" He finished with clenched teeth.

The others began laughing and one asked, "You... What did you just say?" Still about to die of laughter, another one said, "Faggoteers."

"Yes. That is exactly what you are. Faggoteers. The Three Faggoteers." The one without a steak said, looking down at the others who were on their sides laughing. He then saw the plate behind the one opposite of him and walked around to get it saying, "You guys suck. I'm over there doing a quick little job and you guys decide that I just don't have enough already happening in my life to leave me alone in peace?"

"Well, you should've thought about leaving your food here before you left." Another one said as he recovered from laughing.

The legionary picked up his plate of food and walked back around to where he sat earlier and began to eat his food. The others took several more seconds to get over their laughter and sat back up. One of them looked at the legionary eating his food and began to laugh a little bit again.

Chapter

17

The sound of Legio VII Donnious in the distance was, well at first new and then irritating and now everyone was getting used to it. Hierion was always wanting to watch at first, and he still does. He was fascinated by the sight of an army marching, even though he was a prince and was around whenever an army of Jurrunt was on the march, or on the move because they could fly and that wasn't really marching.

What Hierion was really fascinated by was the differences between the armies and how they had their different marches. He would also go out on the platform and tease the Praetorians and Zulkbarians whenever either of the armies began to march and then after they stopped. He didn't do it relentlessly, thank goodness, but he did do it where it was funniest.

Hierion had already come into his ability to use magic, but he wasn't as powerful as an adult, because he wasn't quite an adult. He would, in a way, practice his magic on the armies. He started with bending the light and summoning up a few gusts of wind near where the armies were marching. Mirada didn't like it, but Hevtur, whenever Mirada wasn't around, would laugh at times and tease them himself when he saw it best.

Most of the guards never knew that they would be behind them, so when they did tease the marching armies the scouts who saw the teasing would laugh and ask who did it, but none of them knew, but that never stopped them from continuing to laugh despite their job and training. Granted they weren't guards so that was probably why they could laugh.

Hevtur left for the World Senatorial Meeting a day prior and was not going to return for another week or so. Hierion wanted to go, but a secret is a secret for a reason. Hevtur originally didn't want to keep it a secret from the alliance, but Mirada wasn't having it.

She was smart, but also very paranoid about something, Hevtur never knew why and he didn't ask because the last time he did she just said that she was sorry and didn't go into it any further. At first, even trying to leave for the World Meeting Hevtur had to basically lie and distract her so that he could actually leave without her feeling conflicted about it. Leaving in the middle of the night wasn't an option because somehow someway Mirada knew he was going to leave. The only reason he was able to leave then was because he either got Hierion to help or he was able to get Mirada to go do something else besides worry about it for a moment and snuck off then.

As much as Hevtur loved her, she was still a pain to deal with just to do anything outside the alliance, and the only time she would willingly allow that was every three months when he had a meeting. Thankfully she understood that he wasn't going to be attacked while in friendly territory or else Hevtur wouldn't even be able to go to the meetings, or all of the meetings would have to take place in Jurrunt.

Mirada one day finally let Hevtur go to the World Senatorial Meetings. Before, Hevtur didn't even leave on specific days or weeks, he just left when the time was near and, thankfully told Hierion about it before he left, disappeared into the rest of the world.

Mirada always worried and still worried that something would happen to him, or them, or Hierion, or maybe the kingdom, or possibly the world. That was the kind of chain of thought she had.

The World Senatorial Meeting was to take place in three days, most arrived the day prior and met up with allies before the meeting and then went to what was called the guest quarters and slept there.

Hevtur showed Hierion a secret chamber that Hevtur would go to to watch movements that were happening when Mirada was being relentless with her paranoia and wouldn't let him go outside the King's

Peak. Hierion would go into that chamber when Mirada wasn't looking, that way she didn't know it was there, and attempted some of his magic.

Not magic like summoning a wind stream, but magic similar to bending the light to see farther. There was a stone platform that was flat on the top that Hevtur would use to create a picture of the outside world on. It was like flying over the ground, just you weren't flying, but in a cave looking down at the platform that was showing real time from the outside. Hierion wasn't strong enough to be able to do it, but he kept trying in hopes that one day he could.

Hierion never knew why he was never let outside the kingdom like on one of the meetings with his father, he always questioned it and Mirada would say, "It's a dangerous world and you're not quite ready for what's out there." Or Hevtur would say, "I think it's best if you stay here and get a little bit older before I let you outside the kingdoms borders." As much as Hierion wouldn't like either of those answers, there was nothing he could really do about it since his parents were his parents and were the King and Queen of the faction he lived within. They just had the guards make sure he didn't leave the borders unless they said so directly, and Hierion, being the prince and not the king, could not override that order.

The guards did a really good job at it as well, as much as Hierion might try, they would never let him within thirty feet of any of the borders.

Since his father left for the World Senatorial Meeting, Hierion has just been trying to get an image of the Plaxident Valley, or at least something from the stone platform. Hierion was about seventeen and he figured that he had to be eighteen before he was able to leave the borders of the kingdom, since just about every other family of dragons in the kingdom did. He was almost eighteen and almost an adult, he was turning eighteen in a few weeks, about a month and a half.

He also heard a few weeks before his father left, that a legion from Praetoria was on its way to aid in any fighting that might come. Before, there were two armies near the borders and now there are four. Two Dwarven and two Elven armies, each within their own borders to the north and east. Hierion thought that at last he could see an actual legion up close.

The Kingdom of Jurrunt, like any other faction, had armies of its own; just Hierion knew that human, elven and dwarven armies were different from dragon armies by a large scale in how they looked in their formations, how they wore their armor, and how they fought in battle. And Praetorian legions were not just some regular looking army, they had some of the largest shields and some of the best battle techniques in the world. All armies had different shield sizes for their own size like dwarves had smaller shields compared to that of a human's regular sized shield because dwarves were just shorter than humans. Dragons didn't use shields or swords or spears because, well, they had teeth and claws. Why go through the trouble of trying to get iron from beneath the earth to make a weapon that a dragon is basically hatched with?

Magic's exhausting. Hierion thought, fighting back the pain of a throbbing headache. *I'm beginning to wonder if life is easier with magic or harder. It's convenient to have magic at your side in case of something that it can be used for, but learning and getting used to it are almost worse side effects than the benefits you'd receive.*

His head felt like it was going to explode in white hot flames. He lied down and just tried to rest it off, he would like to go get some fresh air, but the last thing he was going to do was let his mother see him like this. He would never hear the end of her asking him if he was alright. After about maybe a few questions of that she would begin to ask what he was doing and where he was for the past hour or so while he was doing it, and that's where she would never let him hear the end of it.

He wasn't able to even get a glimpse of the outside on the platform, or table, he thought it was very similar to a table of stone. His head throbbed again and he clenched his teeth.

He looked at the table in thought, *I don't know what it is whether I'm just not quite there yet or if I was doing something wrong while trying to perform the magic, or maybe the table just didn't like me in the way it must have liked father. Yeah that must be it, the table is just picky in who is to use it in terms of magic.*

He stared at the table in mild disbelief. He knew he wasn't as powerful as Hevtur in the sense of magic, or more like anything in that matter, but he thought he was at least stable enough to conjure up some portion of the outside.

That must be it. I must have to think, or actually picture, something in my mind and use that to project the image from outside. He thought, then continued thinking, *but that doesn't make sense to me, how would I know what they're doing outside of the chambers walls if I couldn't see it in the first place. I'll just have to ask dad about it when he gets back.*

He stood up too quickly and fell down hard to the ground, or more like let himself down, as another sharp pain stretched into his head. It felt like the pain wasn't even coming from the brain, but from the front of his skull near where his brow was. He didn't want to fall asleep because of how Mirada might respond to him being gone almost all day.

As much as he didn't like that his parents weren't letting outside the borders, he hated the thought of his mother probably going insane about where he was. Luckily for him if he ever did go missing from her sight during the times she came to check in on him and he randomly appeared she wouldn't reprimand him. Instead she would most likely have him next to her or a guard almost all day everyday after that to make sure it didn't happen again.

To Hierion there was three different levels of love from his mother and those were just regular caring for him as he was her son, absolute love where she would probably die if needed for him, and then there was psychiatry level of love where her paranoia took hold and didn't let go like when the dwarven armies first encamped on their side of the border.

That was painful in his eyes, he almost couldn't go anywhere without her knowing. She would either ask him about what he was doing or station a guard on him, and neither him nor the guard liked that. He didn't like being baby sat and the guards didn't like to baby sit either, so when that happened Hierion would just have to try his best to get them both out of that mess before they got into it and wouldn't be able to get out of it until she got back from wherever she went.

When he couldn't get them out of it, he would try to convince the guard to go outside with him and they would tease the dwarves near the Plaxident Valley, and it always worked. The guards obviously wouldn't let him go near the border between Zulkbar and Jurrunt because of how close the dwarven army was. None of the guards saw Hierion as a weirdo or someone who needed to be baby sat like a dragonet that was just stupid absolutely dumb to be around. They didn't really see him as the leader type either, but they saw him as a companion because he mainly shoved that ideal down their throats until they accepted it or else, well, he couldn't do anything about it if they didn't, or actually he could go to his parents and one he wasn't like that and two he knew what they would say.

Mirada would say, 'that's because they're the guards and they are trained not to take too much of a liking to anyone, even the king.' Which actually made sense depending on how one would listen to it. And Hevtur would say, 'Why are you talking to me about this? It's your problem, not mine, and you've got to solve it. That is if you plan on having a brain when you're older.' Well, that's what he thought that they would say, he never actually did that and he was never going to, to him it made him feel like a spoiled brat that had no sense of decency, much less a brain to think about what one was about to say or even wanted to say before saying it.

A few minutes went by of Hierion laying on the stone ground of the chamber before he got up nimbly and walked over to where the exit to the chamber was and poked his head out to make sure no one was looking. He didn't see anyone, but that didn't mean that there was no one there. He sniffed for any nearby scents before creeping out of the passageway and into a large hallway like cave and went over to his personal chambers to await to see if his mother would come looking for him or if she already had.

He passed a few guards on patrol and they moved to the side as much as possible and bowed. He nodded once in response and continued and the guards went about their way as well. He silently prodded across the King's Peak and heard a voice behind him say, "There you are."

He stopped and turned around and Mirada was standing there and it looked like she was nodding thanks to someone, but Hierion couldn't see who. "Hmm?" Hierion asked in response to the previous sentence.

Mirada turned and looked at him and said, "I've been looking for you for about twenty minutes. Where were you?" Hierion almost stopped breathing thinking, *Oh no. Not again.*

"Sorry if I worried you, I was just about to get some fresh air." Hierion said and thought again, *have I said too little, or have I said too much?*

Mirada looked at him with a raised eyebrow and asked, "And where were you before you decided that you were going to get some fresh air?" Hierion choked, thinking of an answer was harder than it should be when trying to mislead.

Mirada began towards him and he choked on more words again as she got closer and finally said, "I... was... just practicing some magic inside. It-It was inside stuff though, so I didn't do anything stupid or anything." Hierion backed up a step and remembered that retreating was usually a sign of fear during a conversation. He stopped and basically froze, looking back, at a little bit of an angle, up towards his mother who was just about on top of him at that point.

She looked slightly down at him and stared for a couple seconds before sighing and backing off a bit giving him some more room to breathe.

"I'm sorry, I was looking for you earlier because I wanted to know if you could handle yourself while I did some errands tomorrow. I'll most likely be gone for most of the day and I wanted to make sure you have everything you need." Mirada said.

Hierion blew out a sigh of relief in his thoughts and said, "I'll be fine, thank you. May I ask what you will be doing?"

Mirada gave him a rye-like smile and said, "Since your father is gone, I am to inspect troops for him to ensure everything is in order. He couldn't check it before he left because it is a set inspection date and it just so happened to land on a day he wasn't here. Which is odd, I'd think that he would've changed it up by now, but every once in a while it happens."

Hierion squinted his eyes at her and asked, "Is that supposed to be an attempt to get me to come with you to inspect the troops so that I can be next to you?" Mirada squinted back and shook her head just the slightest before saying, "I guess it could be looked at that way, I saw it the same way as well."

A smile tried to creep up on her face before she caught it and froze it there. Hierion caught a chuckle in his throat and she lent over a bit and tapped the tip of her snout on the top of his head and walked off.

Hierion got outside on the western platform of the King's Peak and looked out towards the two armies that were thirty miles to the west.

The Valley itself was a mile in width and the Screaming Peak River that led to a waterfall on the west side and down the valley went through the center of the valley at where it was usually lowest in the valley. One point from where he could see the water went underground and back out again on the other side. He couldn't see the other side of the river, but Hevtur always told him about how it split up into many different streams and flowed out of the ground and reformed the river heading to Galadrious Lake in Praetoria.

The lower ground was dark green and the shade of green got lighter as it went up the ridge and onto the flat plains to either side of it, and there was a forest in the distance to the southwest and further to the southwest Hierion could see dust, probably twenty miles away. He stared at it for a moment before breathing in the cool air of the mountaintop.

A wind dragon without wind or some form of breeze was very uncomfortable in any state that they were in at that moment, but when there was a form of breeze then they would usually feel very confident.

The same was with a water dragon with water, an earth dragon with the earth, a fire dragon with fire and a metal dragon with metal. Metal dragons though were hardly ever uncomfortable because of the strength of their scales. Not many things could attack them and give them no chance at fighting back and pulling a victory from a defeat, and they were usually braver than anything else in the world, most likely because of their surety of being able to get out of almost any situation that they found themselves in.

Hierion looked out at the incoming legion in awe. Granted he's seen Legio VII Donnious near the Plaxident Valley thirty miles away, but that was through using magic to bend the light, not seeing it right in front of him. He thought for a moment before realizing that he may not be able to see them up front because he didn't know whether or not his mother would allow it. He never went with his father to the meetings, and those meetings were held in allied territory and this legion was an ally to them, but he was still never allowed to go to the meetings, so he thought that chances of him seeing the legion up close or at least the general or something were very low.

He pondered on that for a minute, still looking out at the cloud of dust that looked like it wasn't moving. He turned to go back inside and found Mirada standing there as she just barely arrived. He froze and almost jumped back as his breath caught in his throat.

She looked at him and then stepped forward and saw the cloud of dust on the midday horizon and looked back at Hierion.

She shouldn't be mad. I did nothing wrong, I think. He thought, returning her gaze.

He turned and looked at the dust and then looked back at Mirada and said, "Looks like an army is marching around, doesn't it?"

She looked at him and a smile grew on her face and said, "You know which direction that is. It's where Praetoria is, and you know that in Praetoria they are called legions instead of armies, Hierion." She sighed and added, "You are not very good at misleading someone yet."

Hierion straightened his back and looked at her as if she had just said something that was blatantly obvious to everyone else but him, and he still didn't get it. She looked at him and said, "You called it an army when you know that it is properly called a legion. It is one of the things you were always very on top of in your studies."

Hierion just looked back at her with utter confusion before realizing what she was talking about and looked from her to the dust cloud and sighed. It usually never took him that long to catch on to something like that.

Mirada laughed a little bit and said, "I was trying to keep it a secret so that I could at least surprise you with something for once." Hierion couldn't tell if she was joking or genuinely disappointed and said, "I'm sorry, I overheard you and dad talking about it one night and coming out here to see it was not my original plan."

"Oh, it's okay. I guess I should tell you that the reason I'm up here is because the messenger from that legion, Legio IX Lavidica, just arrived and I came up here to see." Mirada responded standing next to Hierion and looking out at the dust.

Her head tilted abruptly and looked in confusion out at the legion. Hierion caught the movement and asked, "What is it?" She flipped her snout out at the legion and said, "Look at the legion and tell me what you see that's off."

Hierion arched an eyebrow and turned to look. He bent the light and saw nothing weird or odd at first, but then he saw it. Instead of what was thirty maniples of legionaries, which were one hundred and twenty men in size, what looked like should have been the same, but was only fourteen different standards that were the symbol of a maniple. Since there were only fourteen instead of thirty, that meant that the formations within this legion were larger than what a maniple was in Legio VII, and there were only ten infantry standards among them.

Behind the infantry was the cavalry like what was in Legio VII Donnious, and behind the cavalry was rows of the wooden structures that were also in the other legion. Hierion looked in awe and confusion as to what it meant, whether it meant that the Praetorians switched tactics or they were seeing a mirage out in the summer heat from below, a combination of both. "That's odd. I only see fourteen standards, besides the legion standard." Hierion said. Mirada saw the look on his face and said, "I guess I can still surprise you accidently."

Hierion looked at her and laughed saying, "Yeah, I guess you could." She laughed back and wrapped a wing around him.

She then turned around and back into the cave entrance that led from inside to out there. Hierion turned to go back into the mountain and to his chambers where he was going after he got a look at the outside world for a moment.

Chapter

18

Since it was summer and the days began early, Legio IX could march earlier than any other time of year, therefore making it possible to march farther in one day than in two days when it was winter. The sun was rising over the horizon and the legion was given the order to march. Waking up this early in the morning and marching day to day with breaks at noon and a few hours past made it actually good for the legion. They could now get up and be ready to march in one hour instead of about two and could also be ready for battle in an instant if need be.

"COME ON! GET UP, WE'VE GOT A PLACE TO BE AND A ROAD TO MARCH ON!" A centurion bellowed to his men.

"UP! ON YOUR FEET YOU MAGGOTS! DON'T THINK THE ENEMY WILL LET YOU PLAY FAIRY TALE PRINCESS IN YOUR DREAMS WHEN THERE'S A BATTLE TO BE FOUGHT!" Another centurion bellowed further down the line. "ARE YOU SLUG'S OR SLOTHS?!" Another one said.

One could tell who a centurion was or wasn't by the way you were insulted and reprimanded by them.

"GET UP OFF YOU BUTTOCKS AND FALL IN BEFORE I BEAT YOU ENOUGH THAT YOU WON'T EVER SIT ON THEM AGAIN!" Yet another said, then another followed, "COME ON! ARE YOU MICE OR ARE YOU MEN?! AND WHAT ARE YOU? A SHEEP?!"

They were fourteen miles from the nearest pass into Jurrunt, which was about a half day's march. The messenger went out ahead of them two days before and should've arrived yesterday. General Crassus was on his mount inspecting the cohorts on the road and seeing if they were ready to move after waking up about an hour earlier. He reached the front of the legion and gave the trumpeter the signal to sound the march. A trumpet sounded and the legion began to move again.

Behind him he could hear centurions urging their men forward as they were within the ranks as well. One said, "WE ARE MARCHING, NOT CRAWLING ON ALL FOURS LIKE A BEAST! OR THAT MAY BE WHAT YOU ARE, A SAVAGE BEAST THAT SHOULD BE KEPT ON ALL FOURS!"

Ouch! Crassus thought as they marched and continued, *I don't know if I want to see what will happen when the centurions are inside dragon territory instead of their own and they call a legionary that, or maybe it'll be interesting until I have to get in there and dispute it. That wouldn't be fun at all.*

Crassus was surrounded by twenty Praetorian guards on their mounts as well. The reason there were that many was because they were headed outside of their own territory and into anothers. Not that the dragons would attack, but that if a war broke out he would have twenty guards to protect him from unwanted guests that would be intruding on his life.

They had horses pulling the bolt throwers in the rear of the marching column. They were led by the two cohorts of cavalry that accompanied the ninth legion on the march and into combat. In front of the cavalry were the ten cohorts, each comprised of four hundred and eighty men each including the six centurions in nine of them and in the tenth, or more literally the first, was five and the legion standard that held up the legions name and number along with the symbol that represented it, two pegasus wings connected in the center by a star. The pegasus wings were folded in.

Each cohort had one banner and standard on the same shaft. The banner was lower on the shaft and was the flag of Praetoria, that way one could tell whose side others were on. The standard was at the top portion of the shaft, the standard in the other nine cohorts wasn't like the one in the first cohort.

The standards in the other nine just stated which cohort it was and which legion it belonged to, as where the first cohorts standard was on a completely different wooden shaft than the banner and held the legion name, the cohorts number, and the legions standard, which was the symbol on the shaft.

While they were on their way from their training grounds, they were practicing everyday after a few hours of marching and some rest. It's why it took them longer than usual to reach their destination. On a regular march, they would have reached Jurrunt about two or three days before.

General Crassus often wondered if they'd be pitching tents between mountains or if they would be enclosed in a cave or two, maybe three. He would think that it would be tents, but if winter came they wouldn't do well up in the mountains in just tents.

They would have to make fortifications wherever they camped and he didn't know if that was going to be proper or easy seeing how they would be in the mountains without many trees to work with. That is why he would think that they would be stationed in caves, but then they may not be up there for that long, so maybe it wouldn't be a problem. Latrines might be an issue, unless they get with the city workers, or whatever they were called in the dragon lands, and see about the latrines needed for the legion.

A few hours later they were less than a mile from the nearest pass up to the mountains. The men saw this and the glee coming from their hearts and minds was almost a weather pattern as murmurs came up from the legion. Their pace would've quickened if it weren't for the centurions making sure they stayed at the same pace and together so that they looked like they were meant to actually be a legion of Praetoria, or any army for that matter.

Atop the mountains and throughout them were dragons looking on at the legion march towards them. There were white, red and orange and yellowish, there were also vague outlines of others that were a shade of color similar to the rock of the mountains. The rocks were uncovered of snow during the summer. There was dirt and other soft materials for roads throughout the mountain passes and there were trees on the outer rims of the mountainous region, and there were probably trees within as well. Most of the upper portions of the peaks were gray like rock as well as granite and other stones shaping the mountains of Jurrunt.

Crassus guessed that there was dirt, or something similar to it, within the caves and caverns of the mountains. He knew that dragons would much rather have a softer ground to stand on if possible over rock and metal.

As they got closer they could see more and more dragons looking down at them from wherever they were, whether they were atop a peak or on some form of platform in between the top of the mountain and the base, or whether they were at the base of the mountain.

As the legion came to a halt at Crassus's command just outside the borders of Jurrunt, still within Praetoria's borders, Crassus nudged his horse forward and the Praetorian guards followed him up to a dragon that was moving toward them as well. They came close enough to each other where they could have a mostly private conversation, and the dragon leaned down to look at Crassus on Crassus's eye level.

"I am General Crassus of Legio IX Lavidica of the Praetorian Imperium. I am here with this legion to make camp and await orders." Crassus said to the dragon nearest him.

The dragon sniffed and said, "Make camp here and await your orders here. I will contact the queen for further instructions." Crassus nodded once and turned to the legion and moved his mount towards them. The dragon took off to the sky and into the mountains.

Crassus got back to his men and said to the trumpeter, "Sound the encampment, we will camp here until further notice."

The trumpeter nodded once and blew out a series of sounds and the centurions in each cohort began bellowing out orders to make camp.

I guess this is how the dragons find out how the legions work. By watching one make camp outside their territory and caves and caverns. Crassus thought as he watched the legion get their tents and set them up in the proper places for the camp.

Half of the Praetorian guards went off to set up the command tent for the officers to wait for their personal tents to be set up and the other half stayed near Crassus.

Crassus got curious and turned his head around to look at the dragons to see their reactions, if they were still there or if they dispersed to their daily tasks. There were still a vast number of dragons and most of which he could see were still watching the legion get encamped. Some were smaller and were looking off in something that looked like awe, and others were talking with each other and occasionally looking out at the legion.

He looked up the mountains at the peaks and saw more outlines of dragons looking down. The mountains weren't too tall, about six thousand feet in elevation.

He turned his gaze back to the legion, which was beginning to set up the tents, they were just leveling the ground where they would put the tent as well as around it.

Centurions still balled out orders relentlessly and wouldn't stop until the tents were pitched and the legionaries were sound asleep, which meant the centurions were as well, but when that sun comes over the horizon tomorrow, the legionaries would know no such peace and quiet until the centurions were too thirsty to continue, which felt like would never happen even within a dream, or either the centurions were dead or the legionaries themselves were dead.

Hierion couldn't see the legion from the western platform of the King's Peak and didn't know how to feel about it. A Praetorian legion was right outside their borders and he wanted to see it closer. To see the sheer size of it, but then he kind of lost that chance yesterday when he said that he would just stay inside the Peak all day while his mother inspected the armies. He could ask to go with her, but she could know that there was only one reason that he would and she also would know the reason. That might not be as bad as it would appear, but then it could be worse.

Caring more to see a foreign army over one of your own? That wouldn't look all that great. It's not that I didn't like to see my own, or more accurately my fathers, armies, but I saw them so many times and so many more times than a Praetorian legion. I read all about Praetorian legions from scrolls and other sources I could, and I didn't just read the scrolls that were about Praetorian legions, but Corinosian armies and all others that I could read and learn about. It was the only thing about schooling I liked. All of the others were necessary, I think, but they weren't interesting like history and the military, and I only really liked history for the battles and the action between two armies, or three or four or five. The big battles were the coolest in my opinion, granted it would've sucked to be fighting in it, but it was still the most interesting. Hierion thought as he turned around and into the Peak.

As much as Hierion saw himself as one who would make a decision and stick with it for as long as necessary, he really wanted to see armies all of the sudden, especially the Praetorian's. He looked around the Peak for his mother and it took him longer than he wanted to, but in the end he found her.

She saw him and smiled and asked, "Hi Hierion, what brings you here at this moment?" Hierion could see more than just the smirk on her face, but it was so obvious that she was teasing that he could almost physically feel it resonating off of her. He flinched at it and said smiling, "You do."

Mirada gave him a wry smile and asked, "And what do I have that you would want badly enough to be prancing about on a day you said you would laze around on?"

Hierion didn't realize he was moving any quicker than he usually did, but he was caught in the moment to find her and ask, "Have you inspected the armies yet?" Her smile grew and she began to laugh. Hierion stared at her until she got done and then raised an eyebrow at her.

"No, apparently the generals did and then sent me the reports. I was still going to go, but now it won't take as long since all inventory has been taken recently enough. All I have to do is make sure that they are still where they are." She said with a smile still on her face and continued, "But now another army has presented itself and I must go find a spot for them to encamp and give them directions."

Hierion mused on that and Mirada added, "You can come if you'd like, unless you spent all of your energy trying to find me and now you'll laze around for the rest of the day?"

Hierion narrowed his eyes and said, "I'm not that lazy."

"And how would you know that? It feels like whenever I see you, you're either walking slowly or trying to sleep, or I just don't see you at all and you present yourself later as one of the first two scenarios."

Hierion put a slight scowl on his face before realizing that she was right. Whenever they did see each other, almost every time he was tired or had a headache from magic.

"Huh?" He said, looking up at the ceiling of the cave.

"If you want to go you have to say so soon because I'm about to leave to do those things." Mirada said, semi stretching a wing as a gesture. Hierion looked at her and slightly narrowed his eyes and said, "Are you going right now?" She nodded and turned around to leave. He followed her, to her side and just behind.

A few hours passed and Crassus was in his personal tent resting his eyes, or in other words sleeping lightly, when a voice came from outside the tent asking, "General, messenger here to see you. Shall I permit him to enter?"

Crassus got up out of his cot and walked over to his desk before saying, "Yes, let him in." The tent flap opened and the messenger that he sent out to tell Queen Mirada of the legions coming walked in.

He saluted and said, "Sir, the queen requests an audience." "Where?" Crassus asked, grabbing his armor and putting it on. "In, what they call, the King's Peak map room sir." Crassus nodded and said, "Help me get this on." The messenger saluted and moved to help Crassus put on the armor and his cape.

Once they got his armor and cape on, Crassus walked out of the tent and the guards saluted, he looked at one and said, "Get me my horse." The guard saluted and hurried off to a nearby tent where the general's horse was kept and returned with the general's horse moments later. Crassus mounted and the guards near his tent saluted and stayed there to await his return.

Six guards were stationed outside his tent and the other fourteen were in another tent nearby and got word of the general's horse being readied and got theirs ready as well. They filed up behind Crassus and they began to move forward with the messenger, on his horse, in front.

It took about a minute or two to reach the base of the mountains, from there the messenger led them through the mountains and to one particularly larger mountain than the rest. It was taller from base to peak than any of the others, that Crassus could tell, and therefore was larger at the base than any other he'd seen so far. The messenger led them into a large open cave, or cavern based on the size of it, and every dragon stopped and stared as Crassus's and the Praetorian guards' capes were slightly hovering for how fast they were going through.

Crassus's cape was scarlet and the guards' capes were purple. The scarlet feathers atop Crassus's general's helmet were blowing back and forth as well as the guards' purple feathers atop their helmets.

They rode through the cavern down an open path to a ramp that led up the mountain. There were guards stationed at the base of the ramp and they signaled them to stop. They came to a stop and the messenger said, "General Crassus is here on the Queen's orders." The guards looked from the messenger to Crassus and nodded and one said, "I can't let your guards up there general." Crassus nodded in agreement and turned to his guards and said, "Stay here and out of trouble."

The guards saluted and the lead guard said, "Yes sir." The Praetorian guards moved to the side and out of the path in even numbers on each side and formed up into a line. The Jurrunt guards nodded once and stepped aside for the messenger and Crassus to go through. One of the Jurrunt guards looked down at a Praetorian guard and the Praetorian guard returned the look. They both nodded to each other and looked forward again.

A few moments of a slow gallop up the ramp and they reached the top where two more Jurrunt guards stood guard. They gestured to stop and Crassus and the messenger stopped and the messenger said, "General Crassus here to make an audience with the Queen."

"I'll check in with her and let you know when to enter, for now stay here." One of the guards said, looking from them to the other guard and then turning to tell the queen.

Queen Mirada mustn't have been far because less than a minute later the guard was back and Queen Mirada was next to him. She looked down to Crassus and said, "Thank you for seeing me, general." Crassus bowed his head to her and said, "It was no problem of mine to get here."

Mirada smiled and said to the messenger, "Thank you." He bowed his head to her as well and said, "You're most welcome, your highness."

She said in return, "That will be all." The messenger moved his horse and faced Crassus. Crassus looked at him as he asked, "What are your orders sir?"

"Stay up here and hold my horse." Crassus replied and dismounted. The messenger saluted and moved his horse off down the ramp. Mirada moved aside and said, "Come in general, let's begin on where you will be stationed during your stay."

Crassus bowed to her again and said, "Yes, your highness." And he walked into what looked like an ambassador's hall of some kind and followed Mirada.

"How is the legion doing?" Mirada asked as she walked side by side with Crassus. "Well enough and ready to move on your orders." Crassus said with his hands folded behind his back and under his cape.

"About six thousand. Just under five thousand of that is infantry." Crassus said. "Hmmm." Mirada said as she stopped and gestured to a cave-like room. She turned to go inside and Crassus followed.

The room was lit and there were two guards near the entrance and another dragon near the center. The guards bowed and the other dragon looked from a large table like stone and saw them walking towards him. He sat down as he waited for them to approach the table.

Crassus looked around and saw a staircase that led up to the top of the table. Mirada gestured to the staircase for him to go and he jogged up the stairs and up to the appropriate height for him to see the map on the table.

It wasn't any regular map made from paper. It was a map made by magic so that one could see the outside as if it was a map that was in motion. It was magnified on the mountain range and he could see the legion encamped. It wasn't fuzzy or blurry, but it was perfectly clear as he could see his legionaries marching back and forth as exercise.

"General, this is my son, Hierion. He is the heir and it is about time he got lessons on the positioning of legions. I mean, for him to learn what is needed for a legion to make camp." Mirada said, holding out a wing to point at the other dragon.

Crassus bowed to Hierion and said, "Your highness."

Hierion nodded once in appreciation and said, "General." Crassus looked at the map and said, "So, if you're asking me for a good spot to encamp the legion then…" He studied the map and saw a few points in which they could camp.

The map showed where structures were and where, well, anything was really. He could see the dragons down below in squares and on mountains. The map wasn't magnified enough for him to see details on them, just far enough to see that they were there.

The Kingdom of Jurrunt wasn't really big, in fact it was the same size it was when the piece of land was chosen one thousand years ago. Immigrants came in and out, more out than in, which was the reason they weren't over populated yet.

"I would say that any area that is as big as the camp is now is a perfect spot. Right now the camp is spaced out and can be condensed if needed." Crassus added onto the first portion of his statement. Mirada nodded and asked, "How does this spot look?" And she moved a talon to tap on a particular spot on the far east side of the mountain range.

The map moved with her talon and magnified onto the spot she tapped. It was a good open spot and right where, if needed, they could fight and hold for a very long time. "There are others, but I chose this spot because of the reason why you were sent here. To help protect our borders from threats." Mirada added.

Crassus was almost overjoyed by the spot she had presented because of its strategic value in battle.

"It is perfect. When do you want the legion to move?" Crassus asked.

Mirada said, "As soon as possible." Hierion studied the spot for a moment before Crassus decided to let them in on what he saw saying, "This spot is the perfect spot because it is a gap that can be plugged in a battle. When there is a bottle neck point it makes numbers useless."

Hierion asked, "But you have numbers, wouldn't that affect you as well?"

Crassus nodded saying, "Yes, if we were attacking, but we are defending." Hierion nodded in agreement, understanding what he meant.

"With your permission, I will meet back with the legion and order the march." Crassus said, looking at Mirada.

She nodded and said, "Go ahead, the sooner the better." Crassus bowed and went down the stairs and towards the exit from where he came.

He remembered which way the ramp was and started for it. "I would like to meet again once you are in position, general." Mirada said from behind him. He stopped and turned around to look at her and bowed saying, "It will be done." And he continued out to the ramp.

"What does he mean when he says that the legion will await your orders?" Hierion asked, looking at Mirada. Mirada looked back and said, "He means that this legion has been gifted to us until our borders are secure under our own power."

"So, this legion counts as one of our armies for now?" Hierion asked.

"Yes, and once we don't need their help anymore they go back to being under Imperator Callus's rule." Mirada replied.

"Is it alright if I watch the march with a friend or is there something you want me to see and learn from?" Hierion asked.

Mirada looked at him and shook her head saying, "No, there is nothing else I can think of. Go ahead and watch it."

Hierion nodded and got up to leave when Mirada said, "I don't want you too close to that border, Hierion."

Hierion said, "Okay, I won't go too close to it." And he walked out. Mirada cleared the table and nodded once to the guards at the entrance. They bowed and she walked out with them walking out behind her and stopping at the outside of the room.

Crassus reached the bottom of the ramp to see his guards talking with the Jurrunt guards. The guards heard them coming and stood to attention out of his way. He reached the bottom and said, "Okay, we have a camp to move." And continued after the messenger who led the way again. The Praetorian guards, still mounted, followed in suit.

Apparently some of the citizenry overheard him and got out of the way and spread the word to move down the path they came in on. So when they were going down the path it was cleared for them. They, like before, weren't going too fast, but were still going fast enough for their capes to catch some wind and levitate above their horses.

Once they got back to the camp Crassus turned and told his guards behind him, "Get the centurions to the command tent immediately."

The guards all dispersed to find each centurion. He continued to the command tent and once he got there dismounted and gave his horse to one of the legionary guards stationed there and said, "Get this tied to a post nearby." The legionary saluted and took the reins and led the horse to a nearby post pounded into the ground for any horses that needed to be tied up for a moment.

Several minutes passed as each and every centurion piled into the command tent and saluted. Once every centurion was there Crassus began.

"We are going to march into the mountains today and to our new campsite." He turned and pointed to a map he hung on the wall and continued, "This is where we are to encamp within the mountains. There will be a guide that will lead me there. All you have to do is to get your cohorts to follow me through the mountains."

All of the centurions said, "Yes sir."

Crassus added, "Dismissed, the order to move will sound momentarily." All of the centurions saluted and filed out of the tent and then Crassus walked out and said to one of the guards, "Get me the trumpeter."

A few moments later the legionary guard and trumpeter were running to Crassus who was standing outside the command tent looking out at the legion. They saluted and the legionary said, "Here he is, sir."

Crassus turned to the trumpeter and said, "Give the order to pack up and be ready to move." The trumpeter saluted and blew out a signal. The legionaries were already in their armor and were wide awake and so it wouldn't take them long to be ready to move again. It was about midday and they weren't going to stop until near the evening when they got to their destination.

It took them half an hour to be ready to march again. They began the march for the mountains. As they grew closer the dragons began moving out of the path and to the sides of it as they watched the legion enter into their territory and up through the mountains. The dragons murmured as they marched through the mountains. It looked like they were mimes because of the thunder the legion was sounding out with their feet.

A minute in and Queen Mirada had some guards clear a path and flew down to Crassus. Crassus bowed to her saying, "Your highness." She landed and said, "Follow the path that is being cleared." Crassus nodded and she took off as he followed the path.

More and more dragons, especially younger ones, were watching from the sides of the path that they were just cleared off of. Crassus could feel the pressure on him and his men. He almost wanted to smile and wave, but that would be inappropriate at the moment because the reason he and the legion was there was that the world was on the brink of war and he was sure that they knew that as well.

Hierion found his friend and, with his parents' permission, because that was the way he thought. He wasn't going to just steal his friend when his parents had tasks for him to do, even though he could, but he wasn't going to. They went up to a platform from where they could see the path that the legion was going to take. The path was already cleared, but the legion wasn't quite there yet.

"You know I don't like being looked at like royalty." Wvitun said.

"What are you talking about when you say that?" Hierion asked.

"I mean taking me around The King's Peak as if I actually belong here. It doesn't feel right." Wvitun said.

They were standing looking down at the cleared path. In the nearby distance they could hear the footsteps of the legion growing closer.

Hierion looked at him and said, "Well, stop thinking about it that way."

Wvitun returned the look and said, "How do I not think of it that way?"

"You just don't." Hierion replied.

"Oh, okay, I just won't think." Wvitun said in a rye voice. Hierion looked at him blankly and asked, "How's the family doing?"

"My dad is doing worse and my mom isn't really happy about it. Jarock is still on his scouting tour on the eastern border." Wvitun replied, looking out at the path. "This isn't a bad spot to watch something from." Wvitun added.

"Of course it isn't, I chose it." Hierion said with a rye tone. Wvitun looked at him sideways before barking out a short laugh.

"Am I at liberty to ask where this legion is headed?" Wvitun asked, looking down the path and up at Hierion.

"They're going to the eastern front and encamping there." Hierion said with a smirk on his face, looking over at Wvitun. Wvitun jerked his gaze up at Hierion and asked, "Really?"

"Yeah." Hierion replied.

The legion came into view with General Crassus leading the way, his bodyguards behind him. They were followed by the first cohort. "Woah." Wvitun said in awe. "I never thought that I'd see a legion up close before I did something that involved me going into Praetoria." He added.

Wvitun was a fire dragon, his scales were dark orange to red as each color covered half of his body. The left side and most of the front was orange and the rest was red. His eyes were bright scarlet.

"This is so cool." Wvitun said, looking from the marching legion to Hierion. Hierion smirked and looked down to the legion. General Crassus looked up and saw them standing there and recognized Hierion. He bowed as much as he could while keeping his balance on his horse. Hierion saw the gesture and nodded his head deeply and Wvitun looked from Crassus to Hierion and asked, "Does he know who you are?"

Hierion looked at him and said, "Yeah, we met earlier today."

Wvitun stared at Hierion and asked, "You got to meet him?"

Hierion looked concerned and said, "Yeah, I'm the prince after all. I'm pretty sure that I would be there to meet him when he arrived." Wvitun looked dumbfounded before saying, "I'm so stupid." Hierion began chuckling trying to conceal a roar of a laugh.

"There's no need to remind me of that. How could one forget?" Hierion teased. Wvitun glared back at him and said, "I'm completely lost. I have absolutely no idea what you just said." Hierion looked at him for a moment thinking of a response. Wvitun was staring back.

"I don't know what that look means. I don't know if I want to know what that look means." Wvitun said. Hierion was still thinking of an answer to his previous statement.

"What I meant when I said, 'There's no need to remind me of that', was that everyone knows that you're not that smart." Hierion finally said. Wvitun glared at him again as he was thinking of a response.

Hierion caught his look and said mockingly, "I don't know what that means. I don't know if I want to know what that look means."

Wvitun had a slight scowl, but he knew that if the rules were reversed, that he would do the same thing.

Chapter

19

The World Senatorial Meeting happened every six months at the exact same place and time. It started in the morning therefore most would show up a day or two prior to the meeting and would wait for the day to come.

The Senatorial Building that it took place in was almost beyond measure. It had to be big enough for one representative from each faction to fit comfortably. There were about a fifth of the seats that were empty due to confederations.

The meeting took place on a remote island almost an equal distance from everyone in the middle of the sea. The island was safe guarded by magic and house elves that provided the magic and a seeing eye to look over the place during the World Senatorial Meeting and the six months between each one.

The magic around the island was meant to make all who could use magic not be able to, or at least render it useless while inside the ten mile sphere around the island. It also acted as an alarm system for the house elves. It would notify them if anything crossed the barrier and they would be able to see what it was just by looking at the spot through telekinesis and also be able to divert the intruder away, or kill them if necessary.

The house elves could use magic within the sphere since they were the ones who created it. They never took a side in any matter and always stayed neutral during the meeting. If one tried to do something rash, they would intervene and stop them before they could do it.

They watched over the meeting and also would deliver messages from one side to the other side of the building, but if it was a violent message, like someone wanted a house elf to kill another, the house elf would expose the one who it, and everyone knew house elves didn't lie.

House elves were smaller than dwarves in height and bulk and they had large pointy ears. Larger than high elf ears were. They also had an abnormally large nose. They never wore anything exuberant like the faction leaders would, instead they just wore a simple tunic and trousers so that they were dressed appropriately.

When faction leaders showed up early to the meeting, they were allowed to stay in the guest quarters of the island. The guest quarters were in the same building as the senatorial room, they were just on the outer edges of it. One would walk through one of four hallways and up any number of stairs to get to their assigned seat and the guest quarters all led to those hallways. When one stayed in the guest quarters, the house elves would place a spell on the room to make sure nothing got in or out without them knowing it.

No weapons were allowed there either. If one showed up with a weapon the house elves would advise one to let them confiscate it until the one who brought the weapon was about to leave.

Callus arrived at the island just ten minutes ago and decided to wait on his ship until Agamemnon or Hevtur showed up. He had his lookouts out looking for either of them, Agamemnon was the more likely to be spotted, but there was still a chance Hevtur would be spotted or he would spot his ship.

A few minutes more passed and a knock on the door presented itself. "Yes?" Callus asked, looking up from his desk.

"King Agamemnon is arriving now, my Liege." A voice from the other side of the door said. Callus stood up and pushed in his chair saying, "Alright, I'll be out there in a moment." He grabbed his cloak and put it over his tunic.

It ran from the shoulders to just above the ankles. It covered his back and around his collarbone and fell down. Its background was scarlet with the purple flag design of Praetoria in the center back, large enough to be seen from hundreds of feet away. The design was only on the back and the collar was weighted and clipped together by two silver clips on each side of the top of the cloak.

He put on his crown of silver and gold and walked to the door. He opened the door and the Praetorian Guards saluted. They were standing on each side of the door and began to follow him off of the ship and to the stone docks of the port.

The island was big enough for the guest quarters and the senatorial building to be in the center of it. On the outer edges of the island and its shores were docks for ships to dock and landing areas for dragons to land. Every single non dragon faction had a designated spot to dock their ships and every single dragon faction had a designated spot to land.

What designated the different spots was where they were positioned in the world. Farrius would dock next to Praetoria and Praetoria would dack next to Corinos and Jurrunt would land nearby, so that everyone was near their neighbors during the arrival, and at least some of one's neighbors were usually allies. Callus looked at where Corinos's docking spot was to the left of his own when one looked from the sea to the center of the island.

Agamemnon was followed down off of his ship by four Corinosian guards that wore linothorax. Agamemnon himself was wearing a cape with his armor on. His armor wasn't like a regular hoplites linothorax, matter of fact it wasn't linothorax at all. His armor consisted of a bronze chestplate and bronze shoulder pads that covered his shoulders and neck. His helmet was bronze with a front to back crest that was white and royal blue split diagonally from the top on his left side to the bottom on his right side, like his cape.

His cape bore the flag of Corinos, which was a horizontally elongated C with a star in the center that had longer horizontal points than vertical. The star was white with a royal blue center and the C was white, outlined with royal blue and where the star points crossed the C was also outlined with royal blue.

He spotted Callus and raised his chin. Callus did the same, but furrowed his brows as well. They both smiled and walked towards each other. They met and traded grips with each other.

"Callus." Agamemnon said, smiling.

"Agamemnon, how are you?" Callus asked, returning the smile.

"Good, and you?" Agamemnon asked in return.

"Good as well." Callus said as they released their grips on each other's arms.

"Do you know if King Lithimir had gotten our reply?" Agamemnon asked.

Callus returned, "No, I was going to ask Diplomat Gorronus about it when he got here."

"Ah." Agamemnon said in acknowledgement.

"How is Thessisana doing?" Callus asked, folding his hands behind his back.

"Well, or maybe too well. She keeps thinking negatively about our diplomatic situation." Agamemnon replied, rubbing his hand on the mustache portion of his beard. Callus tried not to laugh, but a chuckle slipped by and Agamemnon raised a brow at him before saying, "I'm serious, she thinks there will be a war." Agamemnon himself was suppressing a laugh.

"She even offered to help with the new techniques I am implementing into my fleets." Agamemnon added turning squarely at Callus.

"New naval techniques?" Callus asked.

"Yes, I was going to tell you and the others all about it at our next meeting." Agamemnon said and Callus nodded in agreement.

A moment later a ship from Farrius docked and a tall lengthy man stepped down from the ship and onto the docks. He had no guards around him. He spotted Callus and Agamemnon and walked towards them.

He had blonde hair and light blue eyes. He was taller than Callus and Agamemnon by about two inches. He walked over to where they were standing and bowed to them both saying, "King Agamemnon. Imperator Callus. How are you both today?"

Agamemnon and Callus both nodded their heads deeply in return and Callus said, "Well enough, and you?"

"The same. I expect that you want to hear about the message for King Lithimir." Diplomat Gorronus said. "Yes, that is exactly what we'd like to hear. Matter of fact we were just talking about it." Agamemnon said.

"We sent the message back and they replied with this." Diplomat Gorronus said, and pulled a scroll from his side pouch and held it up in front of him and reopened it to read:

"This is most excellent news. I agree to meeting with each other before the World Senatorial Meeting. I believe the best meeting spot for our talks will be in a private chamber in the guest quarters. Perhaps the southern wing, and we meet in the main hall and go from there."

"Sincerely, King Lithimir of the Kingdom of Thraldilis."

"Good." Callus said, turning from the diplomat to Agamemnon. "Thank you, Gorronus." Agamemnon said, bowing slightly at the waist. Gorronus bowed to them both and said, "You're welcome, your highness."

Gorronus turned and went to his ship like he usually did before they did anything. They went and got him so that he could do his job for Farrius, but other than that they left him alone.

Callus looked up at the clear sky like it usually was. The sky never had a cloud in it for ten miles, and then when there was a cloud it was abruptly cut off at the ten mile mark. Callus thought that the house elves must not have cared for clouds. He saw Hevtur coming in to land near them where his landing area was and nudged Agamemnon. Agamemnon saw him too and said, "Yeah I see him."

They walked forward to the center of the island to where Hevtur landed. Hevtur landed, saw them and shook his head a little bit before saying, "Hello."

Callus and Agamemnon looked at him and saw that he had sags under his eyes and Agamemnon said, before Callus could, "Have an unpleasant night?" Callus and Agamemnon chuckled as Hevtur looked at them blankly through his almost half closed eyes. "Yeah, just saw something that reminded me of you, that's all." Agamemnon stopped chuckling and stared at him. Callus laughed harder and Hevtur said, "I said you as in both of you." Callus stopped laughing, struggling to keep in a laugh. Agamemnon was also trying to hide and smile to keep his face serene. Hevtur looked at them again and said, "How'd you guys like that comeback?" Agamemnon's shoulders began to move up and down slightly and Callus looked down at the ground holding his eyes shut hard and laughing through his teeth, Hevtur cracked out a slight chuckle and rubbed one of his eyes with his corresponding wing.

"We got news about the alliance letter. King Lithimir wishes to meet in the southern hallway of the guest quarters. From there we'll find somewhere private and discuss matters there." Callus said, looking up at Hevtur.

Hevtur looked at him and asked, "I get to have some sleep first, right? I don't want to be making a bad first impression with our new allies by dozing off every fifteen seconds."

Agamemnon looked at him with a sinister smile and said, "Sometimes there is no time for such pleasantries." He looked at his curled fingers. Hevtur looked at Agamemnon with almost no expression.

"Just a couple hours or more." Hevtur said in a trying-to-convince-someone voice. Callus laughed. Agamemnon inhaled as if he was going to accept it or give him a moral lesson and said, "Be lame like that then." Callus chuckled and the other two stared at each other. Agamemnon gestured with his hands for Hevtur to leave and Hevtur said, "You know what. I just realized that I could squish you like a bug. All but that would be disgusting." Callus laughed and Agamemnon was holding a laugh back. Hevtur smiled and looked smug down at Agamemnon.

"You've got a point." Agamemnon said, turning to look around and added, "It's a dull one though." Callus was recovering from his laughter and chuckled at that. Hevtur looked from Agamemnon to Callus and asked, "And what are you, a hyena?"

"Woah, I'm neutral in this matter." Callus responded. Agamemnon said, "Not any more. You can either decide to join my side or you can fight the both of us."

Callus looked at Agamemnon and said, "That's pretty dumb."

"I know that is." Hevtur said, gesturing at Agamemnon. Callus laughed and Agamemnon said, "Go sleep, you sheep." Callus tried to clear his throat, but it just turned into another chuckle. Hevtur looked at Agamemnon and Agamemnon added, "You're even white like one."

"I'm too tired to continue, we'll resume in a few hours." Hevtur said, turning around to leave. "If you're not here in two or three hours, I'm taking that as a concession of defeat." Agamemnon said to Hevtur as he left. Callus and Agamemnon laughed some more.

"We should head over there to the meeting spot and wait." Callus said. Agamemnon nodded his head in agreement and said, "Which one of us is getting Gorronus?" "I'll get him." Callus said, turning to Gorronus's ship.

Agamemnon stood and waited at the spot they were talking at as Callus walked over to one of his guards and said, "Go notify Diplomat Gorronus that King Agamemnon and I are leaving for the southern hallway momentarily." The guard saluted and hurried over to Gorronus's ship and began to talk to one of the crewmen on the ship. The crewman nodded once and gestured to him to get aboard and the guard went up the boarding plank and onto the ship, following the crewman.

Callus glanced at the other guards and then turned around to walk back to where Agamemnon was waiting. He stopped at Agamemnon's side and looked out at the sea with Agamemnon. There was a cloud in the distance and Agamemnon said, "I bet you can't guess if and when that cloud will hit the barrier." He looked at Callus with a challenging smirk. "I'd say that it would hit the barrier because of how the wind blows outside the barrier." Callus responded, raising his chin slightly. Agamemnon inhaled deeply and said, "I'll guess when it hits first."

They stood there watching the cloud and Agamemnon said, "Right... about... now." Nothing happened. Callus looked at Agamemnon and Agamemnon turned to look at him and said, "You have to wait for my words to reach the cloud. Don't be so impatient." Callus chuckled and said, "My turn."

They stood there for several more seconds before Callus said, "Now." Nothing happened again. Agamemnon turned to him and said, "You suck at this game." Callus looked over at him and stared for a few seconds before looking back at his guard hurrying back to him.

The guard saluted and said, "He'll be out in a minute, My Liege." Callus nodded and said, "Thank you." The guard turned and walked back to where the others were not too far away.

"Now." Agamemnon said, and still, nothing happened.

"Accept it, you suck at this game." Callus said, looking out at the distant cloud and added, "Watch and learn."

Callus took his left hand and pointed two fingers out and pressed them against his temple on his corresponding side and lifted his right hand out to the sea and spaced his fingers slightly and stood there in concentration. Agamemnon stared gleefully and was about to begin laughing. "Patience Agamemnon. Not all things happen within a moment or two of you showing up." Callus said in a mocking voice with his eyes shut tightly. Agamemnon realized what he just did and what he was doing and debated just throwing him into the water.

"Mmmmm." Callus hummed and added, "Oh yeah, right now." And yet again, nothing happened. Agamemnon looked out to the cloud and burst out laughing and Callus joined in a second later.

Gorronus walked off his ship and to the docks and began to walk towards them. Agamenon saw this and tapped Callus on his shoulder. Callus looked over to Gorronus and straightened up his body in good posture. "Shall we?" Gorronus asked, gesturing with a hand to the southern hallway. "Yes." Callus said and they began to walk to the southern hallway.

Their docking spots were on the east side of the island, so the southern hallway wasn't directly in sight. It took them about ten minutes to walk around the island to the south side. They passed a number of each race on their way. They were stopped and greeted by a dwarven lord and king. They exchanged greetings and continued on their way.

One particular dwarf lord known as Lord Dalin saw them and walked towards them. Agamemnon saw him and elbowed Callus gently and Callus alerted Gorronus. They all turned to him and he said, "Greetings King Agamemnon, Imperator Callus and Diplomat Gorronus. How have you three been these past six months?"

Lord Dalin was an older dwarf. His ginger hair and beard were turning white with age and his voice, well, it never really changed, it just seemed like it would with his hair and beard turning into snow white strands of hair. Lord Dalin was always the type of character to call someone out on their bluff without hesitation. Callus liked him for it and had taken a liking to him.

"Lord Dalin." Agamemnon said, bowing at the waist a bit. Dalin did the same and they traded grips with one another.

Dalin turned to Callus and Callus said, "Good day Lord Dalin." He bowed as well as Dalin and they traded grips with one another as well.

"Lord Dalin, how are you today?" Gorronus asked, bowing more deeply than the other two. Dalin bowed and said, "I would be perfect, if it wasn't for what I think may happen in that building these next couple days." Callus tilted his head and Gorronus asked before he could, "What on earth do you mean, my lord?"

"I mean that I do not believe that this world will be at peace for much longer. Whether it be today or another day close by in the future, I believe that there will be a war soon." Dalin replied, looking sorrowful.

"What makes you say that?" Callus asked, repositioning himself to look at Dalin more comfortably. "Since I've gotten here I have seen many things that concern me about our future. Some have changed their appearance to something that it wasn't before, others have scars and scratches, and others are completely new folk. Some of them have replaced some good acquaintances of mine." Dalin said, inhaled and added, "But at least you are the same."

"Replaced, like the representatives you're on good terms with are not here?" Agamemnon asked. "Yes, and I do not believe that they are not here by accident." Dalin said, looking at all three of them. "I always suspected this day would come. Many suspected that this day would fall upon us." He added.

"Well, I will do whatever I can to prevent it, but it may not be enough. This may not be able to be avoided by anything or anyone." Callus said to Dalin. "Yes, I believe you're right. I think it will happen no matter what good is done today or tomorrow." Dalin replied. "The sun always sets at the end of the day, and it will rise at the start of the next." Agamemnon said. Dalin nodded in agreement and said, "And no one knows when the sun will rise. They will have nothing but darkness and whatever we pass down to them through time." They all nodded.

"Well, it was good seeing you Dalin and I hope I will see you again after this, but for now, we've got somewhere to be." Callus said. He stretched out an arm and Dalin took it in a firm grip. Agamemnon did the same a second later and he and Dalin traded grips as well. Gorronus bowed deeply to Dalin and Dalin returned the gesture. Dalin walked off to go somewhere else and the other three continued their journey to the southern hallway.

A minute later they were inside the southern hallway. The hallway was basically empty except for the house elves that were maintaining the hallway. They walked up to the front desk and the house elf there siad, "Good day, gentlemen. What can I do for you as of this moment?" "Is a wind dragon by the name of King Hevtur here?" Agamemnon asked. "Yes, he checked in about ten minutes ago." Agamemnon nodded and said, "Thank you." "Of course. Now is there anything else?" The house elf asked.

Callus said, "I don't think so, we were just going to wait here for some others to arrive." The house elf nodded in acknowledgement and said, "I see. Well, I'll be here if you need anything." Callus nodded, saying, "Thank you."

They turned and walked to a table that was on the left side of the hall from where one walked in. They sat at the table and Agamemnon said, "I was sure he'd fall asleep on the way here." Callus chuckled as Gorronus looked at both of them in confusion.

Another house elf walked up to the table and asked, "Is there anything you men would want to eat?" Gorronus replied almost immediately saying, "Yes, I would like a few ribs with a cup of wine please." "Which ribs and which wine sir?" The house elf inquired. Gorronus mused on that and after a few seconds of thinking he said, "Country-style ribs with some Merlot wine." "Do you want a bottle to go with that, sir?" The house elf asked. Gorronus nodded and the house elf turned to Callus.

"And for you, sir?" The house elf asked. "I would like sirloin steak done medium rare with red wine to drink." Callus responded. The house elf nodded and asked, "Do you want a bottle as well?" Callus nodded his head and the house elf turned to Agamemnon.

"And for you, sir?" The house elf asked. "I would have the same as him." Agamemnon said, pointing at Callus. The house elf nodded and vanished into thin air.

It would've been creepy for someone who hasn't been there before, but for ones who have it was normal for it to happen.

The table was a large table, enough for approximately ten humans to sit there, and was made of marble. The table of marble was white and the seats were made of feathered cushions and wooden supports. The wood was teakwood. The building itself was made of smoothed stone and was painted with pictures of all different faction leaders from the Great War. The southern hallway was painted with faction leaders that went south after the war, the west hallway was painted with the faction leaders that went west, the northern hallway was painted with faction leaders that went north, and the eastern hallway was painted with the faction leaders that went east after the great war.

A few more moments went by and a group of figures walked through the archway leading out to the sunlight of the day. Agamemnon, who was facing the door, stretched to one side to look over Callus and Callus turned around enough to see. Gorronus looked to his left at two elves, a human, two dwarves and a dragon all commuting with one another.

Callus recognized King Lithimir at the same time he looked at the table at the three of them. Callus, Agamemnon, and Gorronus stood up to greet the other six. "Imperator Callus?" King Lithimir asked, looking at Callus. Callus bowed at the waist and said, "King Lithimir, yes?" Lithimir bowed at the waist and said, "I've been looking forward to this day."

King Lithimir was as tall as Callus and had long dark brown hair. He wore the colors of Thraldilis, which were a medium gray and gold, and his cape bore the flag of Thraldilis. The flag of Thraldilis was two gold branches of an olive tree curled up from where the branch would connect to the tree to the tips of the branch over the gray background. The ends that would be attached to the tree were next to each other at the bottom of the flag and the tips of the branches were next to each other at the top of the flag. His crown was made of silver and gems of white. He wore a cloak similar to Calluses and had deep blue eyes.

King Lithimir saw Agamemnon and asked, "And I would guess that you are King Agamemnon, yes?" Agamemnon bowed to him and said, "You would guess correctly." Lithimir bowed back to Agamemnon and turned to Gorronus and asked, "And what is your name. I wouldn't think it to be KIng Hevtur, no offense meant." Gorronus bowed deeply and said, "None taken, your highness. I am Diplomat Gorronus of the

Republic of Farrius. I am the man who comes to the World Senatorial Meeting and reports back to the senate of Farrius about the affairs that took place during the meeting." Lithimir nodded in acknowledgement and asked, "Then where is King Hevtur of Jurrunt?" "He had a long trip here and is recovering just now." Callus said. "I see, yes, we got here yesterday, but King Caladon here was exhausted from his flight as well." Lithimir said, gesturing a hand to the dragon behind him.

"Allow me to introduce you to the rest of us." Lithimir said, turning to his side with his hand out to the others. He looked over and walked closer to the other elf and said, "This is King Volkaire of Kailinis." King Kailinis stepped forward and bowed to Callus and Agamemnon. His hair was long and black and he wore the colors of Kailinis which were magenta and navy blue. The flag of Kailinis was on the back of his cloak as well and it was a shard of navy blue in the magenta representing a shard of ice. His crown was made of magical ice as well. Where Volkaire was from was where a battle against evil took place and in the battle the island was turned to ice that never melted. It covered multiple islands that were all given to the Kingdom of Kailinis. Callus and Agamemnon bowed in return and Lithimir went to the nest closest.

"This is Lord Dunidai of Zailison." Lithimir held a hand out at Lord Dunidai who was a dwarf. His hair was brown as was his beard and he wore the colors of Zailison on his cape, which were green and brown. The flag was divided into a top half and a bottom half with brown being the base for the bottom and green being the base for the top. On each half was a pickaxe of the other color of their colors. The pickaxes were tilted and mirrored and flipped from each other. His crown was of gold and rubies. Dunidai bowed to them and they bowed back.

They went to the next closest and Lithimir said, "This is King Caladon of Malavar." Caladon was a dimmed shade of bronze and had red-orange eyes. He, like all of the other dragons, didn't wear the colors of his faction nor the flag like humans, elves, and dwarves did. Callus could tell that he wasn't just a metal dragon, but he could feel warmth coming from his body indicating that he was part fire dragon as well. His crown held his faction's colors though like other dragon factions did. It was of iron gray and metallic midnight blue. It was a simple cross of both colors, each color having an opposite corner of the flag. Caladon bowed to them and they bowed in return.

Lithimir gestured to the next closest and said, "This is Lord Furrond of Baisla." Furrond wore a cape of his faction's colors of violet and royal purple and was solid violet with an eagle of royal purple in the center. The eagle was perched on an olive branch and was looking to the left side of Furronds body. Furrond was shorter than Callus and had red hair with a shaved beard. His crown was made of copper and had diamonds within it. He bowed to Callus and Agamemnon and they bowed in return.

Lithimir turned towards the last of them and said, "And this is King Narlais of Pargent." He had brown hair and a dark brown beard. He wore a cape of yellow and red and was split into two like Agamemnon's cape with red on the left side of his body and yellow on the right side of his body. There was a red hammer tilted at a thirty degree angle in the center and was outlined in yellow. His crown was made of fire gold, which was red, and had fovaria gems, which were a bright yellow gem, embedded in it. He bowed to them and they bowed in return.

"Well, where shall we wait for King Hevtur to arrive?" Narlais asked, looking at the others.

"We were just awaiting food as you showed up." Agamemnon said, gesturing at the table where they were sitting previously.

"That's a good enough thing to wait for." Dunidai replied. They all walked to the table and sat down. Caladon, being a dragon, lay down next to the table.

They began talking as the same house elf from before appeared and asked the other six what they wished to eat. Once he had that information, he disappeared again and they continued commuting, passing the time by as they awaited Hevtur to awake from his slumber, wherever he was, and meet up with them. They talked about situations and about the meeting that was tomorrow. They all shared their thoughts on the matter of Vasilldir's proposal at the last World Senatorial Meeting and they were all similar, they thought it wasn't as bright as Vasilldir did when he said it. They waited for Hevtur to discuss the terms and whether or not they would align with one another. The house elves appeared again and snapped their fingers as the food they asked for appeared in front of them.

Since house elves use natural magic they have to make the food out of something, so they make it out of the food required to make it and then teleport it to the location of where it is supposed to be eaten.

They began eating and talking for the next two hours as they awaited Hevtur.

Chapter

20

Hevtur awoke at a house elf, instructed to wake him, awoke him. "Sir, it has been two hours as you requested." The house elf said. Hevtur opened his eyes at the house elf and had a hard time keeping them open as he rose to nod and said, "Thank you. Do you have anything to help me wake up by chance?"

"Yes sir, I'll have it out for you if you'd like." The house elf replied.

"Yes I would like to have it in here, please." Hevtur said, still trying to blink his eyes open without them staying closed in mid-blink. The house elf nodded and vanished.

He continued to shake his head and stretch his legs and wings for another minute before the house elf reappeared. "Would you like it now?" The house elf asked.

Hevtur looked at the house elf as he thought that it was a no brainer when and where he wanted it and said, "Yes."

The house elf nodded and raised his hand and snapped his fingers above his head. A dragon sized bowl appeared with some liquid in it and the house elf said, "It is to help you get out of any slumber and be alert again. Will that be all?" Hevtur looked at the bowl and then the house elf and said, "Yes, that will be all."

The house elf bowed and vanished again leaving Hevtur to stare at the bowl of what looked as loose as water, but it wasn't water. Hevtur sniffed the bowl before realizing that he was not going to get poisoned by a house elf. He began to drink from the bowl, taking a mouth full and lifting his snout to above his head and letting the liquid run down to his stomach.

He got done and felt as if he had a whole night and half a day to sleep in. He walked over to where the door was and around a corner to have it in sight and saw his guards. Two were awake and talking to each other to stay awake and the other two were sleeping. He walked over to them and they didn't see him coming. He stopped almost right next to them before one must have seen something in the corner of his eye and looked at Hevtur. He jumped a little bit and alerted his fellow guard. The other guard turned and was startled as well and they both were quick to bow.

"Get some sleep. Both of you and allow the others to stay asleep as well." Hevtur said. The guard that jumped back a little asked, "Are you sure?" Hevtur nodded and said, "Get some rest." They both bowed again and looked at each other as Hevtur walked by and to the hallway. The guards found a spot out of the way and laid down.

Hevtur was about to turn to the main hallway as Agamemnon and Callus came walking towards him talking to each other. Agamemnon spotted him and said, "OH, you're awake. I thought that you were going to have to forfeit our little insult match and that I would win, once again." Hevtur stared down at him for a second and said, "You don't always win."

"I never said I did." Agamemnon replied. Hevtur opened his mouth to speak and shut it again, narrowing his eyes at Agamemnon. Agamemnon returned the look, but was also mockingly doing as well.

Callus stood there and said in a sarcastic voice, "And yet again, one will ask, who will win this insult fest this time?" Agamemnon and Hevtur stared at him. Callus looked at them and said, "Oh, yes I forgot. Three. Two. One. Fight. Or wait. No, no, no. It's three. Two. One. Insult." Callus finished and grabbed his cloak with his right hand and waved it like a flag down near his leg. Agamemnon looked at Hevtur for a moment and then back at Callus. Hevtur a second later looked at Agamemnon and then back at Callus. Callus said, "You guys aren't even in sync with one another."

They stared at him for another moment and Callus looked over Agamemnon's shoulder to the other seven at the table and said, "You guys can either call it a draw or allow me to win this time because we have something to discuss with another seven someones." Hevtur raised an eyebrow and Agamemnon said, "I will never allow you to win an insult match."

Hevtur nodded in agreement and Callus said, "Then it is a draw." Agamemnon and Hevtur scowled at each other and saw that they were scowling at one another and began laughing.

They walked back over to the table where the others were and Callus introduced Hevtur to the others and Lithimir introduced the others to Hevtur as he did with Callus and Agamemnon. Gorronus during that whole ordeal earlier was standing in the back awaiting his turn to greet every single one of the faction leaders separately as they sat down and began to commute.

"Now that we're all here, let us discuss a possible alliance." Lithimir said, sitting down on the seat he occupied before. "We'll start off by saying how our alliances work. Our alliance will go first." Volkaire said, gesturing at the other five in their alliance.

"I should let you know that there is another alliance member that doesn't come to the World Senatorial Meeting. She wished to stay secret until three months ago at our last meeting, where we discussed your proposal." Agamemnon said. "I see." Lithimir said, he inhaled and asked, "Will she be a part of this alliance soon?"

"Yes, at our last meeting we made it a point that we would get her accustomed to our way of meeting, if that changes I will let her know." Agamemnon replied. "Okay, we will continue our discussions and decide on a meeting point or points for our meetings should we become an alliance." Lithimir said.

"The way we have our alliance set up is that we have a meeting point at Zailison, which is in the center of all of our factions, and there we have our meetings when needed." Volkaire said, and continued, "We have meetings every four months and we share what we wish to share at these meetings with one another." Agamemnon, Callus, Hevtur and Gorronus nodded in acknowledgement. Lithimir looked at them for them to take their turn.

"The way we have our alliance set up is that we have our meetings every three months and we alternate our meeting points between each of our factions' home lands. From there we share anything we wish to share with one another and any maneuvers that we are committing. And the way our fathers committed to the alliance is that they would bring us, once we were of age, to the meetings and we would get to know each other. That way when we grew up we were more acquainted with one another." Agamemnon said.

"What do you mean by maneuvers?" Narlais asked. "On my northern border, King Folkhem has stationed two of his armies and I stationed two of mine in response, I told them of the situation and King Hevtur here had the same problem." Callus said, gesturing at Hevtur. Narlais nodded in understanding.

"Hmmm." Furrond said, then added, "I like the way your fathers thought, I agree with it." Agamemnon bowed his head slightly in response. "So do I." Volkaire said and Lithimir said, "Yes, I think that that is a good way to strengthen an alliance." Caladon looked at Hevtur and Hevtur looked back. Caladon said, "It is a good thought and I agree with it." "As well as I." Hevtur said after him.

Furrond said, "So, how will we be setting up our meetings in this case? We could find a meeting point somewhere in between our factions, or we could continue having meetings at Zailison, or we could alternate between our factions the way you do." He gestured at Agamemnon and the others. "Here is the closest point to the center of all our factions and I don't think the house elves would allow that to happen." Volkaire said, folding his arms, musing on the topic.

"That leaves two good options, but we'd be traveling for weeks there and back if we met at Zailison for the meetings. That would leave us on Luminarch not much time to make decisions for our factions to be tasked to as we were gone." Callus said.

"Which really leaves only one known way and that is to alternate between factions, but in the end, most of us would be traveling for weeks anyways." Lithimir said. "We could ask the house elves if they would allow it." Volkaire suggested.

"What if we had our meetings as usual, like how we are having them as of the moment, and meet up every once in a while together for an overall meeting of the alliance?" Hevtur asked. Everyone sat there in silence and thought.

"That could work." Volkaire. said. Everyone nodded slightly, still in thought, and Agamemnon said, "It could very well work." Everyone nodded in agreement and Lithimir asked, "What will we call this alliance for others outside of it to know which alliance it is?" Everyone concentrated on their thoughts. *The Good Alliance?* Callus thought and smiled in amusement.

Narlais looked at Callus and Callus saw and said, "Don't look at me, I'm the one who names his legions after numbers and wherever they were raised." Narlais chuckled. "Where they were raised." Furrond murmured to himself and continued, "We could name it after where it was formed." Callus stared at him knowing where he got that idea.

"The World Alliance. That doesn't make much sense since the whole world isn't in it." Dunidai said. "Since we live across the great ocean from each other, we could call it the cross sea or water alliance." Callus said, and added, "We are the only alliance that would be stretched across the ocean." "The Cross-Water Alliance." Lithimir said, thinking about it and how it sounded. He nodded and said, "That sounds good enough." Everyone else nodded in agreement and Narlais asked, "What will be the colors of this alliance?"

"It could be blue like the water." Agamemnon suggested. "I agree with that." Callus said. Hevtur nodded with Caladon and Volkaire. Narlais thought about that for a moment before saying, "I suppose it is accurate to the name. I agree." Narlais nodded and Dunidai followed. Lithimir nodded and looked at Furrond and he nodded. Lithimir turned his gaze to Gorronus and Gorronus said, "It sounds fair to me." Lithimir nodded and stood up, everyone else followed and he said, "Then that is it, we are now the Cross-Water Alliance." They all began bowing and trading grips.

Narlais walked up to Callus and said, "Now that we're in the same alliance, you don't mind that I call you Callus instead of your full title now do you?" Callus chuckled and said, "As long as I get to call you Narlais without your full title as well." Narlais nodded once and they traded their grips.

Hevtur and Caladon stared at each other for another second before their laughs began to tremble their looks and they wrapped their tails in a grip and Caladon said, "It feels good to actually be an international ally with another dragon." Hevtur laughed and nodded in agreement. "I would like to get to know you more." Hevtur suggested and Caladon nodded saying, "Yeah, we should."

"We should let the house elves know about this therefore they are informed." Volkaire said. They all nodded in agreement and they turned to follow Volkaire to the front desk in the southern hallway.

"I would like to formally announce that everyone behind me including myself is now to be known as the Cross-Water Alliance." Volkaire said. The house elf looked at the ten members of the alliance and nodded saying, "I will let the others know of this." "Thank you." Volkaire said, backing away from the desk to commute with the others.

After a few more moments of commuting, they went their separate ways. Lithimir, Volkaire, Dunidai, Narlais, Furrond, and Caladon all went to the western hallway where they docked and landed and where they usually stayed during the World Senatorial Meeting.

Callus, Agamemnon, Gorronus, and Hevtur all went to the eastern hallway where they docked and landed and usually stayed for the meeting. They didn't walk around the outside of the building this time. Instead they walked through the center near the senatorial room. Others were there and were talking with each other as they either stood in a particular spot or they walked around in their groups.

Every time they would pass another group or sometimes just one loner, they would bow to them since they were almost all royalty there.

They passed one particular group of men, and one of the men said, "Imperator Callus?"

Callus turned to look at him and recognized him to be King William of Mercia. Mercia was a kingdom on the island of Britone off of the north western coast of Luminarch.

King William was just shorter than Callus and had brown hair with a moderately thick beard of brown.

"King William. How are you?" Callus asked, bowing to him. He bowed in return and said, "Better than I was before I saw you. There was something I wished to discuss with you privately."

Callus raised an eyebrow and asked, "Where and when?"

"Hopefully now and most likely a private chamber so that no unwanted ears can intrude on our speakings." William said. Callus nodded and said, "Let us go find a private room for now." He turned back to the others and said, "I'll be along in a moment if you want to continue." Agamemnon and Hevtur nodded and they continued to the eastern hallway with Gorronus following them. The others that were with William stayed and William elaborated, "They're staying because of what we wish to discuss, but not to worry, everything will be peaceful." Callus nodded in approval and they walked to where a house elf was standing near a door and William asked, "May we have this room for a moment?" The house elf looked at him and then the others and asked, "Yes, will this be a private gathering?"

"Yes, just the six of us." William said. The house elf looked into his eyes and opened the door.

Callus relieved himself more because a house elf could see into one's future by looking into their eyes. They could see their intentions and how they would die later in life. They never revealed anything to anyone but themselves. They couldn't see past the death of the one they looked into, but they could see when they were going to die. One's future could always be changed or altered since it has not happened yet, so when they saw that one was going to die during their time at the meeting they would find a way to stop it.

They walked into the room and the house elf shut the door behind them. "So, what do you wish to discuss?" Callus asked. William looked at him and said, "We were looking for you, or really anyone for this matter, so that we could ask something of you."

Callus looked at him and said, "You do not have to fret, tell what it is you want and I shall see if it can be done, and if it can, I will do it."

William nodded in relief and said, "There is an extreme famine in our lands. We have not been able to get out of it for one year, all four seasons. We have come together today and have come to you to ask if you will help us."

Callus asked, "In which way would you like my help?" William looked at the others and they all nodded, he turned to Callus and said, "The famine is not all that we trouble with. Because of the famine our rules are failing and most do no longer have an heir for his kingdom. So we ask you if you will consider a confederation of our kingdoms. If a war is to start, we may be the target of many other factions, but with you as the leader of our lands, not half of them will consider it." William finished with his hands out to his sides and slightly cupped as if they had water within them.

Callus looked at him and then the others individually and breathed slowly. He did not know whether to accept the confederation or not, he knew that William was right on how they would be a prime target for enemies in war. Their people were starving and they could not sustain any army in a famine, no faction could. The army would fall apart and leave nothing to stand in the way of the enemy's forces. He also knew that it would take time and would be considerably harder to stabilize that territory in a time of war.

He thought a while longer before he inhaled and said, "I will confederate your kingdoms, but I would not have a proper army in your lands for a considerable time. You will have to protect the lands that you give me until then. I have fleets in the region that could assist in naval combat. With them I will be able to send you food to sustain your people until then."

William sighed in relief and looked at the other four and they all nodded and he said, "It can be done. The most appropriate time for this confederation to take place is at this meeting tomorrow. If that is good with you." Callus nodded and said, "Then tomorrow, I will welcome you to Praetoria with open arms."

Chapter

21

Callus was fitting his cloak on for the meeting that morning. The meeting never waited for anyone, if one was late then one was late and was looked at as undisciplined. He walked to where his four guards stood on the same side of the door as Callus did, inside the room. There was a passageway that led from the door to around a corner and then to the actual room that someone would sleep in. He made sure his hair was straight and looking like he didn't just wake up even though he did and walked over to the door that led out. His guards saluted and the one nearest the door opened it for Callus to pass through. He walked through and his guards followed him out. He didn't really need the guards because there was magic on the door and all over the room to ensure that nothing got in or out without the house elves knowing. In the morning a house elf would go to each room and alert the current holder of the room that it was morning. The holder of the room would either get up or could tell the house elf that they were going to sleep in a little longer and to come back in however much longer one wanted to sleep in.

When Callus stepped out of the room he occupied he saw Agamemnon already standing there waiting for him. The house elf that awakened Callus had already departed and the house elf that had awakened Agamemnon was gone as well. Agamemnon eyed Callus intently before saying, "It's about time you walked out of that door."

Callus returned his look and asked, "If you're waiting for me then I would be forced to guess that even the meeting would wait as well." Callus lifted his chin and smirked after he was done and Agamemnon scowled saying, "How are you in such a good mood in the morning?"

"Because I'm a good son that listened to his father when he was told to go to bed." Agamemnon began chuckling and then that turned into a laugh. Callus was holding back a laugh as well as he could for the moment.

Hevtur walked out of his quarters and saw Agamemnon laughing and said, "You're not the type to be in a good mood in the morning, or have you abruptly changed overnight? What have you done with the real Agamemnon?"

Agamemnon turned to look at Hevtur and suddenly stopped laughing. There was no slowing down the laughter or chuckling before coming to a complete stop, he just stopped laughing and stared at Hevtur with a sober face. They stared at each other and Callus broke the silence with, "Today, is going to be a good day."

They both looked from each other to him and Hevtur said, "And you're just unnatural in the mornings. Almost always happy or in some type of pleasant mood."

"That's because, unlike you two, I'm not married." Callus said, putting his hands on his hips and looking extremely smug and amused with his comment. Agamemnon began laughing again and Hevtur stopped in his tracks trying not to laugh.

"I'm too tired for this, Callus." Hevtur said finally after containing the laugh that was in his throat. "Well then wake up while I go take care of something." Callus said, Hevtur looked at him and Agamemnon stopped laughing naturally this time and looked at him as well saying, "What do you mean, 'take care of something'? What thing would want your care?"

Hevtur began chuckling and Agamemnon continued to stare at Callus. "I mean that I have a life." Hevtur stopped chuckling and inhaled slowly and said, "Callus, sometimes I think that you want to be taught a lesson." Since Calluses guards were used to such behavior they didn't move. Callus mused on that and responded, "Probably because I keep teaching you two lessons and I want life to be more fair."

"You're so stupid that killing you would just stupify the one who killed you." Agamemnon said. Hevtur nodded in agreement and Callus said, "Whatever, you're just jealous that I am able to wake up in the morning and you're not."

"You know that's not true, you liar." Hevtur said. Agamemnon saw an opportunity and said, "Hevtur, you're just in denial because it's true for you. As for me I didn't deny it as fast as you did, therefore it is less true in my case. It is how liars lie." Hevtur looked at him in confusion and sweeped down to him saying, "Alright, who are you really Agamemnon because I know that you're never in a good mood at the start of the day and I also know that you're not that smart." Callus nodded his head in agreement. Agamemnon stared back at Hevtur and inhaled.

Callus said, "Well, I'm going to get going on this task and I'll see you two at the meeting." He began walking away and Hevtur moved his tail in his path and said, "Care to share any secrets before you leave? Particularly this one that you are trying to leave to." Callus looked up to see Hevtur looking back at him intently.

"You're not tired at all are you? You're the real liar around here." Callus accused, pointing a finger at Hevtur. Hevtur narrowed his eyes and Agamemnon strode around him to see Callus. "I think you could tell us." Agamemnon suggested.

Callus looked at Agamemnon then back at Hevtur and said, "It won't be a secret for long. All you two have to do is show up at the meeting and pay attention." Hevtur began to chuckle saying, "Oh no, the vote on you telling us right here and now is two to one. It's democracy. Now tell us." Callus scowled up at him and said, "You guys have no patience." Agamemnon nodded with a smile on his face and Hevtur nodded as well.

"I'm going to talk with King William, that's all." Callus said, moving his arms out from his sides and almost horizontally with the ground.

"I thought you talked with him yesterday?" Hevtur asked. "I did, I'm just going to talk with him some more to clear something up." Callus said.

"So you don't mind if I come as well?" Agamemnon asked, his arms were folded. "Okay, you don't do that either." Hevtur said, looking at

Agamemnon. "Don't do what?" Agamemnon wondered, Hevtur stared at him and said, "Fold your arms."

"Yes I do, you just are too blind to see it." Agamemnon complained in reply. "I'm the blind one? The one who can use magic to see farther is the blind one?" Hevtur asked.

Hevtur must not have known it, but as he was arguing with Agamemnon he moved his tail out of the path of Callus and Callus walked past and into the hallway. Not that his tail was too big to step over, but Callus just didn't want to.

"Where does he think he's going?" Agamemnon asked. Hevtur turned around to see that Callus wasn't there anymore and that he was walking down the hallway to the center to meet up with William.

Callus looked over his shoulder and Hevtur asked, "Where do you think you're going without us?" Callus stopped and turned fully around to look at them and said, "I'm going to leave you girls to continue arguing with one another so that I may think more clearly, and then I am going to talk with King William."

"Callus, don't you remember me telling you yesterday that I would never let you win an insult match?" Agamemnon said.

"And I didn't. I won two insult matches." Callus returned and kept walking saying, "See you both at the meeting."

"Whatever." Hevtur said, turning back to Agamemnon and added, "We have a common enemy." Agamemnon nodded and said, "Yes we do." They both looked at Callus walking away and gave each other rye smiles and turned to their quarters and entered them leaving the hallway.

Callus walked around the Senatorial Building and to the north hallway where William was quartered. The hallway was almost crowded with leaders of factions from the north. Most of the leaders were dragons from Drakenmor, but there were still many others from the northern island wall and Britone and other islands along the north of the world.

After a minute of walking through the north hallway he spotted William and the other four with him. They saw him as well and walked towards him. "Imperator, I'm glad to see you again." William said, bowing at the waist.

Callus returned the gesture and asked, "Shall we discuss our matters further?" William nodded his head and began walking towards a room, gesturing to Callus to follow. Callus followed him and they walked into a room that was guarded by what seemed like Williams guards and a house elf was there, most likely at Williams's request. The door shut behind the six of them and William picked up a paper from a desk and a pen as well saying, "I've written up the papers like you asked and we've all read and signed them. All that needs to be done is for you to sign as well and to discuss it in the meeting today."

Callus nodded in approval and said, "Okay." William held out the papers for Callus to grab and he grabbed them and walked over to a desk to read them thoroughly. He got done reading over them a few minutes later and signed the papers at the bottom of each one.

He stood up and said, "Welcome to Praetoria, Governor William." He turned to the others and said, "Governor Alfred, Governor Felix, Governor Richard, and Governor Jared. I welcome you all to the newly reformed Empire of Praetoria."

They all bowed to Callus and Callus said, "For today's meeting you will take your original seats. I will announce at the meeting of this confederation and we will go from there."

"Yes, my Liege." They all said in unison. Callus nodded once and walked to the door and said, "I'll see you all at the meeting." They bowed again, still getting used to it and Callus walked out of the door.

He turned around and closed the door again and said, "I would wish that you will inform your people of the laws and your soldiers of the salutes when you return to your governed lands." William and the others nodded in the affirmative and William said, "Yes, it will be done."

"Thank you." Callus said, before walking out of the door again and to the western hallway back to his quarters for the next half hour while he waited for the meeting to start. Late last night he gave each of the new governors, of his new land, documents of the laws of Praetoria. They were to read over them and fulfill them to the best of their ability. Callus now had to ensure that that land was not lost, or not too much of it anyways, to any possible enemies from the north. He knew that if a war broke out that anyone that wasn't a dragon wouldn't attack because of his amassing of his fleets in Port Reaver. The dragons were a whole different problem all together. If they attacked, not much could stop them from taking a vast majority of the land and turning the inhabitants of that land against him in an effort to cripple Praetoria as much as possible with raids and riots. The only things that he could hope for is that one; the dragons distracted each other enough to keep themselves off of his land. Two; the dragons decided not to attack him at least until he had some legions up there to help protect it.

A half hour later he was sitting in his designated spot for the meeting with Gorronus below him and Agamemnon above him, and Hevtur to his right. To the left of him were the savage marauders from across the river who would occasionally stare at him and others around them in secret discussions with one another. He looked across the senate building and saw Lithimir and the others at their designated spots for the meeting as well. He looked to the north and saw William and the other four governors with him. They sat next to each other like their factions did on the world map. The southern factions were in the southern portion of the building and the northern factions to the north. They were positioned like they were on the world map as well with Hevtur being closer to the north than Callus and Agamemnon being more to the east of Callus. The way everyone was seated was east to the top of the building and west to the bottom of the building. Where the speaker would stand was, on the map, where the island itself was. Callus was closer to the bottom of the seating than the top, he was five rows from the bottom and about fifteen from the top. The meeting would start out with a house elf by the name of Dorly and he would start off each meeting with a greeting to all the leaders in the seats of the building.

"Greetings leaders of the world. Today we come together for the World Senatorial Meeting to discuss and dispute any troubles or worries that we may have. To prolong peace and justice through the world and through time to hopefully many years in the future. We will start off this meeting with something of peace and unity. Emperor Callus, will you please come to the stand and share what you have done recently." Dorly stated.

Hevturs gaze shot to Callus and so did just about everyone else in the building. That's when Callus knew that he didn't really think about the changing of the words Imperium to Empire and Imperator to Emperor very thoroughly.

"What did he say?" Agamemnon asked, leaning forward to look down at Callus. Callus stood up and looked at him as he walked to the stairs that led down to the floor and said, "You'll see."

"I'll see your hide on a roasting stick if you did something stupid." Agamemnon said, a little harshly, but that was how he was when something large was at stake. Callus walked down off the stands and to the podium to speak through the wind magic that was in place to allow the whole of the building here his words. He stood on the podium base and looked up at Hevtur, still staring at him as he pulled out the documents of the confederation. Hevtur saw them and used wind magic to see what they were and his eyes widened.

Callus put the papers on the podium and said, "This morning I and five others made an agreement. An agreement that will change the world. Many of you have heard of the forming of the Cross-Water Alliance that was formed yesterday between the Diamond Plains Alliance and the Adriatic Alliance." He fell silent for a few seconds swallowing while murmurs spread like wildfire through the stands.

He continued, "Today I, King William, King Alfred, King Felix, King Richard, and King Jared of Britone have made a pact. Here it is:

> "I, King William of Mercia, declare myself to make an oath to someone of new interest, Emperor Craesious Callus, and I make this oath on my people of new and of late to serve under one flag and to be a newly found governor of this state to protect and fight for its people and my new Emperor, I, if need be, will bleed and die for this oath in any case of righteousness and clarity, but will not in any case bleed and die for unrighteousness and disclarity. Signed, Emperor Craesious Callus of Praetoria."

He paused as his gaze went upon the next page and continued:

"I, King Alfred of Larkan, declare myself to make an oath to someone of new interest, Emperor Craesious Callus, and I make this oath on my people of new and of late to serve under one flag and to be a newly found governor of this state to protect and fight for its people and my new Emperor, I, if need be, will bleed and die for this oath in any case of righteousness and clarity, but will not in any case bleed and die for unrighteousness and disclarity. Signed, Emperor Craesious Callus or Praetoria."

Callus paused again, swallowing and looking to the next page saying:

"I, King Felix of Fundaland, declare myself to make an oath to someone of new interest, Emperor Craesious Callus, and I make this oath on my people of new and of late to serve under one flag and to be a newly found governor of this state to protect and fight for its people and my new Emperor, I, if need be, will bleed and die for this oath in any case of righteousness and clarity, but will not in any case bleed and die for unrighteousness and disclarity. Signed, Emperor Craesious Callus of Praetoria."

Callus went to the next page and read:

"I, King Richard of Lionhart, declare myself to make an oath to someone of new interest, Emperor Craesious Callus, and I make this oath on my people of new and of late to serve under one flag and to be a newly found governor of this state to protect and fight for its people and my new Emperor, I, if need be, will bleed and die for this oath in any case of righteousness and clarity, but will not in any case bleed and die for unrighteousness and disclarity. Signed, Emperor Craesious Callus of Praetoria."

Callus went to the next and said:

> "I, King Jared of Winex, declare myself to make an oath to someone of new interest, Emperor Craesious Callus, and I make this oath on my people of new and of late to serve under one flag and to be a newly found governor of this state to protect and fight for its people and my new Emperor, I, if need be, will bleed and die for this oath in any case of righteousness and clarity, but will not in any case bleed and die for unrighteousness and disclarity. Signed, Emperor Craesious Callus of Praetoria."

He put down the papers and looked up at the crowd all staring at him. Some were in awe, others were in content, and the rest were in terror for they knew what that just did.

"Thank you, Emperor Callus. Go sit down please." Dorly said. Callus bowed in appreciation and walked to the stairs that he walked down before and looked up to see Hevtur, Agamemnon and even Gorronus staring at him in disbelief. He got back up to his spot as Dorly began saying, "And now, anyone who wishes to speak will, in an orderly fashion, come down to speak their minds and we will continue this meeting."

Callus reached his spot and couldn't help but smile at Hevtur and Agamemnon who were staring at him with something Callus couldn't identify.

"You what?!" Hevtur asked.

"How many others have you confederated with?" Agamemnon asked. Callus looked at both of them and sat down and said, "Relax, it's not like you're going to be affected by it."

"Pfft." Hevtur scoffed and continued, "You're now the biggest faction in the world and you act like it's no big deal. If you were to take a look at everyone in this building you would find that they are either looking at you then turning to talk with one another about you or the other way around."

Callus shrugged and said, "It's just fame, get used to it." Hevtur was taken aback by that response and Agamemnon blinked several times to comprehend what Callus just said.

"You are going to be the reason why this war starts, aren't you?" Hevtur claimed. Callus looked at him mildly and raised a finger to his mouth for silence. Hevtur blinked and shook his head and said, "You know exactly what you're doing and you're okay with it." Callus looked back at Hevtur and put his finger to his lips again and turned back to look at the floor. It was Vasilldir.

Callus almost rolled his eyes before he caught himself as he knew that he was now being watched by many across the building.

"Thank you, Dorly." Vasilldir started as if he was just the coolest thing alive and continued, "Impressive Emperor. Very impressive. I'm sure everyone at this meeting knows what I mean by it."

He put his hands on the podium and rested upon them and continued, "We have witnessed history, we now have seen the largest faction in the world be formed on this day. I wonder, how will you sustain such a territory?"

Callus signaled for the house elf that stood with him so that he could speak from where he was in the stands. The house elf got closer and listened to Callus say, "Get me an amplifier." The house elf nodded and snapped its fingers and Callus stood up and said through the magical amplified air in front of him, "The five previous kings are now to be my governors for the territory that I have acquired from them. They have already sent out word to the people in their provinces that they are now under Praetorian rule. Their messengers went out this morning after the signing."

"Ahhhh, I see. Many may think that you forced them into such a decision." Vasilldir said. Right before Callus could respond Governor Richard spoke up saying, "Then they would be mistaken." Callus nodded in approval to Richard's remark and the other governors nodded in agreement with him.

"Now they might say that you are being brainwashed into saying such a thing." Vasilldir said, looking from Richard to Callus. Callus looked dumbfounded and said, "I can assure you that they have not been brainwashed into anything."

Mmmm." Vasilldir hummed.

"You are trying to mislead, Vasilldir, you are trying to contort a good thing into a bad thing. You are trying to start a conflict." Dalin spoke out into the building. Vasilldir turned to look at the dwarf with an 'are you challenging me' type look. Dalin was standing and leaning forward when he said it.

"Why would I ever…" Vasilldir was cut off by Dalin saying, "Because it is something too great for you to accept was done by someone who didn't use magic to do it." Murmurs ran through the building.

As much as everyone here was a leader of a faction, they sure acted like senators in a senate, like true politicians. Callus thought.

"I never underestimated Imperator Callus at any time, or I mean, Emperor Callus now, but now he has done something that makes others wonder. I do not wonder about these things, I am merely trying to speak on the behalf of the ones who do think of such things." Vasilldir said, putting his hand to his chest as if what he was doing was so hard and caring. Callus was able to keep down a laugh and instead was able to put his hand over his mouth to make it look like he was considering that Vasilldir had a point in the matter, he was actually putting his hand there to cover a smile of amusement.

"And all you try to represent are the ones who resent Emperor Callus for what he has done without magic. Say you do not resent the Emperor for deciding to go against the movement you started years ago about converting the world into nothing but magic users." Dalin pressed. Vasilldir inhaled, trying to buy time for a response.

One would think that someone would call Dalin out of line for how he is pressing a matter onto Vasilldir, but then again, many thought that Dalin would either expose them in some way or would have the backing of Callus and Praetoria, who was now the largest, most populated faction in the world at least two times over in both categories now. Praetoria would now be able to raise and fund more legions than most factions and each legion could have the potential of being twice as large as any other faction's armies.

Many were not terrified of a war happening, but were terrified that if they chose the wrong side to fight with or against they would end up pitted against Praetoria on the battlefield. Praetoria already had one of the best trained land forces in the world and now they had the ability to have the most men in each force and more forces than any other faction, many of the factions put together wouldn't match up to the amount of troops that could be mustered by Praetoria.

Vasilldir said, "I am disappointed that the Emperor has not sided with me in my efforts to make a better world, but that does not mean that I resent him in any way. My followers may resent non-magic users like you say, but I do not push that ideal onto them." Dalin nodded once and sat back down to listen.

"So, about the discussion of why this has happened I will elaborate on. Yesterday they came to me with a question, a request more like, and asked if I would confederate them into Praetoria. They said that they were and still are going through a major famine and have been for the past year. They for a year barely sustained their people from utter death. They came to me for help and suggested that they be confederated, they were also worried of their neighbors who saw their weakness and that they would exploit it when the time was right. A confederation made it where the chance of an attack would be less likely to happen, but the chance is still not zero. The confederation, the way I saw it, was a scare tactic to the ones who made them feel threatened. There was no brainwashing of any sort." Callus said to the other faction leaders within the senate building.

Murmurs ran around the crowd and Vasilldir said over them, "I understand the point from where you come from. Five kings were worried for their people, their people that they could no longer sustain and properly protect from their point of view. They asked you for help and you offered, but I wish to let you know, that anyone who still doubts your ability to rule and carry on with the hardships of life without magic, are not under my control." More murmurs spread and Vasilldir thanked Dorly again and left the floor. Callus sat back down.

"Is there anyone else who wishes to take the floor?" Dorly asked, looking out into the stands and one stood up and walked to the floor announcing, "Yes, I would like to take the floor for a moment." Droly nodded and Callus saw King Folkhem walk out onto the floor and to the podium.

"I come to you today for insight upon a situation that has and still is occurring on my borders." Folkhem said and then abruptly pointed to Callus and Hevtur saying, "They are amassing their armies and legions to war."

Callus froze seeing what Folkhem was trying to do. He looked over at Hevtur and Hevtur must have seen the same thing because he was frozen as well. "My scouts have recovered sightings of mysteriously new equipment in the Praetorian legions nearest my borders. More of my scouts have reported that Praetoria's two fleets are on the northern border of their lands. Praetoria makes ready for war!" Folkhem said, still pointing at Callus and Hevtur.

Before Callus could speak another voice cut in and said, "Yes, my people have been losing their lives while fishing in the Alzeirs River. There are never any survivors from these fishing trips. I believe that Corinos is destroying them to claim the river as their own." Calluses head snapped to his left where the marauder states from the south of the Alzeirs were standing in protest.

Agamemnon's head snapped there as well and he shot up from his seat and said, "You exaggerate such things. I have never sent a ship from my ports out into your waters. Ships from your people travel into my waters, my waters that I have rightfully claimed in this very building. Those ships have attacked my trade galleys and allied trade galleys and transport ships. Just three months ago I received a report from my men that two of your so-called fishing ships attacked a transport ship from Farrius. The attack wounded an ally that was on his way to my capital of Corinthus!"

Callus didn't know how the house elves kept up with the arguments without being able to look into the speaker's eyes for foresight into what their intentions were.

"King Folkhem, I call you out on something you are withholding from this senate! You withhold the information that your own armies are at your borders and that they were encamped there first! You came to this senate today in fear that you made a decision that you could not support if a war started, you decided to encamp armies at your borders where you bordered these other factions and when your situation was desperate you came to cry unto this meeting to help free yourself from your own mistakes! Own up to your own dealings and settle it yourself instead of making everyone else's mind quake and tremble with the thoughts that you think!" Dalin bellowed into the building. Folkhem turned to look at the other dwarf in shock as if he forgot that Dalin existed.

"You try to hide the truth of the matter! You try to tell me to own up to my own decisions and yet you stand in for someone else who is supposed to stand up for their own decisions! You are a hypocrite Lord Dalin! You are a misleader of information! You are a deceiver unto the world and the minds and ears of the ones who listen unto your words! You are a plague that corrupts the hearts and minds of the ones you speak unto! Why do you do this to others? Why do you spread misinformation about subjects? Why do you spread deceivings unto the minds and hearts of the ones you share bread and water with?" Folkhem protested.

Before murmurs could even be thought of, Dalin bellowed back through the building, "I do not do such things! I have seen what happens around the world I live in! I watch what happens to those who are right and to those who are wrong! I do not spread such deceivations unto you or anyone of whom I speak to or with! I speak of what I see! I speak of what the prophecies of old have said and what they have told me to look for in the world! The prophecies say unto us that the evil our ancestors fought and destroyed started because of such twisting of words! They say that the evil started with such withholdings of information! They say that evil will regrow its strength in the future and will rise again to threaten the world, and that if we are not nimble and careful unto what we say and do, that the evil will consume us all and we shall all perish underneath its darkness and wickedness! Have you not read the prophecies? Have you not been true unto all thine words? Have you not been keeping a watchful eye unto what you act upon? Have you not seen what evil can do to one's mind, body and soul? Have you not been told the stories of old about the greatness of the wicked and the power of the evil they serve? I say unto you, nay! I do not think you have taken those words and prophecies and stories of old soberly! It was the evil that started the Great War! Not the good and righteous! Did our ancestors not defeat this evil one millennia ago so that we may live on to be free and to breathe in free air and our own air and eat our own food and drink our own water and sleep in our own beds and under our own roofs and love our own loved ones? Did our ancestors not create this meeting so that we may come together to commute and speak to one another? Did our ancestors not sweat, bleed and die for us? Did our ancestors not stand up against such idiocracy to eliminate it from the world so that we may know of peace? The prophecies and teachings say that we were not the only people to be attacked by evil, but that others were as well and they did not do as our ancestors did and they fell and they bleed and they sweat and they cried and they were slain by the evil and now the evil rule over their lands!" Dalin stopped for a moment to catch a breath because he was getting old and tired to continue his preaching.

"You claim that we are not one! That we are divided upon ourselves. That we will fall into ruin and die upon the blades of evil! You say that we have committed evil in our own rights! I say that you are mistaken and that you must be punished for your attempts to mislead us and mistake us for something that we are not! You are the evil you speak of! You are the evil that the prophecies have taught us! You are the wrong among the righteous and you must be plucked from our world before your weed grows any farther! I call you to war! To end this wronging and this treachery unto our ears and minds! And I say unto you that you will die and you will not receive a grave for a grave is for the ones who are not wronging others, but are righting them and encouraging them and standing with them, not over them!" King Folkhem claimed, pointing at Dalin and continued raising his other hand from behind him, "Who will stand with me against this evil that attempts to rise within our world and sight? Who will help me pluck out this evil from the earth and cast it out into the fire to be burned and churned to ashes?"

The building erupted into roars of defiance and rage. Leaders from all factions stood up and roared out their defiance and ferocity and with that, the world was at war.

Callus looked over to where Governor William and the others were and they were staring at Callus. He gestured to them to go and they fortunately knew what he meant and sprung to their feet to run out of the building.

Hevtur looked from Callus to the governors and back and said, "We have got to go now! I will take word to my people and tell them of this news."

"Wait!" Agamemnon said to Hevtur. Hevtur turned to look at him and Agamemnon said, "Get to the pier where you first met Cora and tell her of what happened and to please send someone to speed our arrival back home." Hevtur nodded once and darted to the exit. Callus looked across the building at Lithimir and the others and they were up and moving to leave as quickly as possible.

"Come on!" Agamemnon said. Callus turned and almost ran into him as he headed for the exit.

Hevtur awoke his guards and said, "We are at war! Let's MOVE!" And they sprung up and followed him to the open ground outside of the building. They went to take off.

He took off and was struck from the side and hit the ground hard. The guard saw this and rushed to his aid. One minute into the war and he was already attacked. An earth dragon from the looks of it went for his neck. He ducked and one of his guards pounced on the dragon and was followed by another guard.

As Callus and Agamemnon got to their guards, the guards were on high alert and one of each asked simultaneously, "What's going on sire? Are you alright?"

"We are at war, so we've got to move quickly." Agamemnon responded to both guards. The guards all nodded once and began to follow them.

"Come sir!" Another one of his guards called and he looked around before taking off and saw that the coast was clear and lifted off of the ground.

Callus saw the endeavor that Hevtur just went through and shouted, "Be ready for anything!" They were still in the eastern hallway and were slightly jogging to the exit. The intensity of the moment, or past few moments, was so inducing that sweat was forming on the brows of everyone there.

They didn't have weapons with them at the time because they were inside the Senatorial Building. They had weapons on their ships though.

They reached their ships without any contentions, but they did see the two wind dragon guards that stayed behind kill the other dragon. They ensured that the dragon was dead and went to fly off. They saw Callus and Agamemnon and their guards getting to their ships and the two dragons looked around for anyone that could be a threat.

Callus had no idea where Gorronus went or where he was at that moment. He worried that he may have not exited the building and that he may have gotten killed. He didn't really know Gorronus all that well, or as well as he knew Daentious, but he knew what would happen if Gorronus didn't return word to Farrius.

Callus knew that he could send word to Farrius, but that they may not listen too easily. He knew that the senators of Farrius and almost any other politician there had something against someone or something, but he didn't know who or what they were against.

The ships of Corinos and Praetoria cast off and were under way toward home. The Jurrunt guards took off at the sight and flew over the ships to make sure that nothing was coming for them.

It was a few days sail back to where Cora could send any help out safely and then about another one or two days to an allied port.

PART THREE

Chapter

22

Two Days Later

After almost a three day flight, Hevtur was arriving in Corinthus to alarm Cora about the situation.

I may just need some more of whatever that house elf gave me. Hevtur thought as he landed on the pier where he first met Cora. His two guards landed after him and one asked, "My Liege, may I ask what we are doing here?"

Hevtur turned his head to look at the weary dragon and said, "I am spreading the word of the war. You do not need to come." The guard nodded tiredly and yawned and blinked his eyes a few times to try to stay awake. All three of them were panting heavily as Hevtur walked up to the door and knocked with a wing, almost falling over due to exhaustion.

The door opened slightly and Hevtur said, "War has started. I need to speak with Queen Cora on behalf of King Agamemnon." Hevtur couldn't quite see who or what was on the other side, but the door opened wider and a water dragon peered out at him and the two wind dragons behind him. The guards behind Hevtur whipped their heads up slightly trying to see who it was, but they were too tired to see as well. The water dragon guard looked at all three of them and said, "You wait here. I'll see if she can make it." Hevtur was too tired to complain or argue and just nodded his head.

The door shut and he could hear faint voices on the other side. Hevtur tried his hardest to keep his eyes open and found that staying still was not going to help. He began walking around in random shapes of circles, triangles and squares while he waited. His guards were beginning to drift off every once in a while and when they caught themselves they would snap their heads up and shake them. Other times when they didn't catch themselves falling asleep, the other one would wake him and they would both continue to attempt to stay awake.

It felt like they waited an eternity. Hevtur thought of knocking again to see if they had even gone anywhere. At one point he got too tired so he went to knock to see if it would just wake him up a bit more when they opened in front of him and Cora stood there on alert.

He snapped his head back in surprise and she went to him and asked, "What happened? Are you hurt?" Hevtur was too tired to respond properly and just said, "Agamemnon wishes that you aid in his return back here. The war has started."

He bowed his head in exhaustion and swayed and said, "I must go to my home to protect it. Farewell." Cora stopped him and said, "Are you sure you'll make the flight?" Hevtur nodded tiredly and said in a barely audible voice, "Yes, yes I'm sure."

"No you won't." Cora said looking from him to his guards, who were too tired to even respond to her moving closer to him to stop him from going. She turned to one of her guards and said, "Get a force ready to go out to find King Agamemnon and the others." The guard nodded once and darted away to complete the task. She looked at the water and focused. The water stirred and shot out of the river and at Hevtur and the two wind dragons behind him. The water hit them like a hammer blow and Hevtur shot to attention and almost attacked Cora in reflex. He stopped himself, remembering where he was and what he was doing. His two guards shot up and one fell over in surprise.

"You are in no condition to go anywhere. If you are attacked, you will most certainly get killed. All three of you." Cora said to Hevtur and continued, "You need to get some rest."

"NO! I can't. I've got to get back to my people, my kingdom, and protect them. I cannot rest yet." Hevtur blurted out.

"A dead king is not going to protect anyone." Cora said in response and added, "If you go, and we are at war, you will be targeted. I know that you can camouflage and hide, but you are in no state to be able to camouflage and fly that distance. You MUST rest." Hevtur was stunned at that response. Only Mirada had talked to him that way and well, his parents as well.

Cora turned to the guards behind her and said, "Get the other two in here." She gestured with her head to Hevturs two guards. She led Hevtur into the building and set him in a comfortable spot. When one is tired, any spot is comfortable.

Her guards led the others in as well and guided them to the sides so that they were out of the way of anyone who went past. It didn't take over a couple seconds for the guards to pass out. Hevtur was still in rebellion to the fact that he was going to be made to stay there.

"I need to warn them." Hevtur said, trying to get up onto his talons.

"You need to rest." Cora said calmly and added, "Agamemnon and Callus will be here in about a few more days, if my party finds them."

"IF!" Hevtur said. He didn't know where that came from, but he was very tired.

Cora looked at him sharply and said, "You are too tired to fly that distance. If you were to go, when you got there you would be too tired to warn them anyways. The only difference is that this way there is no chance of being harmed by an enemy." She ended harshly, baring her teeth.

Hevtur almost jumped back as he knew he was too tired to control his responses and that if she was provoked in a violent way, he wouldn't be able to stop her from literally disabling him from flying for another however many months or even years depending on where she attacked. If he continued to contend with her and she got over it, she might just go after his wings so that she had a legitimate reason as to why he couldn't go and not that he shouldn't go.

Hevtur tried to get up one more time and she pounced on him saying, "I am NOT going to let you get yourself killed because you thought that something else was more important than your own life and health. You ARE going to stay here and you ARE going to get some rest. I know you have already been targeted because it is standard practice for everyone who went to that meeting to have four guards, not two, and you have a fresh scar on your wing and your side that was not from rough-housing with a friend." She paused for a moment before adding, "I know that four is standard for that meeting because my husband used to go to them, until one day he didn't take the four guards and he never came back." She bit off most of her words and released her grip on Hevtur.

Hevtur lay there stunned and said, "Alright, you win."

She nodded once and said to her guards, "Make sure he sleeps." They nodded and bowed as she semi-dove into the water and disappeared. Hevtur shut his eyes and shifted his weight to a better position to sleep. Since he was cold and wet it was harder than usual to fall asleep. His left side also was in a bit of pain. He curled around and formed himself into a ball-like shape with his tail wrapped around him and his wings folded tightly against his back and within another few seconds he fell asleep.

Several minutes later Queen Thessisana stepped out of a coach and onto the pier where she saw Hevtur land. She was followed by four guards and she walked to the edge of the pier and rounded a corner and walked up to a door that was the size of a dragon and she knocked on the door. The door opened slightly and she could see an eye looking out and down at her.

"I am here to inspect the arrival of three dragons from the west." The dragon stared at her and moved to look at someone else and back and said, "Okay."

The door opened and she and the four Corinosian guards followed in behind her. She looked around and saw two wind dragons in one spot near the wall asleep, and another was across the building on the other side curled into a ball-like form.

"They're resting, Queen Cora doesn't want them awakened until they're fully rested." One of the guards said.

Thessisana nodded in agreement and asked, "May I speak with Queen Cora?" The guard nodded and went into the water. She watched as the guard left and turned to her guards and said, "Be sure to stay quiet. Make sure no one comes near this pier today nor tomorrow." The guards nodded once and went out onto the pier to watch for ships that may come near the pier.

Cora was seeing to the party that was to go and find Agamemnon's ship as well as Calluses. Fifteen was the number that was the party to go. She made sure that they were well rested and that their strength was up to their best.

She saw one of the guards from the building where Hevtur was and she turned to him. He bowed to her and said, "My Queen, Queen Thessisana wishes to speak with you. She arrived to see what King Hevtur was doing here." Cora nodded, she turned to the fifteen and said, "Go find them, be careful and vigilant." The fifteen nodded once and went on their way. She turned back to the guard and nodded once.

They went back up to the building and Cora emerged from the water in the building and stepped onto the floor.

Thessisana turned around and saw her. She smiled and bowed to Cora. Cora bowed back with a smile and said, "Thessisana, you wish to see me."

"Yes, I wanted to see why Hevtur is here." Thessiana said. Cora inhaled and laid down saying, "He came to warn me of what happened at the meeting. War has started. He came to ask me to send a party to Agamemnon's aid, to help him arrive sooner."

"Agamemnon didn't send for me?" Thessisana asked in a rye voice. Cora smirked, looking at her and began to giggle. Thessisana sighed and shook her head jokingly. "I cannot let him get away with this. I may have to send some ships, or some fleets." Thessisana said, touching one of her fingers to her lips. Cora began to chuckle.

"Maybe I will." Thessisana added.

"More troops wouldn't hurt." Cora said in the same tone of voice as Agamemnon would, mocking him. Thessisana began to laugh and caught herself and looked at Hevtur, still resting in the ball he was in when she walked in. Cora looked over to him and began to lightly chuckle as well as Thessisana.

Chapter

23

Four Days Later

Daentious was sitting at his desk as the sun was going down in the west. He was studying the maps and formations of their neighbors to the west of Farrius. He was leaning back in his chair thinking about what happened at the meeting.

He wanted to know whether it was time for war or if the world still kept peace. He stood up and walked to the tent flaps and opened one to look outside to the setting sun. It was beautiful, especially if one looked at the moons as well. One moon was about thirty degrees above the sun, there was a slit of lit up moon that Daentious could see. The other moon was not on the same side of the world that he was on. The second moon was nowhere in sight of him. He knew that the world was bigger than anyone knew, or at least guessed.

Many years ago the merchants of the far east sent out ships to try to sail around the vast ocean and to the island wall that they supposed was on the other side of that ocean. Those ships were never seen again. Many thought that the ships had sunk in a storm or that they fell off the edge of the world when they sailed too far that way. Many people believed it, they believed that the world had its limits in the way of just looking like a map on a table. The air was nice and warm at the moment, and since it was still summer, there was no worry of waking up in the morning to find frost, ice, or even snow on the ground. There could be rain, but not any of the other three.

He took in a long deep breath and walked back into his office. He sat back down at the desk for the next two hours, studying papers and drinking coffee. Coffee beans came from the south where they were grown and ground into coffee grounds that were then mixed in with supposedly hot water. If it wasn't hot water that one mixed his/her coffee grounds in then that one was off their rocker.

He picked up a paper to look at it more closely and heard horns blowing not too far away. They were Farrius horns, they were horns of the elves that they bordered and they sounded as if they were right outside of camp. He shot up and heard footsteps approaching his tent. He picked up his sheathed sword and unsheathed it, holding the sheath in his left hand and his sword in his right. "Sir! Sir, we're under attack!" Daentious's eyes widened and he darted to the tent opening and held out his sword to the soldier who warned him and once seeing who it was he lowered his sword and asked, "Who and Where?"

"The Njori sir, and they've got dragons!" The man said, still panting mildly. Daentious looked up and said, "Get the trumpeter and sound the call for battle!" The soldier saluted with a hand to his forehead and bolted off to find the trumpeter. Daentious stalked down through the camp and found everyone he could and formed a phalanx with them. "MOVE!" The newly formed phalanx took positions and marched forward into battle.

Daentious still hadn't seen any elves and was beginning to wonder if the chaos around him was a bad dream. He could still hear the horns blaring and a moment later a trumpet picked up on the air and carried throughout the camp.

Men began bursting out of their tents and to their captains ready for orders, forming into their phalanxes with their swords and shields, and their spears and shields, and their pikes and axes. That's when Daentious saw what was happening. A phalanx of men with pikes was engaged in close quarters with elves that carried dual blades. The elves began to cut down and through the phalanx like paper. Daentious took hold of a phalanx that had lost its captain and said, "WITH ME!" The phalanx shifted and began to follow Daentious into battle.

The pikemen routed and the elves pushed forward into the camp with swift furocity. They saw Daentious and the phalanx around him and charged with howls and screams of battle. They engaged and the phalanx of axemen cried out their own screams and howls of battle.

It was almost pitch black, except for the torches that had been lit inside the camp for light. Visibility was almost at the minimum for sight, but when one was in the military for long enough, he could feel where the enemy was. Daentious brought up his sword and brought it back down upon the unguarded neck of an elf. He carried his sword around and to the temple of another elf's head. He was close enough to be able to see through the darkness and see a Farriusian strike down on an elf and then moved to the next without support and was killed by it. Another Farriusian soldier beat down an elf with his shield and continued to cut open another's gut, spilling the elf's intestines onto the ground. Another Farriusians oval shield was not in position to protect the holder and the man went down with a shriek of pain.

Cries and sobs went up all around as men and elves alike were slain and put down to the earth. Daentious saw through the darkness, between him and a lit torch, another elf come for him. The elf swept his first blade at Daentious and he evaded and caught the second blade with a parry of his sword. He kicked at the elf's knee and his foot landed with a crack and a scream from the elf. The elf fell grasping his knee and Daentious saw pity enough to put him out of his misery.

As the battle raged on, Daentious slowly was able to conjure up many of his remaining force to a better defensive position just outside of the camp.

He was also able to get bolt throwers into the position and set up for any open window of attack. They were on a ridge near the edge of camp and had their backs to the open country of Farrius. Cries and howls and screams of defiance roared up from the raging battle and Daentious was atop the ridge seeing to the bolt throwers and any who wanted to run away.

He turned routing men around and into the mix of battle to fight for their homes and lives. The bolt thrower crews were still not profitant in their works, but were still able to lay low many of the enemy. He still

SECRETS AND PROPHECIES | 193

had not seen any dragons as of yet, but did not doubt that they were out there ready to strike from the shadows where they may have lurked.

"NO! FIGHT AS ONE! FIGHT TOGETHER AND WE WILL GET OUT OF THIS MESS!" Daentious bellowed to weary soldiers. Daentious led a routing spearmen phalanx back into the enemy lines and fought for several minutes with them before departing to watch over the rest of the remaining army that he knew was still alive. They were pushing the elves back and Daentious shouted at the top of his lungs, "THEY'RE RUNNING! THEY'RE BREAKING UPON OUR SHIELDS, SPEARS, SWORDS, AXES, AND PIKES! KEEP LAYING THEM LOW AND PUSH!"

The Farriusians burst into bellows of war and battle and pushed forward into the enemy ranks and cut them down like vines in a jungle. A pikemen phalanx paralleled their pikes with the ground and charged forward into the elves and impeded an elf counter-attack. Their pikes broke and snapped under the pressure and weight of the elves falling to the ground and the men holding them rushing forward over the carpet of dead that covered most of the ground of that ridge. Daentious saw a glimpse in the corner of his eye and recognized it as something bigger than an elf or human.

A dragon burst into the battle lines and tore the unprepared phalanx apart from itself, throwing men six feet through the air to land down upon the ground or other Farriusians. The dragon stomped on the smaller humans and batted them aside to clash into the ranks of either elves or their fellow humans. The dragon whirled and brushed the ground beside it with its tail, snapping legs and leveling men into the dirt and rock of the ground. The earth dragons' spiked tail flailed the Farriusians and tore them like paper.

More dragons charged into the ranks of the men and attempted the same, but for some it was not as successful. One dragon was targeted by the bolt throwers. The bolt throwers had trouble penetrating the dragons' scales, but some aims were true and they struck the dragons in their weak spots near the end of the tail and wings and eyes and the mouths. Dragons struck by the bolt throwers roared in pain and agony as they snapped back from the attack. One dragon, unlike the others, must not have seen the pikes of one phalanx and charged into them.

As strong as dragon scales were, they would not stop a sharp, thinly pointed tip at a high speed. The bolt throwers loosed their bolts at high speeds, but were not the weight needed to penetrate their scales with one volley.

The dragon came in at high speed like the others and was heavy enough for its scales to not protect it from the pike tips that awaited and it was impaled by twenty pikes and the pikes shafts broke under the impact and the dragon reeled back in pain and surprise. The men saw this and roared in hope and tenacity and charged the dragons with their weapons and assaulted the dragons that laid waste to their companions and they drove the dragons back and out of the battle lines and they continued their advance upon the elves who were now wavering in fear and troubled minds as to what to do in their situation.

A metal dragon rolled into the battle ranks and smashed through the ranks of Farriusians and began to break the morale of the men it attacked within an instant of arriving. Daentious saw this and darted towards the dragon and rallied as many men as he could to his flanks and pressed into the gap that the dragon was creating. The men still fighting the dragon saw Daentious coming and gained new hope as they charged the dragon in the gap and they fought off the elves that attempted to spring through the weakness in the line. Daentious arrived seconds later after the Farriusian counter-attack to the dragon and he led three hundred men into the gap to take it back and plug it.

He cut down two elves with a down stroke and a vertical thrust from the knee into the elf's head. The dragon saw him coming and began to make its way to him. Daentious turned to the dragon, who was being targeted by the bolt throwers, but was not deterred in any way. Daentious selected several men to aid him in the fight against the dragon and they made their way to the dragon. The others around Daentious and the dragon saw what was about to happen and they fought the elves out of the way for Daentious to arrive untouched to the dragon. The sword in Daentious's hand warped and cried in bending into an unusable state. Daentiouses armor began to creak and contort on his body trying to crush him. He without a second thought picked up a spear from the ground near to him and launched it at the dragon's eye.

He deterred the dragon from its metal bending for long enough to rush it and pick up another sword into his hand and with one swift movement ran at the dragon's leg and used his speed to leap atop the dragon's back. The dragon felt him and panicked as Daentious took his sword in his hands and thrust it down into one of the wings of the dragon and cut it open. The dragon howled in pain and Daentious took that opportunity to reposition the sword in his hand and hook it into the eye of the dragon.

Blood was drawn and the dragon bellowed in agony and thrashed around and Daentious, with his sword still in the dragon's eye, used his strength to move the dragon to a better used spot where it would not crush his men, but would trample the elves in its wake. He left the sword in the eye and lept down off the dragon to near his men and darted behind them as they reengaged in combat with the enemy. He got out of the battle line and went behind his men to survey the battle again. That time the enemy was targeting him. Elves tried to rush towards him as he picked up another sword and engaged with them. The first of the four elves that slipped through attacked ferociously, but was blinded by that ferocity and Daentious took his blood as payment for it by cutting open the elf's neck and almost completely severing it. The next elf waited for a companion to attack and they attacked in unison from two different sides.

Daentious waited for the last moment to leap out of the way and towards the last elf. The two elves who attacked misstepped and slammed into each other. One of the elves incidentally killed the other with one of his swords and the other nicked him and drew blood from his wrist in a spray of red.

Daentious attacked the last elf, blowing one of its blades from its hands and parrying the other to the side and glided forward within the elf's guard and with his helmet, beat the elf's head into its brains with one hard swift blow to just above the eye socket. The elf screamed in pain for a split second before he crumbled to the ground and died. The other elf who was not dead as of yet, looked at Daentious in terror and tried to flee, but could not outrun Daentious and he caught up to the elf and sliced down his back and across his legs at the back of the knee, crippling the elf to the ground as the elf screamed in agony and terror as he looked up at Daentious who stood over the elf. Daentious couldn't take the crying wails of the elf and killed him.

Daentious saw that his army was pushing the enemy back and off of the ridge entirely and was beginning to reclaim the camp. He was down near the front lines and two more elves saw the opportunity to strike at him and he averted his gaze upon them. He engaged with them and was in the open away from the rest of his army. More elves came from small momentary gaps in the line.

He continued to strike them down one by one as he pushed forward with his men and back into the camp. He swung his sword left and right, up and down at the elves, and with almost each stroke, added new blood to his sword and armor. Then with a single vibrating thud of the earth, a dragon hit the ground behind Daentious and darted low and fast and turned its head ninety degrees, opened its mouth and clamped down on Daentious's unaware body and cut him in half at the waist and his lower body fell to the ground as the dragon of pure red scales ate and swallowed the top half of his body.

Some men saw this and went to take revenge for their fallen leader's death and the dragon turned and breathed fire from its mouth and burned the men to ashes. The fire spread to the battle lines and engulfed a portion of the lines as well. The bolt thrower crews targeted the fire dragon and, without a moment's notice, was attacked by more dragons and were helpless to stop them. Now with a fire dragon behind them and no leader to look to, and them not knowing where their initial general was, the Farriusians' wills began to wane and their morale began to waver. They began to flee one by one, then three by fours, then by the tens and twenties, they fled from the battle in defeat.

Flags of purple and gold began to fall to the bloodied ground and burn in the wake of fire. Men began to throw off their armor in an attempt to flee faster. The elves and dragons saw this and began to run them down like dogs after stray sheep in a pasture.

The Farriusians were picked off by the fives and tens. Many of the Farriusians surrendered to their enemy and others were either killed or were swift enough to flee with their lives and alert the rest of Farrius that the war had begun. Fires raged at where the camp once was and it was the only light for miles and miles, and the stench of death filled the air in a thick hue of destruction. The Second Great War had begun.

Chapter

24

Callus was standing on the port side of the ship and was looking out at four ships that were enroute to cross their paths. Callus looked from the incoming ships to Agamemnon's ship and saw Agamemnon staring at the ships as well, he turned and looked at Callus and smiled saying, "Are you ready for some fun?!"

Callus grinned. Agamemnon unsheathed his sword and Callus unclipped his cloak from around his neck and reclipped it upon the outer edges of his shoulders. Callus was wearing his armor for that morning and had a sword sheathed at his side. He unsheathed the sword and saluted Agamemnon, duelist style, and Agamemnon returned it, lifting his chin as well. Callus lifted his chin in return.

"I'll be counting my score. How about you?" Agamemnon asked.

"I don't know if you should, I don't think it'll matter much since I'm going to win anyways." Callus said back boastingly. Agamemnon laughed and turned to his men to prepare them for battle. Callus did as well.

His men were standing in a formation of six men by fifteen men and they were all wearing the purple capes of Praetorian Guards. They had their shields in front and their swords within their sheaths as they awaited the enemy to arrive.

"Today we will meet the enemy aboard this ship, above these waves, upon these deck boards. We will meet them and we will spill their blood to soak into the boards and mingle with the water. They will pay to visit us with their blood and lives." Callus said to the Praetorians aboard his ship.

They burst out into roars of defiance and unsheathed their swords and readied for battle. Men on Agamemnon' ship also roared their defiance and raised their spears up to the sky.

A few moments passed and the ships were almost on top of them. The first two ships targeted Agamemnon's ship and the other two went for Calluses.

The first ship hurled ropes at the Corinosian ship, the ropes grabbed hold and they pulled their ship in against the Corinosian ship. Agamemnon stood in the front of his men and as the first marauder hurled himself onto the Corinosian ship and onto a waiting spear. More and more marauders jumped onto the ship and they fought aboard the ship. Agamemnon blocked an attack with his shield and cut off the arm of his attacker with a swift movement.

Callus watched as both ships boarded Agamemnon's ship and battle raged from the ship. The two ships coming for Calluses slowed and threw their ropes to board. Callus positioned his men in two different groups. As the marauders began to board they were met by Praetorian steel. The Praetorian Guard fought with fierceness and great coordination and they killed many of the marauders within the first two minutes.

Callus watched the skirmish unfold and thought, *I should get down there if I want to at least compete with Agamemnon in this bet.*

He stepped down from the rear tower and headed to the closely quartered fighting. There were ten Praetorian Guards protecting him and they followed him. He looked over to Agamemnon's ship and saw him knock a marauder's sword arm away and brought down his sword into the marauder's neck. He brought his round iron shield to his side and blocked another attack as one of his men came and thrust his spear into the marauder.

Agamemnon turned and swept his sword at another marauder and missed. The marauder moved inside his guard and slashed at his armor and thrust. The slash didn't penetrate the armor and the thrust barely went into the armor, but did not harm Agamemnon in any way. Agamemnon looked down at the stunned marauder's face and swept his sword down and opened his skull, splattering blood all over his armor.

Another marauder came from behind and tried to cut down into his neck, but the sword was stopped as it met Agamemnon's armor and he turned around to face the marauder. The marauder tried to evade, but Agamemnon seized the marauder by the hair and drove his sword into the eye socket of the marauder. A high-pitched scream of pain came up from every marauder he slew and he looked up at Callus and smiled shouting, "Eighteen!"

Callus grinned and shouted in return, "Watch this!"

Callus unsheathed his sword and a loud hissing sounded and half a dozen marauders dropped dead with surprised gasps and streams of blood. Agamemnon widened his eyes and shouted back, "That's cheating!" There was a trickle of a laugh in his voice.

Callus laughed and stalked into the chaos and cut down three marauders in a couple seconds. Agamemnon went into the fighting as well.

Callus swept his sword out across the chest of one marauder startling the man and Callus continued through his Praetorian Guard and into the marauder's undignified ranks. He brought his sword back and cut off the head of another within his range and swept his sword from his bottom left to his top right, cutting off another marauder's hand and he thrust his sword into the previously injured man and laid him low. His men followed in front of him and created a shield wall to protect their Emperor.

The marauders were being slaughtered by the couples and the triples. They began to break and tried to flee and Callus and his Praetorian Guard made another push and cut down the remaining marauders and the ropes between the ships were cut. The marauder ships fell back and they made an attempt to run from the Praetorians.

Agamemnon and his men also pushed the marauders off and slew many of them as the marauders retreated. The ships fell off of the ship and turned to flee with the rest of their lives and they began to run away.

Callus and Agamemnon stayed on course to their destinations and allowed the marauders to flee with their lives. Corinosians and Praetorians cheered and roared in glee as their attackers. Agamemnon walked to the starboard side of his ship and Callus walked to his port side to talk with Agamemnon.

"Will I have to beat out the secret of how you did that or will you tell me?!" Agamemnon asked, shouting for Callus to be able to hear.

Callus grinned and shouted, "I'll tell you if you tell me a secret of your own!"

Agamemnon grinned and shouted, "I can do that!"

Callus tilted his head towards Agamemnon and shouted, "And it better not be something useless or stupid!"

Agamemnon laughed and shouted back, "Not to worry, it won't!" Callus nodded once and laughed.

In the distance the marauder ships were attacked. One of them was shattered into the air and debris flew through the air over the marauder ships. Another ship was hit by something and it split down the middle of the ship. Cries came up from the ships and the crews and men of Agamemnons and Calluses ships turned to look at what was happening.

Agamemnon and Callus turned as well to look out at the retreating ships. A wave rose up from the surface of the water and crashed down on another ship, smothering it and sinking it under the waves. The last ships' crew cried in terror and pleaded for the sparing of their lives, but nonetheless, the ship was destroyed by the waves that tore it apart and shredded the boards from each other.

Callus and Agamemnon looked at each other and they both knew what happened, water dragons were there near them. All they could really do was hope that they were friendly.

A water dragon emerged from the water to see which ship was the correct ship and headed towards Agamemnon's ship. Agamemnon noticed the dragon and stood near the starboard side of his ship, looking at Callus for him to stay there.

Callus looked back and the dragon swam up to between the two ships and emerged above the water, looking at Agamemnon and said, "King Agamemnon, we have come to your aid per your request."

Agamemnon inhaled and nodded saying, "Thank you. Are you able to speed up our arrival back?"

The dragon nodded and said, "Yeah, we can do that." Agamemnon nodded as did Callus. The dragon nodded and submerged.

Nothing happened for several minutes until Callus could slightly tell that the ships began to move faster. He looked up and walked over to his cabin and walked into it and shut the door behind him and sat down in his bunk and sat there for a moment. He laid down after a moment.

Later that same day, Callus was standing on the bow of his ship and looked out at the horizon that was full of distant sails. Agamemnon was also on the bow of his ship and was looking out at the thousands of ships that were on the horizon and heading straight towards them. They were close enough to be able to see the sails clearly without any magic of some kind. The sails were white and royal blue with the flag of Corinos at their center.

Thousands of ships, quadriremes to be precise, were sailing right towards them and Agamemnon shouted, "Thessisana has decided that she is now the coordinator of my fleets!" Callus laughed and Agamemnon looked over at him and stared and shouted, "You'll stop laughing when you're married and your wife is something of the same nature!"

Callus stopped laughing and looked at Agamemnon and shouted back, "Not if I marry a woman that is less... Thessisana than Thessisana is!"

Agamemnon laughed and shouted, "Even if you do, I'm sure Thessisana will convert her to the appropriate chain of thought!"

Callus laughed and looked back out at the incoming ships.

Chapter

25

It was dawn in Jurrunt and the legion camp was still lit. Legionaries talked with one another and also with the occasional dragon scout that was embedded into the legion while they stayed.

General Crassus was given command of thirty scouts that were in the area of his camp. He would never send them out of the mountains, but had them on the very edge so they could spy on the elves to the east. They were of much help, they spotted many different movements across the border and reported them in fine detail, something a legionary scout would almost never do.

Everyone there knew that the World Senatorial Meeting took place a few days before and in a few more days they would know whether or not the world was at war. Tensions were quite high among the legion and dragons about war.

As much as the legionaries would boast about how if they got in a fight with those elves that they would mop the floor with them, none of the legionaries wanted to fight and possibly die for it. A bet went around about whether there would be a war when King Hevtur returned. Everyone, or most everyone was betting that there wouldn't be and that the world leaders would figure out a middle ground and peacefully dispute it, but everyone knew that that wasn't going to happen.

The only things that would happen were either nothing would happen and they would all be stuck there until something did or a war would start and everyone would go home at some point, whether they were slain or were either lucky or possibly skilled enough to survive and see their families again.

"What do you think is going to happen?" A legionary asked.

Another legionary looked up and said, "I don't know, I just work here." They began laughing around the little campfire they had built.

"But seriously, do you think that we're going to fight?" The first legionary asked.

"I don't know Vellious, anything can happen." The other legionary responded. Vellious looked at him and said, "Yeah, anything can happen, so tell me what you think could happen, Manorus."

Manorus looked at him and asked, "Can't you think about anything else? Can't you be unlike the others and think about something positive?"

Vellious shrugged his shoulders and said, "Well, I'm here because I'm like everyone else. We're all legion."

Manorus looked up at the sky and cursed. Vellious had a joking smirk on his face as he looked at Manorus. Manorus looked at him and asked, "What, have you never heard a curse before or something?" Another three legionaries walked up from the darkness and to the campfire.

One said, "Are you guys just going to hog up all the heat?"

Vellious turned around and said, "If you want any, then yes."

The legionary scowled and said, "Maybe we could use you to fuel it and help it grow." The others began laughing.

Vellious stared at the legionary and said, "No, Aspisius, I think that you would be the proper fuel. You're nice and fat." The legionaries around burst into a laugh and others at other campfires overheard what he said and laughed as well.

There were four campfires along the Urkidest Pass that the legion was guarding. The camp was further inward into the mountains so that in the case of an attack they could be prepared and be able to fight by the time the enemy force reached them.

Four teams of five watched the pass and kept an eye out for any unwanted guests that might think that they're welcome. One dragon was assigned to every five legionaries making the group's total six team members. The dragon that was a part of their group was off getting some wood as it was his turn to go find some.

The sun was rising in the east, but the day was still going to get colder by the minute until the sun crept over the horizon and shared a bit of its light and warmth. The whole time the legion had been there they have grown very fond of being where it was warmer.

Although it was summer, the temperature in the mountains was still not the funnest as the nights would get cold and the days would be windy and the sun was relentless in its pursuit to make the legionaries blind every time they would look at something that had the possibility of reflecting its light. The wind was almost always blowing, usually at a steady rate, but that did not change the fact that it was still blowing.

Often when a legionary was done with someone in his group, he would pick up his sword and angle it to shine the light of the sun into the eyes of whosoever bothered them, humans and dragons included.

When the dragons got bored, if they were a wind dragon, they would bend the light so densely that it would reflect the light and shine it into the eyes of whosoever bothered them, or they would summon some wind and make everyone's lives miserable. As for the dragons that weren't wind dragons, well they didn't know what they would do because only wind dragons were embedded into the legion for the temporary stay.

As for the guard outpost that monitored the traffic that went next to the pathways between the legions camp and the rest of Jurrunt, they would have their fair share of passersby and they would sit there and make sure that no one entered.

Often enough, little dragonets, when they would pass by, would try to see the legion. The guards at the posts didn't even care at that point because they would do it no matter what they told the dragonets.

When the legion first got settled in, some of the dragonets were interested enough to try to talk to the guards. The guards, trying to get them to leave, would talk to them and tell them to leave, but then the guards realized what the dragonets were doing and they talked as little as possible to try to avoid contact with the little buggers. Well, they weren't little compared to a human, but they were little in comparison to another dragon.

The guards at one of the posts were chatting as a group of dragonets passed by, one of them saw this and notified the other and they both abruptly stopped talking and looked over at the dragonets and stared back at them. They stared at each other for a moment and the dragonets whispered to each other and every now and then look at them.

The guards recognized this as a tactic of trying to get the guards to talk, or so they thought, and would usually ignore what the dragonets would say and continue their staring contest.

The dragonets split up and the guards looked at each other as they had never seen that one before. One of the guards leaned towards the other and whispered, "What do you think they're doing this time?" The other guard shrugged and looked back out at the partially empty streets. The legionary guards could swear that some of the older dragons or dragonets were bidding the younger into doing something to the guards, but they never knew for sure.

There were two guards per post and shift. When the shift was up for the two guards at the post, two more guards were supposed to show up and relieve them. The two guards watched the dragonets until they were out of sight and continued talking quietly.

Another dragon, still basically a dragonet since he was under the age of adulthood, would regularly stop by and talk for a minute or two. The guards at that post came to realize that he was funding the dragonet expeditions to try and outsmart the guards at the post. They always wondered if he just lied about his age or something and everyday wished that he would get older and be old enough to do something else for a change, hopefully be drafted for a term or two, but beggars can't be choosers at times.

He stopped in his regular spot and waited as one of the guards slumped out of his seat very dramatically and walked out to him.

"Good morning." The guard said, trying to sound and look cheerful even though he was the opposite.

"Good morning, Waixus." The young dragon said, or old dragonet depending on how one looked at it.

"What is it this time Vieron?" Waixus asked, stretching just so he could feel like he was doing something productive.

"You've heard all about how there might be a war, right?" Vieron asked, looking down at Waixus.

Waixus was about five foot ten inches and had brown hair with a slight beard forming on his jawline. Vieron was a metal dragon of silver and what was called, "Water Iron". Water iron was just iron that was resistant to water corrosion and when reflecting off of the sun, or when the dragon chose to, had the colors of the rainbow.

"And what makes you ask me that?" Waixus asked, stretching some more.

"Because that's what's going around." Vieron responded.

Waixus looked up at him in the eyes and said, "What, you want to have some fun in battle?"

Vieron squinted his eyes and accused, "You're avoiding the question."

"And you're now avoiding mine." Waixus said.

The guards on the posts got more than enough training with their fellow dragon counterparts as they guarded the posts and were now almost professionals at what they did there. They were not supposed to really talk with the public, but not talking didn't work once when an apparently very lonely dragon showed up one day and wouldn't leave until the guards responded, and now the guards were looked at as something one could talk to when one was bored.

The dragonets didn't help at all with the questions and some of the most discipline that the legionaries have ever seen, same with their determination to get an answer when they asked one, they never left them alone until they answered.

The legionaries now talked, but didn't reveal anything that could be brought back at them. So they mainly avoid questions, or they would lie when they couldn't see a way out of the situation.

Waixus and Thrasis, the other guard on duty with him, drew straws that they had prepared the days before and the one who got the shortest straw went out. Waixus got the short straw and Thrasis got to watch as he had to basically dance to avoid well put questions.

"I asked first." Vieron said.

"And I asked second, two is greater than one." Waixus said back.

Vieron eyed him and said, "But one comes first because it supports two in the number line."

"Nerd." Thrasis murmured just loud enough for Waixus to hear. Waixus turned his head around and smiled at Thrasis, barely concealing a laugh.

"Okay, answer my question and I'll answer yours." Waixus said.

Vieron looked at him and said, "We just had that previous discussion about who would answer first and you seemed not to listen."

"Who do you think you are, my primary school teacher?" Waixus asked, putting his hands on his hips. Vieron smirked.

"The reason I said to answer my question first is because, if I answer yours, my question may just become irrelevant." Waixus said.

Vieron nodded and said, "But it won't."

Waixus nodded and said, "Yes I have. What about it?"

"I've just been thinking and I have realized that when the King usually went to the World Senatorial Meeting, he would have returned by now."

Vieron said, looking up at the sky. Waixus almost stiffened, but caught himself before he could and said, "He's probably just making a pit stop or something."

Vieron looked over, far over, Waixus's head and said, "Maybe."

And shrugged his wings. Thrasis came out of the post and asked, "Waixus, what in the blazes are you doing?" Waixus turned around to look at Thrasis storming towards him. Waixus stood up straight and looked at Thrasis head on.

Thrasis was around the same height as Waixus and had brown hair, his facial features were different, but he also almost had the same beard outline growing on his jawline.

"Get back to the post." Thrasis ordered.

"You're not my superior officer." Waixus said, pointing a finger at Thrasis.

"But you're going to get us both in trouble."

"Trouble?" Vieron asked.

Waixus and Thrasis looked at him and Waixus said, "None of your business, and don't try to get smart." He pointed a finger at Vieron and turned back around to look at Thrasis.

"I'll finish up." Thrasis said, folding his arms and standing in front of Vieron. Vieron arched one of his eyebrows and said in a joking tone,

"Whatever." Waixus almost chuckled but remembered who the true enemy in this situation was and stowed it. Waixus nodded and began to walk back to the post.

"So, what is it you want, Vieron?" Thrasis asked.

Vieron looked from somewhere behind them and down to Thrasis and said, "I wanted to know what you thought about the current situation in the world of politics."

"That is an interesting way of putting that." Thrasis replied.

While Waixus was walking back to the post, he caught a movement in the corner of his eye and looked up. There was a little dragonet trying to hide. He looked back at Vieron and the crowd behind him. The crowd was occasionally watching as they walked by. Vieron caught his eye and began to hide a smile.

Waixus turned back at the slope and shouted, "What on earth are you doing up there!?" Thrasis turned around to find Waixus looking up at the cliffside. He looked up as well and saw one of the dragonets from earlier and his mouth almost dropped.

The dragonet wasn't moving all that much, but Waixus could see it and said, "I can see you!"

The figure didn't move and Vieron said, "Maybe you're just seeing things." Waixus turned and stared at him before looking back up the slope and said, "You. Ehh." He stopped and pointed up there and asked Vieron, "Which one is that?"

Vieron shrugged his wings and Waixus said, "Don't you dare! I know that you know which one that is and you are going to tell me or at least tell that one yourself that your gambit is over. You lost." Vieron was beginning to chuckle and Waixus said, "Alright! I give that dragonet the count to three before I climb up there myself and expose the mastermind behind this operation, which I know to be you Vieron, and then I will find out how many more you have sent on this task and get them down here as well." Waixus turned to look up the slope and shouted, "One last chance before I start!" Waixus stopped and realized that it was one of the dragonets from before that split up. He looked to the ground and picked up a chunk of dirt and hurled it at the dragonet. It hit the rocks and the dragonets head snapped up and turned to look at

Waixus. "I have found you. Now get down here." Waixus said, pointing to the ground.

The dragonet eyed him and said, "I can't get down until he gets down." The dragonet gestured behind him and Waixus squinted up at the cliffside and saw a small movement.

"Both of you get down here now!" Nothing happened for a moment and Waixus added, "I see you as well. You're gray like the rock." He pointed up at where the dragonet was and the dragonet said, "Okay." Two forms began to move and they came down the side of the cliff. Waixus and Thrasis stared at them and Thrasis signaled them to stop. They did and looked like they shrunk and Thrasis asked, "Is that guy being mean to you?" Waixus stuttered and stared at Thrasis. One of the dragonets shrugged and the other said, "It was a better response than what you gave us earlier."

Waixus stared at Thrasis in disbelief and said, "Thrasis, I swear, if you do something stupid I'll kill you in your sleep." Thrasis formed his brows into a line and looked at Waixus and said, "There are young present." Waixus relaxed and stared at Thrasis with mild discontent.

"You think you're funny, huh?" Waixus asked, tilting his head slightly with the last word.

"No, I think I'm the good guy." Thrasis said, with the most rye smile ever seen on a man's face ever before. Waixus's eye twitched and he shook his head and began to walk backwards, his eye was still twitching. Thrasis turned to the dragonets and said in a threatening, teasing voice, "Run." They bolted up and darted. Thrasis smiled and turned to Waixus and he began to chuckle and Waixus said, "You sly brat. You're going to give those poor things paranoia."

Thrasis laughed harder and asked, "Didn't those guys look like some of the dragonets from earlier?" Waixus nodded and he froze for a few seconds before whirling around and looked up at the other slope and walked towards it.

He stopped at the base of the slope and said, "Come on down." Nothing happened. He looked at the dirt and the ground. It was quite soft and malleable. He looked to his left and saw a pitcher of water and said, "If I have to come up there and get you. I will personally give each of you a mud bath. I will make sure the mud gets in every crack and crevice and that it may never come out and that you will have mud in your scales for the rest of your lives."

A voice from above said, "Nope. Not worth it." He looked up and saw another dragonet that he saw earlier and asked, "Where's the other one?" The dragonet pointed with a claw at a spot and Waixus stepped back to get a better angle.

Thrasis walked over to Vieron and said, "I see that you have new recruits. And that they are still…" Thrasis looked from the slope to Vieron and said flatly, "Recruits."

Another dragonet appeared and said, "I guess it's not worth it either."

"Don't guess!" Waixus shouted. He pointed to the ground and added, "I said that if I had to come get you I would give you both mud baths, not if you revealed yourselves!" The dragonets shot back and began to race down the slope to the ground. Waixus nodded and turned to look at Thrasis and then walked back inside the post.

"One day, I will get them through." Vieron said, looking at the slopes that the dragonets were just found on. "Whatever." Thrasis said mockingly. Vieron looked down at him and said, "I almost did it."

"Almost doesn't cut it. Now we'll just have to be on the lookout for all manners of dragonets, even you." Thrasis said, walking back to the post. "Challenge accepted." Vieron said jokingly. Thrasis turned to look at him and said, "Bring it on." They laughed and Vieron went on his way. Thrasis walked into the post and Wiaxus was glaring at him.

"Wwhhaatt?" Thrasis said as if he were talking to a child and holding out his hands with the palms up. "I'm going to kill you." Waixus said, barely keeping a laugh and smile in. Thrasis's lips quivered and he began laughing. Waixus couldn't keep a straight face anymore and began laughing as well.

Chapter

26

Hevtur awoke and it hurt to keep his eyes open and he just wanted to go back to sleep, but thought it best to get up. He remembered where he was after a moment and then remembered why he was there. He shot up and almost fell over with a headache.

"You're certainly not going to get back that way." A voice said. He blinked and realized that the reason he didn't fall down was because someone was holding him up and stabilizing him. He looked around and the voice said, "I'm over here." He looked the other way and saw Cora sitting there looking at him. She was holding him up and was looking into his eyes and said, "You need to wake up a little more first." He looked at her and asked, "What?" He was going to ask more, like 'how long have I slept' or 'what time and day is it', but nothing else came out.

"Keep resting, Hevtur." Cora said. She almost had to force him to lay back down. He struggled as hopelessly as a child.

Hevtur felt a sharp pain in his left side and winced. He flinched to it and was smacked and Cora said, "I said to keep resting, Hevtur." Hevtur curled his snout and shook his head saying, "Ouch." Cora was at his side and some doctors from Corinthus were tending to his wound at his side. The doctors almost couldn't believe he flew all that way from the World Senatorial Building to there and was still awake, much less still in the air with his injured wing.

Hevtur flinched in pain again and Cora batted at him with her wing and said, "Go back to sleep."

"What are you doing?" Hevtur asked, opening an eye to look at Cora.

She looked down at him and said, "I'm not actually doing anything, I'm making sure you don't whip around and hurt the ones that are helping you."

Hevtur looked at her confused and then realized what she was saying and said, "How long have I been sleeping."

"About two days, which surprised me. I thought that you would wake earlier." Cora said, looking from.

Hevtur to the doctors at his side. "I shouldn't have. I need to warn my people."

He went to get up and Cora pushed him back to the ground with her front talons and said, "You can go when the doctors say you can." Hevtur looked up at her and asked, "And when is that?"

"I don't know." Cora said, shrugging her wings. She looked down at the doctors and one said, "We're just about finished rebandaging it. He will be able to go once we're done, but he cannot involve himself in any form of fighting of physical contact with another for at least a couple more weeks."

"A couple more weeks?!" Hevtur demanded.

"Yes, whatever, or whoever got to you a few days ago cut you open and almost gutted you. You should be glad that you even made it here alive, much less awake." The man returned. Hevtur tried to get up again and Cora almost fell off balance and repositioned to place most of her weight on him.

"Once we're done here, are you going to continue to push me around?" Hevtur asked.

"No, because you'll probably be too strong for me to do so. You'll be at full strength then." Cora responded. Hevtur huffed out a breath. Cora looked down at him and said, "I don't like this either."

Hevtur glared up at her and said, "Whatever."

"Maybe I shouldn't hold you down, but to keep smacking you when you try to get up, or move." Cora said. Hevtur considered that for a moment and Cora said, "That's what I thought."

"I didn't say anything." Hevtur replied. Cora looked at the doctors and then back at Hevtur and said, "Good." Hevtur stared at her in disbelief.

No wonder why the king of Alzeirs went off and got himself killed. She was probably the same way with him. Hevtur thought, still glaring at her in disbelief. She caught him looking at her and smirked. "You're crazy." Hevtur accused. She looked at him and thought for a moment.

"Done." The doctor said. Cora looked down to him and got off Hevtur so he could stand. He lifted his head and winced as he stood on his talons.

You'll have to take it easy. If you get in physical contact, like a fight, you might rip it open again and you'll be in a lot worse pain than you are in now." The doctor said. Hevtur looked down at him and the doctor said, "I am a doctor, when it comes to injuries no one outranks me, not even a king." Hevtur sighed and nodded in agreement.

Cora was there looking from him to the doctor and back to him and said, "Your guards are ready when you are." Hevtur gave her a skeptical look and said, "Thank you." Cora nodded once and Hevtur bowed as much as his wounds would allow and strode to the door. The guards opened the door and he walked past and out to where his guards awaited. They saw him and rushed to his side and one asked, "Are you alright, my Liege?" Hevtur nodded and said, "Let's go home."

It was a couple hours before midday as Hevtur and the two guards took flight. Hevtur winced and grunted in pain and spread his wings and lifted off the ground. The guards were helping Hevtur stay in the air with him using minimal effort. He focused on camouflaging and his own wind stream to help get them back as swiftly as possible. He looked to his left down the river and couldn't see anything for the moment. He turned his gaze back to look forward.

About an hour into the flight and he could barely keep his attention on flying and camouflaging with the sky and clouds. He dropped his focus on his wind stream and it slowly dissipated as they entered the second hour of their flight. The pain at his left side was becoming almost unbearable whenever he flapped his wing to stay aloft. He wanted to stop for a moment, but thought about that decision. It would enable him to feel better and not feel like he was about to pass out from the pain, but on the other hand he was already late for returning home and there was a war, he had to get word to his kingdom and his generals as quickly as possible. He worried about Mirada and how she was feeling about him being gone longer than usual. He worried that she may panic about the fact that he was gone. He knew that she would freak out about the wound at his side and that it would be frustrating to get anything done after she saw it, which would most likely be right when he landed.

"Your Majesty?" One of the guards asked. Hevtur looked at him and said, "Go ahead." His voice was strained by his attempts to nullify his pain.

"You should rest, we still have about an hour to go." The guard said. Hevtur thought on that for a few seconds and said, "There's no time, we must get back to warn the rest."

"But sire, you're injured." The guard protested. Hevtur shot back a look and the guard nodded once and backed off.

Hevtur thought it over some more, *Maybe he's right. I am injured after all and making it worse won't help anyone, but then again, it's been two extra days that have been lost and, well, a half hour or so wouldn't change anything. Or it could, but it most likely wouldn't.*

"You're right. Find us a good spot to land." Hevtur said. The guards nodded once and began scanning the ground below for a secretive spot.

"Here your Majesty." One of the guards said, gesturing to the ground with one claw. Hevtur looked down and saw what he thought the guard saw and said, his voice still rough with pain, "Lead the way."

They landed and Hevtur winced in pain again as he pulled his wing back in and looked around the spot they were in. It was a thick swamp in the lands of Corinos. There was much fog in the area making it hard to see fifty feet away.

"Your Majesty, do you need anything?" The other guard asked. Hevtur turned to look at him and said, "Just a place to lie down."

The guard nodded once and said, "I think I found a spot." Hevtur looked at him and he pointed with a wing to a shallow cave. Hevtur nodded and the guard stood by his side and helped him over to it. The other guard was watching their backs and slowly crept backwards to the shallow cave with them.

As much as guards were trained and looked like they knew nothing but royal posture, it was almost an entirely new feeling of fear that hung over the place. Hevtur could basically feel the fear from the guards, or he thought that it would've been them.

It felt like something was watching and waiting for the right time to strike. Hevtur was sure that the guards felt the same. They didn't just look around differently, like one would when one is higher alert than usual, but they moved differently. They moved almost completely foreign to the way they usually would when they were patrolling the Kings Peak, or when they would be his escort when he went to meetings. Granted two of their buddies fought off an attacker and they haven't been seen since then. It was a wonder as to what happened, whether they made it out and were safely resting and ready to move at home, or whether they were killed or taken prisoner, or whether they were just missing or hiding from sight and were too afraid or cautious to move.

The guard cleared out a large spot for Hevtur and helped Hevtur into it. "Here you go, your Majesty." The guard said, laying Hevtur down onto the cleared spot of soft, wet, marsh ground.

"Thank you." Hevtur said, laying down on his right side to keep the left side off of the ground and relieved.

The guard nodded once and turned to look at the other guard and whispered, "Come on." The other guard looked at him and quickly stepped over the ground between the two. They took up positions around Hevtur and sat on alert. Their eyes scanned the swamp endlessly and Hevtur said, "We'll leave in an hour." The guards nodded once and continued their scanning of the area.

Mirada was pacing back and forth and she was doing it for hours non stop. Hierion watched in worry as she continued muttering to herself under her breath. He didn't know whether she had seen him or not. He stood there watching for almost five minutes before her alternating course led her to look up at Hierion. She jumped back with almost a breathless yelp and said, "Don't do that."

Hierion flinched as she turned around and continued her pacing between the walls of the cave section. Hierion cleared his throat and asked, "What's the matter?"

She turned to look at him and asked, "What's the matter? How could one not know what the matter was? How could you not know what the matter was? Or is, or... ugh."

She continued her pacing again and Hierion inhaled deeply and said, "I'm sure dad's fine. He's probably ju..." She cut him off and said, "Probably? Probably still leaves room for anything." She turned around and paced again.

Hierion stared at her and said, "On his way back." She stopped and looked at him and asked, "Really?"

Hierion looked at her blankly and said, "I was finishing my sentence." She tilted her head and asked, "What?"

"The sentence you interrupted... about five seconds ago." Hierion said, with a somewhat irritated tone.

She looked at him in utter confusion and said, "Oh, oh right. What were you saying?"

Hierion stared at her utterly confused and said, "That he..." He stopped and thought about his answer carefully and continued, "That he..." He couldn't think of a way to finish the sentence without her catching something in it to be paranoid about.

"That he what?" Mirada asked.

Hierion finally thought of what to say and said, "That he wouldn't want you to do this to yourself." Mirada went to speak then stopped before any sound came out.

She retracted her chain of thought and said, "Clever." Hierion didn't know what she was talking about and didn't know whether he wanted to or not.

He nodded deeply once and backed away to go out on the western platform to watch for his father to return. He was also worried for him, he didn't want to know a life without a father. He knew that one day he would know a life without a father, but he didn't want that day to be so soon.

Hevtur was back in the air one hour later and there was only about half an hour to go. The sun was just past its highest point in the sky and was now on its way down to the west. It was still hot in the air and was getting hotter. This made the wound on Hevtur's side burned without relenting, but he did his best to push it down. The mountains were in view and they were almost there. The guards made sure that Hevtur was well before they entered the airspace of the kingdom and one of the first ones to greet Hevtur was Hierion, who disobeyed orders or wishes and came outside the borders of the kingdom to greet Hevtur.

They reached the platform and Hierion wrapped his wings around Hevtur and said, "Dad. I was beginning to think something happened." Hevtur wrapped his wings around Hierion as much as he could and said, "That's just your mother in you."

More guards showed up and more. Hierion looked and said, "She just about went insane."

Hevtur chuckled and said, "I just about did as well trying to get back here."

Hierion looked slightly up at him and asked, "What did happen?"

Hevtur looked at Hierion and said, "I'll tell you later, for now I have something to do."

"Not until you tell me where you were." Mirada said in a stern voice.

The very air pressure almost shifted as Hevtur stiffened and looked up to see Mirada standing there. He thought that he even saw a guard flinch when she spoke.

Hevtur turned to the guards that were with him and said, "Get some rest." The guards bowed and turned to leave until Mirada noticed that there were only two and she stopped them. Hierion noticed it as well and looked around for the other two.

"They're not here, Hierion." Mirada said, still staring down Hevtur. Hevtur wanted to flinch just for her look, much less her tone of voice.

He stared back and said, "They've had a long trip, they need rest." Mirada thought that over and lowered her wing to let them pass. They looked at her and Hevtur and slowly got on their way.

Mirada studied Hevtur and noticed that he was keeping his wings tight against his body, as if he were hiding something. "Come inside, please." She said.

She moved out of the path and Hevtur gestured to Hierion to come closer to him. Hierion listened and Hevtur lifted his left wing and did his best to conceal his grimace of pain and he wrapped his wing around Hierion and began walking inside. Hierion upon making contact with Hevturs body felt him flinch and could also feel the deformity on his body. Hierion thought that there was just something there or something that he didn't know what to think of and moved to look at it. Hevtur held him closer and tighter as Hierion tried to look and he saw Hevtur almost wince. Hierion didn't catch on to what Hevtur was trying to do, but didn't fight him on it and went along. He looked over to see his mother and she was staring at the both of them skeptically. Hierion wanted to help in some way but didn't know how to and just kept his mouth shut and followed Hevturs lead. Mirada followed them in and half of the guards followed and the others stayed outside on the lookout.

They walked into the dinning hall and Mirada told the guards to wait outside the section of cave. She walked into the section and said, "Hierion, step away from your father." Hierion looked at Hevtur and Hevtur turned a hard eye at Hierion and just slightly shook his head.

Hierion thought of an excuse and said, "He's tired, can I at least get him somewhere comfortable?" Hevturs eyes stayed hard and he just slightly nodded in approval. Hierion barely saw this in the corner of his eye as he looked at Mirada. Mirada looked at both of them skeptically and after a moment of silence she said, "Okay, then step away."

Hierion looked back at Hevtur with a sorry look and Hevtur returned the look with thought. Hierion walked him over to an edge of the section with Hevturs left side to the wall. Hierion winked slightly and Hevtur smirked back.

Hierion set Hevtur down, or fake set him down, and walked away and went to leave when Mirada said, "No, stay here, Son." Hierion stopped and looked to her and to Hevtur and back to her. The moment he looked at Hevtur, he and Hevtur made eye contact. Hierion walked over to a side of the section and stood still. Mirada kept her gaze on Hevtur as he shifted closer to the wall.

"What happened?" Mirada asked. Hevtur finished sliding nearer to the wall, keeping the pain concealed. Hevtur looked at her and said, "Ah, thank you for reminding me. I need to speak to the generals and…" "WHAT happened?!" Mirada began with a snap.

Hevtur blinked and said, "If I tell you, will you let me speak with the generals?" Mirada huffed out a breath through her nostrils and Hevtur took that as a sign as a yes and said, "War has started and I was delayed in Cor…" "DELAYED!" Mirada shouted.

Hevtur blinked again and said, "Yes. I was in Co..." "Hevtur, I..." Mirada stopped and took a deep breath through her nostrils and closed her eyes and turned her head away in frustration.

"Mirada, pleas..." Mirada cut him off and said, "No, Hevtur, I will not let you outside this peak." Hevtur wanted to get up and argue, but was too comfortable and in too much pain to do so. He closed his eyes and looked to the ground.

"You are the King and you will be targeted if we are at war. I will not let you go out and be a target for our enemies!" Mirada said, her voice raising in the end. Hierion wanted to leave and was even leaning towards the exit as she spoke. Hevtur looked at her for a few seconds before she asked, "What happened?"

Hevtur inhaled to speak and hesitated for a moment before saying, "I was attacked at the meeting."

Mirada stared at him for a few seconds before saying, "And?"

Hevtur looked from the ground and up to her eyes and said, "I was injured."

Mirada took a deep breath and said, "Hierion, leave." Hierion swallowed and got up to leave and Mirada looked back at him and shouted, "NOW!" Hierion backed up at first then turned to leave, giving his father one last sorry look before disappearing outside the cave section that they were in. Mirada turned her gaze from Hierion to Hevtur and stalked towards him. Hevtur went to get up and winced as he strained his wound.

"Why be so hard on him? He didn't do anything wrong." Hevtur said as he was still trying to get up. He grunted with pain and finally stood on his talons and Mirada was there right in front of him. He looked back at her as she stared into his eyes.

"Move." She said in a not as hard voice as before, but it still wasn't gentle. He shifted to his right and lifted his left wing so she could inspect the wounds on his side and wing. She looked at the wounds and studied them for a few seconds and her voice began to break as she said, "Just days into something dangerous and you're already hurt."

Hevtur looked at her with worry in his eyes and said, "Mirada, I do need to talk to the generals so that they know what has happened."

She sat down, looking at the ground and said, "I'll send for them."

"They shouldn't leave their posts. If we are attacked while they are here, it could be devastating." Hevtur responded. He sat as well and looked at her and said, "I must do this. I promise you that when I do this, I will stay here and will not go anywhere until I am fully healed."

She shook her head and said, "No."

"Mirada, I…" She cut him off, "NO!" Hevtur wanted to shout back, but that wouldn't be very good of him to do so. He leaned forward and touched his snout on hers and said, "Please, let me do this."

Tears slowly crept out of her eyes and to the ground and she said, "Not this time. I will find a way to get the generals the word and have you stay here where you can be safe and the armies will not be left leaderless. I do not want to take the risk of not having you around anymore. I will not take that risk."

Hevtur blew out a breath of disappointment and said, "Please hurry. I will help in any way I can to make it go faster."

Mirada began to sob softly and said, "Thank you."

Epilogue

A Week Into The War

"What do you think will happen?" A female voice said. "I don't want to think about it all that much, Weira. It's too... political." A male voice said. "Dailer, be serious. This is a serious question."

The sun was rising and the ground was lush and green with the grass of the summer. There weren't many birds in the sky and there were plenty of clouds. Two dragons lay on a ridge top and were looking towards the sun as it rose higher in the sky. Mountains stood all around and caverns that were miles deep split the ground here and there. Never too close to each other.

Dailer had red orange scales that looked like molten, his eyes were fire gold red. He looked slightly down at the dragon laying next to him. She was looking at him with intent eyes waiting for a response to her question. Her scales were silver and water iron. Her eyes were silver.

"Well?" She asked. Dailer looked at her and said, "Politics." She scowled at him and asked, "Why aren't you serious when I want you to be serious?"

"Because you don't control how I respond." Dailer responded. She scowled at him again, inhaled and asked, "What did I do to deserve this?"

"You liked me back." He responded again. She looked at him with a rye smile and asked, "Who said you liked me first? What if I liked you first and you liked me back?"

He looked at her, trying not to laugh and said, "I just did."

She bowed her head, shook it and rested her head upon his shoulder and asked, "Don't you like how pretty the sun is?" "Yeah, sure, but

223

I don't like how it tries to blind me whenever I look in its general direction." He responded. She sighed.

He looked off into the distance and a couple seconds later was shook side to side. He blinked rapidly and looked to his left where he was being grasped.

A brown and dull gray scaled dragon was there and he was looking at Dailer with confused eyes. Dailer blinked a few more times before recognizing who it was. It was Hextiun, his friend. Hextiuns eyes shifted from confusion to comprehension and began to silently laugh, like usual.

Dailer sighed and said, "Yes, I was thinking of her again." Hextiuns shoulders and wings were bobbing up and down with laughter, but no sound came out.

Hextiun was mute. He never spoke around anyone or at least not around Dailer and Weira. Hextiun had earth and metal dragon blood in him. Dailer had fire and metal dragon blood and Weira had plain metal dragon blood.

They were now within a cavern and were also surrounded by other dragons of much diversity. The world was at war and they were in the military. Hextiun and Dailer never talked to any of the others that were around them unless it was necessary, just as none of the others around them ever talked to them, unless it was necessary.

They were in line to get an armor set up for battle and Dailer said quietly, "We've got metal blood in our blood. Why do we need to be fitted with armor? We have scales after all, if the scales won't protect us from something, what makes them think that the armor will change that?"

He was tapped on the side by Hextiun and Hextiun shrugged and bopped up and down in his four legs. Dailer, after knowing Hextiun for thirteen years, understood what he was trying to say.

"Extra weight? What would extra weight do for us, have us plummet to the ground faster when we fall off an edge or something?" Dailer asked, rather mockingly. Hextiun shook his head and knocked into Dailer just slightly. Dailer thought for a minute before getting what Hextiun was trying to say.

"Oh." Dailer said. Hextiun nodded and looked forward.

They were citizens of Garradant, well, actually soldiers now. The world fell apart and now almost everyone was at war with at least one other faction. They had just finished their beginners exams for the military and were now receiving orders as to which training camp they would be going to.

"I don't want you to go." Weira said looking at Dailer.

"It'll be okay. I'm just going for a few months, or several, and then I'll be back." Dailer responded looking into her eyes.

"Yeah, you'll be back, all mangled and twisted and dead." She said looking at the ground and away from Dailer.

He inhaled and moved a wing to return her gaze back to him and said, "I have to go. I don't have a choice in the matter."

"Death is always a choice. As you would say whenever you didn't like the choices you were given." Weira responded.

"Death is still a choice, but then that wouldn't change the fact that you would still go against that choice as well." He said.

"What if I told you that there was another path to take?" Weira asked, leaning into Dailers wing and looking into his eyes.

"I would ask you what that path was." Dailer responded.

She smiled back at him and said, "Then I would tell you what that path was." She paused for a moment before adding, "We could run away." Dailer stiffened and choked on his breath and backed up a bit.

He never really knew how much words could feel like physical blows until now. He stared at her and asked, "How long have you thought of that?"

She sat down and looked at him squarely and said, "Ever since you were drafted." She looked around and at her wing as if what she just said was too little of an answer to be deemed worthy of emotional response.

"Well, I don't want to fight either, but I don't have an escape plan and I most likely won't have one while I study for exams." Dailer said and continued, "I'm sure Hextuin wouldn't have a plan either."

She looked at him and said, "But I do. It may take a little bit longer for me to solidify, but I still have one."

"And how would you get in contact with us when you have it solidified? We'll most likely be in a training camp, or worse and the front lines depending on how well we do on the exams." Dailer pressed.

"That's the part that I haven't solidified yet." Weira said, her tail moved a little bit. He looked at her and his eye began twitching as it normally did and he broke eye contact as she laughed and he rubbed his twitching eye with his wing.

"NEXT!" A voice shouted. Hextuin bumped Dailer out of his flashback and they walked forward and to the officer that shouted. "Names please." The officer asked.

"I am Recruit Dailer of the Eastern Province and this is Recruit Hextuin of the Eastern Province as well." Dailer stated.

The officer looked up and asked, "Why didn't he introduce himself?"

"He's mute, it's why I'm always with him." Dailer responded. The officer looked at them both skeptically and looked down at a paper that had names on it and other writing next to each name.

The officer inhaled and said, "Okay, you two are going to get your equipment from over there and then will be forming up on the southern platform. Understand?" The officer pointed at another section of the cavern where armor was being assigned to other dragons.

Dailer looked at where he was pointing and nodded once saying, "Understood." Hextuin nodded once as well and turned to follow Dailer.

They reached the inventory section and were greeted by an inventory officer who already had their armor ready. "Here you go." The officer said, pushing the armor forward and into the reach of the two dragons. They grabbed the armor and left for the southern platform. They placed the armor on their backs and began walking.